PLANNED OBSOLESCENCE

A Manuscript of Life

Lorin Brandon

LOUDHAILER BOOKS

All Rights Reserved

Copyright © Lorin Brandon 2022

This first edition published in 2022 by:

Loudhailer Books
13 Lyminster Avenue
Brighton
BN1 8JL

www.loudhailerbooks.com

This is a work of fiction. All names, characters, businesses, places, events and incidents in this book are either the product of the author's imagination or used in a fictitious manner. Any resemblance to actual persons, living or dead, or actual events, is purely coincidental.

Dedicated to,
and in defense of,
my wonderful Bianca.

'The wages of sin is death.'
The Bible

* * *

Only a slave owner would blame you for your death.
Only a slave would believe it.

Contents

Chapter 1. A Different Path 1
Chapter 2. Para-archaeology 5
Chapter 3. All That Glitters...13
Chapter 4. Marvelous Manny..17
Chapter 5. Striking Gold...31
Chapter 6. A Good Woman 39
Chapter 7. Theodicy..47
Chapter 8. Seek and Ye Shall Find 55
Chapter 9. Incognito 67
Chapter 10. Saved by Myles 71
Chapter 11. Seeing through a Glass Darkly 77
Chapter 12. Magic...87
Chapter 13. Freethinkers...97
Chapter 14. Men in Dresses..111
Chapter 15. Laying the Groundwork 125
Chapter 16. Wine Bibbers...131
Chapter 17. Propaganda 141
Chapter 18. Gnosis..153
Chapter 19. A Hidden Veil 167
Chapter 20. Fancy Coats of Many Colors 181
Chapter 21. Salvation..189
Chapter 22. Manuscript of Life 195
Chapter 23. Meet the Overlords 213
Chapter 24. Planned Obsolescence 223
Chapter 25. The Cure 245
Chapter 26. Meet Moses 265
Chapter 27. Rule-Maker 285
Chapter 28. Debriefing..303
Chapter 29. Kangaroo Court...327
Chapter 30. Bully Begnini 337
Chapter 31. Excommunication...343

Chapter 1

A Different Path

Early spring at Cambridge University, the sun was high in the sky, and the clock had just struck thirteen. A panicked research assistant bolted from the laboratory of the archaeology department, piercing the calm early spring afternoon on the usually serene campus. In sheer terror, he raced across campus towards the security office with confused and bemused students looking on in halting anticipation.

The assistant reached the security headquarters and flung the door open, demanding assistance in the archaeology department. He breathlessly beckoned two security guards to return to the lab with him where there was a serious emergency.

'What happened?' mocked one of the security workers. 'Did someone break a nail on a dig?'

'We need help! Now!' the assistant screamed. He was pale and shaking; clearly this was no keystone cop call.

The terrified young scientist implored the security officers to assist him immediately. He told them that they should also call the police and medics and ordered the secretary to call for help. As the officers ran back towards the observatory, they were met by a strange entourage playing out across the previously tranquil campus. A well-known professor was plodding across the campus being followed by a cadre of cohorts attempting to help.

Despite his great consternation, the assistant attempted to explain to the security guards what was thought to be the problem. His professor had examined an ancient manuscript and had fallen into a trancelike state, unreachable and catatonic. All the electronics had failed, including their phones, so they couldn't call out for assistance. Now the rogue professor was on the run, even if the run was a slow walk.

'How could an ancient manuscript cause that type of reaction?' demanded a confused security officer.

'That's what we're trying to determine,' the assistant shot back. 'Now can you help us out?'

As they approached the rogue professor, the research assistant ushered them out of the way as he explained that no one could touch him or they would get the same reaction.

Incredulous as they were at hearing this, the officers did as told and stepped back to allow the professor to pass.

They stared in amazement at the blank face of the professor and noted that his eyes were completely blackened.

'This is demonic!' exclaimed one of the officers, but the research assistant assured them this was part of the reaction. The entire entourage was frantically trying to figure out what to do to stop the professor without touching him.

As the professor slowly made his way across the campus, the security officers and the approaching police cleared the path to protect the professor from himself and others. The approaching police officers demanded to know the situation, but the research assistant waved them off and explained to them as well.

'What kind of drugs are you doing on this campus?' one of the officers demanded. 'Someone has to know what caused this and how to fix it.'

But the looks on the faces of the scientists told the whole story. Their scientific examination had caused the reaction, and the effect had been catatonia. What were they going to do if they couldn't touch him and he never came out of this? How were the scientists to know what to do in this novel situation that none of them had experienced or prepared for before?

Students were confused and bewildered as they observed the situation: a well-known professor slowly crossing the campus with an entourage of scientists, police, and security protecting him and guiding his path. Was he drunk? Why weren't they giving him medical attention?

At that moment, medical personnel arrived, only to be told that they couldn't get near the patient because he couldn't be touched. What crazy notion was this? The confusion on their faces was clear, but all they could do was join the entourage and hope that an opportunity would reveal itself.

As the professor approached the far end of the campus, it became clear that he was headed towards the subway, presumably to take the tube back home. The scientists wondered aloud if this was a good idea and how could they possibly stop him since he was unreachable and untouchable.

Approaching the subway platform just in time for the train to enter the station and before anyone knew what was going to happen, the professor leapt off the platform directly into the path of the oncoming train.

'No!' screamed his colleagues, but it was too late.

Chapter 2

Para-archaeology

On the surface, the archaeological world has always seemed to be a slow-moving discipline that has yielded few interesting finds to the public. It has been thought of as a world of old men and women in hats, digging in the dirt and discussing their finds in conferences and scientific journals that would be of little interest to most people. These quirky individuals, who could dig at a find with a toothbrush for days, had patience that we could not even imagine because they realized they only had one chance to get any relic out intact.

It would probably be a fair statement to suggest that archaeologists were thought of as stodgy and rigid, with little imagination about the finds they were pulling out of the ground. It was hard to imagine an archaeologist pulling something out of the ground or discovering a megalithic find and breathlessly describing the potential ramifications of this find in an interview with speculative anticipation of the possibilities it possessed. Generally, they were much more conservative and plodding as scientists would be.

As a result, it could be rare to find an archaeologist with the character of Dr Consuelo, who broke that mold. Oh, he was no Indiana Jones or anything like that, but he could not be described as stodgy or stiff in any sense of the word. Gregarious and outgoing, he enjoyed teaching and interacting with his university students at the University of New Mexico in Albuquerque, which inspired a sense of wonder, he thought. What else would you expect from a city with 3 Us and 2 Qs?

From the sprawling Sandia Mountains that majestically gazed over the city, to the history of Route 66 running through it, and to the singing highway, he embraced the allure of this city and the Southwest. Despite his affection for Albuquerque, it was not so central to his identity as his birthplace, Taos, where he had grown up in the pueblo of his ancestors. New Mexico was an intriguing place, the land of enchantment, and he was not afraid of mysterious finds and strange artefacts, such as the one that had been recently discovered in a gold mine in South Africa that had the archaeological world buzzing with excitement.

'So, what do you think about archaeology now that you've had your first university class?' Dr Consuelo asked his students.

The students in the auditorium glanced around at each other, wondering if this was recess and why their professor wanted to engage in post-educational review once the class was over. There was no answer, and the students avoided the question and looked uncomfortable. They had been warned not to answer because that would drag out the class even longer.

It was the first class of the fall semester, and it was mostly a freshman-level course, so most of them had little familiarity with the profession.

'I get it,' Dr Consuelo said. 'There may be a lot to take in. But what I want you to know is that archaeology has the potential to transform history. I know that's a big statement, but it is completely true.'

The students continued to stare blankly, wondering if their new professor was taking mushrooms.

Archaeology was the profession that had always called Dr Consuelo, and he had felt drawn to it from his earliest memories. He had been aware that humanity was placed in a puzzling world with surprising mysteries that always seemed to hint at something greater, yet humanity never really found out what that was throughout their isolated lives.

'So, what is the purpose of archaeology?' Dr Consuelo continued.

He rarely got an answer of course.

'It just so happens that human beings are a curious bunch, and they are naturally enthralled with their history since they have been placed on this confusing planet with no idea as to where they came from. Human inquisitiveness and the paucity of clues as to who we are has led humans to dig in the dirt and search the earth to find out more information on our history, and this process is what we call archaeology.

'Archaeology is one of the few disciplines wherein our history can change with a single find and that allows for a certain mystery that I think makes archaeology exciting and intriguing. Any questions? Okay then. You are set free.'

Dr Consuelo often concluded his lectures with a message to his students about life in general or the purpose of archaeology. When he was a student, he would often grumble about having to learn certain things without ever understanding why he had to learn them. Home economics. Social studies. Even sometimes math and science. They all seemed stupid at the time. He hoped these little monologues helped his students to focus on the purpose of learning what he was teaching, and he wished his high school teachers and university professors had done the same thing. Then again, he had no idea if his students now were even paying attention.

Dr Consuelo had been a professor at the home of the Lobos for twenty years, thirteen of those as a tenured professor. The tenure afforded him the ability to dabble in the mystery of archaeology without fear of losing his job. He had always been a spry and outgoing younger-looking individual, but he was starting to become chiseled around the edges, and he looked closer to his actual age now that he was in his fifth decade on this earth.

Archaeology was his passion because he could see no bigger question than the ones humans still faced daily with insufficient answers: 'Where did we come from?' 'What are we doing here?' 'Where are we going?' Archaeology was the vehicle that allowed him to explore these questions further, not only for his professional benefit, but also for his personal satisfaction. If he was going to be honest, he did not care quite as much about the occupation of archaeology as much as the potential of the discipline to answer deep-seated questions about the human condition.

The mystery of life had deepened for him when, as a child, Dr Consuelo had seen some strange lights over Pueblo Peak that had seemed mysterious and nothing like anything he had ever seen. When he had asked his dad about them, his dad had acted very strangely. His dad's reaction had only served to pique his interest since he had been sure of what he had seen, and both his parents had reacted like he was being a silly child who did not know what he had been looking at.

Instead of quelling his interest, which had been their intention, this reaction had only served to heighten his curiosity, and he had read and researched as much as he could on the topic. The way he'd thought about it, there must have been something there if his parents had tried to convince him there was not. As an adult, he was forced to suppress most of these curious endeavors because now he was a serious-minded professional who was supposed to be focused on strict science and materialism. There was no place for his curiosity in his chosen discipline. After all, he was now a scientist, and no committed scientist could consider such silly issues.

As a result, he kept these interests to himself and rarely discussed them with anyone except his closest confidants. At least that was how he had intended it, but then the paranormal came and found him. It should be no surprise that archaeology would occasionally have strange finds that would be difficult to explain and could often be described as paranormal. It was not his fault that New Mexico had an enchanted and paranormal tinge to it, and he had had several occasions to be exposed to the phenomena.

Since these experiences occurred on professional digs that would naturally be of interest to the community, he published a few white papers that described his experiences in the hopes that some of his colleagues had had similar encounters. Unfortunately, these did not go over so well, and instead of starting a dialogue about it in professional circles, he simply got marginalized by the community who was either too cloistered to admit their encounters or had never had any experiences themselves. Many of his colleagues began referring to him derisively as a para-archaeologist, and his institution was not terribly happy.

As a result, Dr Consuelo had no choice but to downplay the phenomena as well. If he was marginalized for even reporting them, then he couldn't be taken seriously in professional circles, and this would diminish his credibility with his peers. Not that he really cared anymore because he had grown somewhat listless about his career and could not seem to find the motivation to care how seriously he was taken by colleagues. It was not success that drove him but answers. He had suffered a deeply personal tragedy that had nearly knocked him out of his game, but now he wanted answers to the mysteries, and he felt the only way to get those was through archaeological connections.

Chapter 3

All That Glitters

The discovery had taken place half the world away, in a gold mine in South Africa, in the deepest gold mine in the world. Gold mining was a demanding and dirty job, physically taxing to anyone who dared put themselves in the ground to take on the challenge. Mines had always been dusty, dirty, and loud, and this one was especially dangerous since it was two miles below the ground. It was also difficult to access due to the maze of elevators, trolley cars, and narrow alleyways needed to get there. The heat and humidity in the mine were stifling, and those issues got worse the deeper you went into the earth.

South African Ndinge Bwana was nearly done with his shift, and he was especially excited because he was going on a holiday for two weeks. It had been a long day at the end of a long week, and he should have been exhausted, but the thought of vacation was invigorating. The jackhammer in his hands felt like a stylus as he deftly managed it despite his aching muscles.

Suddenly, his jackhammer hit on a soft spot, and as he pulled back, he was shocked to see the dirt collapse, exposing a purplish haze peering at him through the dusty little cavern. As the dust began to settle, he noted a gently glowing artefact of some sort, which he thought to be impossible from where he was at this depth. The glow was eerie and oddly threatening, and he backed away instinctively. He breathlessly called over his fellow miners. As they approached the area, most of them paused as they saw the glow coming from an area where there should have been no power source. They had the same reaction Ndinge had.

'What the bloody hell is that?' Ndinge asked.

The other miners said nothing and just stared with mouths agape, shrugging their shoulders in mass confusion. Some of them looked frightened as this was a surreal thing to find in the ground this deep.

'I don't know,' one of the fellow miners said. 'But there is no way there could be something with a light this far down, and I would not touch that because that is a menacing glow.'

The dust had settled some, and Ndinge pulled out his phone to take a picture. As the view became clear, they noticed a metallic-looking artefact that seemed quite shiny and new, which confused the miners even further.

The object was shiny and rectangular. One of the miners thought it looked similar to an iPad, but it had writing on it, and it looked like there might be thin and flimsy metallic pages. The miners had imagined an ancient artefact like this would be rolled up as a scroll, but this looked like a tablet that had pages that could be turned and examined. It certainly did not look old and almost looked like a modern artifact.

'How does something like that get way down here?' Ndinge pondered as he gazed at it. The other miners nodded in agreement. 'What should we do with it?'

'Nothing, if you ask me,' another miner said. 'I'll go get someone.' He hurried away to find the manager.

Shortly afterwards the shift manager arrived and asked, 'What's this crazy talk—'

He stopped midsentence as he laid eyes on the glowing item. He paused, looked around at the other miners, and exclaimed, 'What the fuck is that?'

There was no answer as the miners again shrugged and looked at him.

'Who found this?' he asked further.

'I did,' Ndinge said. 'My hammer broke through, and the soft dirt collapsed away, and there it was.'

The shift manager cleared the area and instructed all the miners to leave this alone. He said he was going to call administration and have them quarantine the object until they could get someone to look at it.

Before he was able to do so, the rest of the miners pulled out their phones and took pictures so they could share them with their friends. Their astonishment was slightly overshadowed by their fear as they felt like they were gazing at a relic of eons gone by.

'Knock it off,' the shift manager yelled, 'and you better get on the elevator, or you'll miss it.'

The dusty and dirty miners all clamored for the elevator as it did not wait for anyone.

Chapter 4

Marvelous Manny

Dr Consuelo had grown up being a religious Catholic in the Taos pueblo where he was raised. As a result, he had not always asked such deep questions about life—until tragedy struck.

He had married his childhood sweetheart, Sylvia, and they had finally decided to start a little family once he graduated and established a career. Manny was their wonderful little boy who thrilled them in ways difficult to describe for first-time parents who were surprised by how much love and joy a child brought. But Manny was different. His spark was enthralling, and all of Dr Consuelo's friends and relatives agreed. He couldn't help it, and he was especially in love with his boy who Dr Consuelo felt was the most special soul he had ever met.

Manny had smiled and interacted with his parents at such a young age, and Dr Consuelo thought he had the most engaging personality that he had ever experienced. It did not occur to him that most parents thought their kids were quite special because he knew that Manny was the most special kid ever, and like any first-time parent, he was smitten. Manny's giggle and laughter would peal through their little cabin in the pueblo, and the warmth from his laughter would permeate the cabin, even on the coldest of winter days. His throaty voice and vibrant spirit endeared him to his parents, and they couldn't have been happier with their little family.

Manny's favorite television show was *SpongeBob SquarePants*, and he loved to watch it while he ate his favorite meal, Lucky Charms. Dr Consuelo and Sylvia were horrified by how much he wanted to eat it for every meal and would gag just a little when they saw him drinking the sweet milky nectar leftover at the bottom of the bowl. They did not know it at the time, but these were some of their best memories, and the laughter and giggles were all that mattered to his parents.

Dr Consuelo was anxious to show Manny the outdoors. He taught him to ride a bike just about as soon as he could walk. He was looking forward to the years ahead of fishing, hunting, biking, and hiking. He had never been sure if he wanted kids, but now that he had Manny, he did not know how he'd ever lived without him.

One day at his office in Albuquerque, he got a call from his wife that would forever change his life and set him on a path he could never have imagined. Manny's preschool teacher had called his wife in a panic to say that Manny had just had a seizure. The teacher had asked her if she could come get him and take him to the hospital. Sylvia called Dr Consuelo on the way to picking Manny up, so she did not have many answers, but it was quite alarming.

'I'll be right there,' he told Sylvia, and he jumped into his car to get to Holy Cross Hospital as quickly as he could. It was where Sylvia took Manny to be examined.

Dr Consuelo completed the two-hour drive in under an hour and a half. When he arrived, he found Sylvia comforting Manny. He had a little IV in his hand and a tired look on his face.

'What happened, little man?' Dr Consuelo asked.

Manny just shrugged and said he did not know and could not remember.

The doctors had run a variety of tests, and they were unable to determine the source of the seizure. Dr Consuelo had sought out the doctor and grilled her as best he could to try to find an answer, but there was nothing to be gained. They eventually left the hospital and brought Manny home despite their deep concern.

Manny returned to school a few days later, and things seemed to be back to normal. Dr Consuelo thought perhaps it was just an isolated event that meant nothing, but Sylvia continued to harbor a grave concern as a seizure in a three-year-old could mean a lot of scary things.

'Our boy is going to be just fine,' he told Sylvia, trying hard to put on a brave face.

Sylvia's furrowed brow and deep concern showed on her face and told a story that Dr Consuelo did not want to hear.

After an uneventful weekend, Dr Consuelo got the dreaded call on Monday that would prove Sylvia right and devastate their world indefinitely. Manny had suffered another seizure, and this one had been violent and lasted several minutes. Manny's eyes had rolled back in his head, and he had convulsed for minutes that had felt like hours. Finally, he'd lost all the Lucky Charms in his stomach, and his teachers had been horrified at how helpless they had felt.

Manny became very listless after this event. He began to act strangely as well, as if he were losing muscle control, and he seemed to be growing weak and uncoordinated. They found the top neurologist they could find in Albuquerque, who happened to work for the neurology department at the UNM School of Medicine. Life became a bit of a blur from that point on. Manny was put through rigorous tests until the horrible day arrived when they were told the news that Manny had Tay-Sachs disease.

'Tay-Sachs disease?' Dr Consuelo asked the neurologist. 'I've never heard of that. Is it bad?'

The neurologist took a deep breath and said, 'I'm afraid so.'

Dr Consuelo froze in terror as he heard these words. 'How bad?'

The neurologist went on to explain that Tay-Sachs was a devastating genetic disorder for which there was no cure and very few treatments. Manny was likely to decline steadily and die at a young age.

Dr Consuelo and Sylvia were in shock as they heard this, and Sylvia sobbed as the doctor explained the devastating news.

'There must have been a mistake,' Dr Consuelo begged the neurologist. 'How can this be possible?'

'I'm afraid it's not a mistake,' the neurologist said. 'We always run multiple tests and consult with the Mayo Clinic before we give this kind of devastating news because it is the worst part of my job.'

'Well, what do we do now?' Dr Consuelo asked as he searched the face of the neurologist for any possible hope.

'Take him home, and love him for all the days that you have him,' was all the doctor could say.

At the time this kind of angered Dr Consuelo, but in the months to follow, he would realize it was the best advice that could be given in the moment. Tay Sachs disease, he wondered, who would come up with such an evil condition? Did they have a contest to see what disease they could perpetrate on humanity and there was a prize for the worst? The condition was confounding to Dr. Consuelo and worse yet, it was his precious Manny.

Why had he ignored the evil in front of his very eyes all these years?

Sylvia and Dr Consuelo did take Manny home and love him, but the devastation was overwhelming to them, and they could hardly categorize their feelings and thoughts. Dr Consuelo had researched the condition and grew enraged as he realized what was going to happen to his boy. This disease was so cruel and capricious that it was hard to imagine how such a hideous thing could happen, especially to his amazing little boy. Dr Consuelo could not have conceived of such a horrible thing if he had set out to torture people intentionally, and he wondered how it could even happen. It was a condition so odious as to defy logic.

'How is it that people think this is even possible in a world with a supposedly good god?' he yelled at Sylvia.

He knew he shouldn't be yelling at his poor, innocent wife, but his growing rage at the unspeakably cruel condition that was so callously visited upon his innocent little boy filled him with despair, and he had no outlet for his anger. Oddly, he also felt incredible guilt that they had even brought Manny into such an evil existence. Suddenly life took on a sinister tone.

Dr Consuelo had never thought much about his faith, despite his upbringing, but he now felt as if God were an uncaring monster who would not save his beloved child from the horrors of disease and death. Dr Consuelo immediately knew that this experience meant the Bible was a lie and God was a monster. According to his church's teachings, humans suffered because they lived in a fallen world, so it was their fault—whatever the hell that meant.

Dr Consuelo knew this could not be an explanation for Manny's condition since he had been born with the disease and was completely innocent. Dr Consuelo knew such church teachings could not stand up to scrutiny if looked at objectively and wondered how they had gained such a strong foothold. He now recognized these teachings for the evil that they were.

It was not clear whether a god would intentionally tell people these things or if humans had convinced themselves of these beliefs after studying holy books. Or was the church using guilt to coerce and manipulate believers for its benefit? Whatever the case, these beliefs seemed to Dr Consuelo to be built on faulty logic, and they made his faith seem silly. Dr Consuelo simply could find no way to reconcile the tragedy of his son's disease and impending death with what he had been taught about God and faith.

One especially cruel outcome of Manny's condition was that he had deteriorated remarkably quickly, as he seemed to succumb to the disease rapidly. His doctors were shocked and could not fully explain why his condition had been so aggressive. Tay-Sachs was always devastating, but some of the neurologists began to test for other conditions since his decline was so precipitous. They never settled on the exact source of Manny's rapid deterioration.

After his diagnosis at nearly four, his parents were horrified to watch as he quickly lost his physical capabilities. He was in a wheelchair shortly before his fifth birthday. Along with the cruelty of watching their precious child deteriorate, Dr Consuelo and Sylvia would become his caretakers and deal with every horrendous event in this torturous process. His body became contorted with scoliosis, and his muscles wasted so quickly they could almost watch them atrophy.

Their house became a virtual nursing home, where they had a handicap van, wheelchair ramps, lifts, hospital beds, shower chairs, oxygen tanks, and the occasional caretaker they would hire when possible. Sylvia did most of the care for her son, but her face showed the strain as time went on, even though she would always care for her child if she were capable.

The world of disability was all-encompassing, as Dr Consuelo and Sylvia had discovered, and they felt alone in their tragic spiral with no one to blame and no one to help them. Except that Dr Consuelo blamed God to anyone who would listen since he did not think there was anyone else to blame, and his rage grew as Manny declined.

One especially dark day, Dr Consuelo had come home early to relieve Sylvia and give her a break. He spent the afternoon caring for his son and loving him as best he could. Manny had lost his speech at this point, but he still had his beautiful laugh, which came from the best laugh factory ever. They lay in Manny's bed and watched his favorite show, and Manny giggled away as Dr Consuelo rubbed his poor, aching muscles.

After a few episodes, Manny fell asleep, and Dr Consuelo snuck out of the room so he could get a good nap. Upon checking on him about an hour later, he was horrified to find that Manny had soiled himself while he slept. A sedentary child could have awful bouts of constipation, and they would give Manny laxatives to prevent him from getting too constipated. Apparently, this one was explosive because Manny literally had feces from his shoulders to his shins, from the middle of his back all the way down his legs.

Dr Consuelo was horrified to see this, and he hardly knew where to start. He pulled the poor little soul out of his bed while Manny was screaming in pain. He put Manny in his shower chair to clean him off, trying to ignore the fact that he was also now covered in explosive diarrhea. After cleaning him up as best he could and changing the sheets, he placed Manny back in his bed. Manny fell asleep again, exhausted from the whole episode.

Once Manny was resting peacefully again, Dr Consuelo escaped into the basement, grabbed a chair, and flung it into the wall where all four legs stuck into the drywall. He then grabbed a pillow off the couch and screamed into it as loud as he could. It incensed him to no end that his little boy was treated with such indignity and given such a ghastly disease. It was not just that he was going to die, but the agony of going through this was heightened by these horrible complications of the disease. His child was being slowly tortured to death, and he was just watching.

This was not the worst indignity either one of them had suffered, but it was emblematic of the evil process. It was not enough that he was destined to decline and live the life of an invalid; the disease was slowly breaking them all down with its relentless progress. Dr Consuelo decided that being covered in shit was better than being full of shit, and he abandoned his religious teachings with fervor.

He wanted to find the person or persons responsible for this disease and slowly burn them to death while sticking needles into their eyes. There was no way he could tolerate this, but he had no choice, and he was not going to abandon Manny for any reason. He raged in that moment against the incalculable cruelty of life and cursed God in his darkness.

It offended him so much that when he described the cruelty of this disease to his peers, most of his friends and colleagues could listen to him about the unbelievable cruelty of this disease and yet continue to proclaim there was a good God. Dr. Consuelo now recognized that anyone who could defend such evil was also evil. If you can't call bullshit on an obvious faux pas, then you are as bad as the perpetrator. Whoever 'invented' these diseases were evil and if you defend it, you are as guilty as them. I don't care that you've been threatened with eternal damnation, speak out for the helpless. It felt like they were just saying to him that his Manny did not matter that much because there would've been no way they could feel that way if their own child had been struck with such a tragedy.

He attempted to gain some insight by having a counseling session with his childhood priest, Father Donald Lujan, who had been his spiritual mentor when he cared about that stuff. Father Lujan was very understanding and concerned about Dr Consuelo because he saw the extreme strain this was putting on him, and he genuinely wanted to help.

Father Lujan had always been a wonderful, kind-hearted individual, and he was a perfect fit for the Catholic Church in the Taos pueblo, having grown up where poverty and tragedy were rampant. He had gone into the ministry out of a sense of deep care and concern for his people.

'Why would you blame God for this?' Father Lujan asked. 'Don't you know that suffering is part of a fallen world and that every tear will be wiped away?'

'That's what I would tell suffering people as well,' Dr Consuelo replied. 'Our entire lives are tinged with pain and tragedy, and ultimately, we have to die. Not a very uplifting world, and yet we are told it is for our own good. Well, what do I care about that? That is simply a controlling god who blames it all on us for living in a fallen world, in which he put us, according to your theology, and then pretends like it's going to be wonderful when we die. Why would I trust a god who could do this to Manny?

'Can't you see how manipulative that is? We must die to obtain any reward, and we must trust this controlling entity who caused our sickness to make it right. As if any reward would be worth that amount of suffering. It is clearly a ploy to keep us compliant and complacent. I don't care about a reward, and what good will it do to wipe my tears away? God blames us for our condition when it is clearly the other way around, complacency be damned.'

Father Lujan was not sure what to say for a moment, but then he thoughtfully mused, 'I cannot compete with your intellect, Dr Consuelo. But I know God loves you and loves Manny, and logic can sometimes be a hindrance in these matters.'

'The only reason you would suggest logic is a hindrance is that your faith has no logic. Shouldn't your faith comport with some sort of logic?' Dr Consuelo asked. 'Otherwise, it's just propaganda, and we know frightened parishioners aren't very good at detecting propaganda. Blind faith will do that to a person.'

'That is a good point,' Father Lujan said, 'but I'm concerned about your anger.'

'Let me worry about my anger,' Dr Consuelo said, 'because I think that is the only appropriate response when a tragedy like Manny's occurs. My son is dying, and if I have an ounce of care for him, I should be angry. Otherwise, I'm selfishly concerned about my well-being instead of Manny's. Besides, I'm working through my anger as best I can, and giving me trite answers only intensifies my rage.'

'Perhaps I'm not the right counsellor for you,' Father Lujan said, 'despite my great compassion and care for you and your family.'

'I think you would be a fine therapist for me if you would just think through your banal answers and how bankrupt they are logically. At least Job's friends tried to understand his deep questioning when he felt he was innocent, but even they failed ultimately because of the fear of the monster that had a supposed bet on Job's fortunes.

'It may be that it is impossible to understand someone else's pain. Even though I think you are a very caring person, you are unable to go outside the script. Some people say that the purpose of pain is to increase one's empathy, but what good does that do when our suffering is so isolated that even you can't fully understand? I like you very much, Father Lujan, but you must understand how impotent your answers are in the face of Manny's condition.'

Dr Consuelo came away from this conversation with a greater understanding of how faith could lead to brainwashing, and he could understand that brainwashing because he had been brought up in it. But when it came to answers to the tough questions, faith was often a hindrance to proper insight. Father Lujan was doing his job as best he could, but his answers were hollow in the face of Manny's fate.

Manny declined and ultimately passed away at home in his bed, with his loving parents at his side helplessly watching him slip away. Dr Consuelo had never felt such despair and uselessness at his inability to do anything to stop the relentless progression of the disease. As Manny took his last breath, all they could do was hold him and cry. Manny had disappeared, and their lives were silent. Without Manny there as the glue, they eventually drifted away from each other as well.

Chapter 5

Striking Gold

Dr Consuelo was in his office at the university when he first caught wind of the find. It had been an exhausting day on campus, as this was the day he taught several courses. It was a typical sunny day in Albuquerque, and the only things stirring on campus were a gentle breeze and the students coming and going.

He had come back to his office to get some work done, but instead of working, he was on the computer, once again distracted by the most amazing of time-wasters, the internet. As was common knowledge, when work beckoned, the internet's pull was stronger, and this day was no different.

He was perusing the website of *Archaeology* magazine, which was a publication put out by his professional society, the Archaeological Institute of America (AIA). He loved to view the news on the site, which told of the latest finds around the world, piquing the interest of professionals and occasionally the public.

It was a short piece, very scant on details, that told of a strange manuscript that had been unearthed in a gold mine in South Africa, at a depth of two miles down, where no human-derived manuscript would've ever been expected. The miners had been so excited about it that they had immediately contacted the AIA with news of the find and had even sent them a picture. Dr Consuelo knew from the brevity of the piece that there was a lot more to this find than what was being stated on the website. He was hooked.

These kinds of finds were fascinating to him, and this one seemed especially intriguing given the depth at which it had been found. Manuscripts of this type were nearly unheard of and often extremely difficult for the archaeological world to secure because they got taken and sold on the black market, eliminating the possibility of it being examined fully. The fact that it had been found in a mine, where none of the miners could take anything out without being detected, certainly was a positive, but contacting the AIA was proof that the mine was sincere about securing the provenance for scientific examination.

Dr Consuelo wanted in. He was not the top scientist in the field, but he knew the top scientists, and he wasted no time in contacting them. He phoned his colleague, Dr Myles Hawking of Cambridge University, and informed him of the find.

'Trust me,' Myles said. 'I know all about it, and I'm suspicious of the report, but I'm not even sure who is going to be the lead on that. I'll have to check into it and get back to you.'

'Bullshit, Myles,' Dr Consuelo blurted out. 'You guys are sitting on this, and you know they're calling you.'

'I'm shocked at you,' Myles said, holding back a smirk. 'I would never hold out on you, especially not after last time.'

He was referring, of course, to the last find in Turkey, approximately ten years earlier, when Dr Hawking had essentially run interference on him so they could get to the dig before he had a chance to get there, and now Dr Consuelo was a little skeptical as to whether he was forthcoming.

'Exactly, Myles,' he retorted. 'You probably wouldn't even tell me if you were looking directly at this find sitting on your desk. With your reputation, you guys are bound to be contacted first by the society. I don't know if I can trust you on this one.'

'Don't be a whiny little bitch,' Myles said with a chuckle. 'You know that I had to hold you off in Turkey. It's not every day that these things pop up, and we were determined to be first on that one. Being in an institution like this doesn't guarantee that you get all the top finds, but it helps. Besides, we are stretched pretty thin right now, and I don't know if we have the bandwidth to take the lead on this one.'

Myles was right, of course, and he had the name and the institution to back it up. He and Dr Consuelo had become close confidants over the years, collaborating on different finds. Myles was a fair-minded, lighthearted individual, who had to come across as austere from time to time to uphold the integrity of the institution he was representing. Dr Consuelo liked him a lot, but he was not sure if he should believe him this time.

Not only did Dr Hawking work for a prestigious organization, but he also came from an impressive pedigree, which gave him more clout as a scientist. He would not say how, but he was related to the great physicist Dr Stephen Hawking, and he downplayed that fact because he did not want to name-drop or be overshadowed by such an immense figure. Dr Consuelo was a huge admirer of Stephen Hawking as he had grown to think of him as a hero after having witnessed neurological decline in Manny. How could a man suffer from the deadly condition of ALS as long as he did and still be such a fertile investigator and scientist?

Dr Consuelo sighed, 'You better tell me if you hear anything, Myles,' he said. 'I don't want to find out that you covered up your involvement on this one as well.'

'Don't worry, my esteemed Dr Consuelo,' Myles responded. 'I will let you know when I hear something.'

Reluctantly Dr Consuelo hung up and went back to perusing the find on the website. He pulled up another browser to research about it for himself. Typing 'strange manuscript in South Africa' got a million hits, with nothing specific to this find. He tried another one, 'Manuscript in South Africa two miles deep,' but once again the search yielded little that would specifically tell of any new find about to set the archaeological world on its head.

Maybe I'm reading too much into this, he thought to himself. But his instincts told him differently, and he wanted to find out more.

Pulling out his personal laptop so his tracks could not be traced on his work computer, he decided it was time to go to his favorite conspiracy chatroom, which, unfortunately, required that he went to the dark web. He knew his colleagues were not likely to frequent chatrooms and consider conspiracies, let alone entertain the dark web, but he could not help himself, as the mysterious had a rather strong grip on him.

He pulled up his Tor browser and got straight to the site, wherein he knew someone had to be talking about it. Browsing through the different discussion topics, he was getting frustrated when he finally saw the thread he was looking for: 'STRANGE FIND IN ACTIVE MINE IN S. AFRICA.'

Clicking on it, he started reading through the comments and discussion with bated breath. Most of the comments were no help until he came across user 818radar818, who claimed to know a friend of one of the miners who had discovered the artefact in the mine. His comment sent a chill through Dr Consuelo. According to this conspiracy junkie, who practically lived in this netherworld, the artefact had only been discovered because a miner's jackhammer hit a soft spot and the dirt collapsed around a purplish glowing document of some sort.

Dr Consuelo closed the Tor browser and slammed the computer shut. He knew there was something about this find. He was so excited he was almost shaking. What could this strange artefact be? And why would Myles lie to him? Dr Consuelo was sure that he knew more than he was letting on.

'I am going!' he nearly shouted to himself in his office.

He was getting on a plane and heading to the mine, just as soon as he could find out who was going to examine the artefact and remove it from the mine for proper examination. Maybe it was a dumb idea because if he were not invited on a professional level, he probably would not be able to get anywhere near it. He didn't care though because he had to try to get all the information that he could. Besides, he had never had the opportunity to go to South Africa, which was where his profession got its beginning.

Instead of making plans straightaway, Dr Consuelo remembered that he was employed by an institution that expected to be kept informed of what he was studying. All universities had oversight of their professors, and his university was no different, though they were different with him. They had not been pleased with his reputation as a para-archaeologist, something of which they often reminded him. Worse yet, it was the University of New Mexico's own publication, the *Anthropological Journal of Research* (*AJR*) that he had convinced to publish one of his white papers on his strange finds.

This was problematic for the university and his colleagues because it tainted the entire university with a paranormal tinge, which was already the reputation of the region. His department chief was especially wary of anything Dr Consuelo got involved with, so Dr Consuelo reluctantly contacted him to meet for lunch and get some sort of approval for his plans.

Thomas Riordan was a straight shooter who was not interested in monkey business, and Dr Consuelo thought he was one of the reasons archaeologists had such a stuffy reputation. The first thing out of his lips was, 'What ludicrous find are you looking at now?' And that set the tone for the whole meeting.

The conversation was terrible, as usual, with this guy because he could not get past the small talk. Dr Consuelo could kick himself for trying to have a discussion with this fence post. Why did he even make an effort?

Dr Consuelo informed Dr Riordan that it was a stunning find and gave him all the adjectives he could come up with to gain some interest from the robotic form across the table, but nothing seemed to puncture his veneer.

'Regretfully, we gave you tenure,' Dr Riordan said. 'That means you have some level of autonomy. I will not endorse your pursuit of this artefact, but as long as you do it on your own time, I will not oppose it. Do not, under any circumstances, appear to be speaking on behalf of the university on this endeavor,' he finished with his wonderfully monotone speaking voice.

'Wouldn't think of it,' Dr Consuelo said.

Chapter 6

A Good Woman

It turned out that it was easy enough to find out when the artefact in the mine was going to be examined because the media started to catch wind of the find, and Dr Consuelo took his cues from them. There was to be an archaeological examination in situ, and the fact that they were reporting this indicated that he was not the only one who suspected something about it.

He wanted to make a trip of it and decided to bring his long-standing colleague and closest intellectual sparring partner to provide some company on the trip. He picked up his office phone and dialed her straightaway. This was a great opportunity to spend more time with her and enjoy a trip abroad. Dr Tegan Mallory was his compatriot and colleague who was as intellectually curious and stimulated as he was, and he could think of no one else that would enjoy this trip the way she would.

Dr Consuelo had known Tegan for almost as long as she had been at the University of New Mexico. He had met her the same week she'd started as a professor in mathematics twenty-five years ago. He was a student at that time and fell in love with his math professor at first sight, especially since she was not married. Dr Consuelo was engaged at the time, and life had taken him on a different journey. They had kept in touch after he was married and always had a cerebral affair but were never romantic.

Tegan was a beautiful woman, and despite being petite, she had a presence about her. She could carry a room just by entering it although she did not seek attention. She had the appearance of someone who could be easily intimidated, but nothing could be further from the truth.

Tegan had recently taken early retirement, which afforded her great freedom in her mid-fifties. Dr Consuelo was intrigued by her brilliance and open mind, given that she had been educated at Harvard and had chosen the University of New Mexico for the enchantment she felt in the region. Being an early adopter of Bitcoin and other cryptocurrencies had set her up to retire early, with occasional consulting jobs.

She spent much of her time at casinos in the area, playing poker with large, intimidating men who would often hit on her to throw her off her game. Tegan would always ignore the cocky advances and parlay the distraction into some serious winnings. These cocky assholes were not so smug when all the chips were shoved her way and her stacks were always growing.

Tegan lived in Santa Fe, where she felt she best fit in because she loved the deeply artistic culture and history of the oldest capital city in the United States. As a mathematics professor, she had understood the investment world and had done quite well for herself, investing in stocks, real estate, and the occasional art piece, but it was her cryptocurrencies that had really cemented her wealth.

Another reason Dr Consuelo was so infatuated with Tegan was that she was a long-standing atheist who did not see the need for a god and felt it was unlikely there was one. She seemed to be less atheistic than she used to be as she got older because after studying all the top thinkers she could find, she realized that although atheism might be the opposite of theism, they both had their own problems.

To hear Tegan tell it, atheism seemed to be a discipline critical of theism, but most of the arguments were aimed at a specific religious theology, and even if you could prove that theology wrong, you still would not have proven there is no god. She decided a better term for *atheism* was *a-religion*, but since that was not a term, she settled on *agnostic*, but preferred *freethinker* which she felt described her best since she despised the way that both theists and atheist pretended to be so certain about things they couldn't possibly know for sure.

Some people found it odd that she had never married, but Dr Consuelo found that made her even more intriguing since she did not feel compelled to conform to societal norms. She had dated an obscure and mysterious CIA agent for years, but they had never tied the knot.

When she picked up the phone, she was surprised and elated to find it was Dr Consuelo; she had not recognized the number since he called on his office phone.

'So glad you called,' she said. 'I was just thinking of you. I really enjoyed our retreat last weekend, and I really appreciated you taking me. I must admit that your discipline seems mundane sometimes, but there is an underlying mystery I can't deny.'

They had gone on an archaeological retreat the previous weekend, and while she was skeptical that she would find any interest in the topic, she had been surprised by the potential of archaeology to answer difficult questions about human history.

'Well, that's exactly why I'm calling,' he said. 'I know you sometimes pretend to be interested, but I have something that will really get you excited.'

'I'm not pretending,' Tegan said. 'The more I'm exposed, the more I'm intrigued.'

'I know you are,' Dr Consuelo said, 'and that's why I was hoping you would accompany me on this trip.'

Dr Consuelo jumped right into it and told her in almost breathless whispers about the find and his plans to travel to South Africa.

'Wait, where are you going?' she asked. 'To South Africa? Why?'

'Because I can't resist this mystery and I have to be there,' he blurted into the phone with childish excitement.

'Why would I go with you on a dig?' she queried. 'I said I was intrigued by archaeology, but I'm not interested in digging in the dirt with you.'

'No, that's just it,' Dr Consuelo said. 'I'm not doing any digging or examination for that matter. I'm just going to observe what I can while the manuscript is being examined in the mine.'

'So this is just a curiosity for you, or what?' she asked.

'Yes! I mean, no!' he again nearly shouted. 'I am professionally interested, but this will be an excellent adventure for both of us, and you must imagine the possibilities. Come on, get excited!'

The truth was that Tegan was kind of excited because of her great fondness for Dr Consuelo and the close friendship they shared. But she was confused about traveling halfway across the world for a find which they might not even be able to get near.

'Why do you care about going to the site when you probably won't even get near the damn thing?' she asked. 'Is this going to be another of your paranormal finds?'

Dr Consuelo chuckled because he could not hide anything from Tegan. She knew his reputation for being a para-archaeologist, and she was enthralled by the finds he had discovered with his colleagues that had led him to write his white paper.

'Look,' Dr Consuelo said, 'I only study things that are right in front of me, and I'm not like all the other sheep who won't talk about something just because they can't explain it.'

'Yes,' she said. 'I do know that, but I also know that you are determined to prove there is something there when most of your colleagues want to pretend it didn't happen,' she gently chided. 'Are you really intrigued by this on a professional level, or are you simply trying to restore your reputation? I know you have been less motivated since Manny's death, and getting your reputation back might be a great motivator.'

That one stung just a little bit. He assured Tegan it was not the case and that he did not care about his reputation anymore.

'I know I've told you this before, Tegan,' he said, 'but I just can't care about those things anymore. I have one driving motivator, and that is to find answers to these deep questions that have swirled around me since Manny's death. That is the only motivation I have in the unknown and mysterious, and that is what drives me to be curious about this. I can't bring myself to give a damn about my reputation, and I consider most of my colleagues to be sheeple who can't talk about what is right in front of them. I want answers, and I feel I can only get them in the mysterious. My world will never be the same with Manny gone, and I am driven by one question: what could possibly cause a world to be so cruel that even the most innocent are tortured and ultimately must die?'

Tegan was briefly silent on the other end of the line. She felt bad about even saying anything.

'I'm sorry I said that. I know you have been reeling since Manny was torn away from you, and you would be a robot if you weren't. I'm glad that you put it that way because I thought it was a desperate attempt for you to get back in the game, and I see now that your motivator is Manny, and I am touched by that.'

'Please, you don't ever need to be sorry. Listen, you know me and my passion for this kind of thing,' Dr Consuelo explained. 'I can glean information about this just by being there and observing the media and might even be able to see who the archaeological team is that is chosen to examine it. That will give me a lot of information that I couldn't get otherwise. Even if it's a whiff, I can always have a great trip to South Africa with my best buddy.'

'Well, you and I are of the same mind there, Dr Consuelo. I spend much of my time trying to figure out the exact questions you have, and I don't want to let some priest or preacher give me unsatisfying answers. I suppose it would be a nice trip, and I haven't been to South Africa again since I went on that hunting trip, so let's do this. It's not like my calendar is full,' she said with a laugh.

'That's the spirit, Dr Mallory!' Dr Consuelo said. 'I can expense this thing anyway and claim you as my assistant, so get your passport and jump on a plane, you crypto-hoarding atheist!' he teased.

Prior to departure, Dr Consuelo got an unexpected gift that confirmed the manuscript was real. The miner who had discovered the artefact, Ndinge Bwana, gave an interview to the *Daily Sun* newspaper that discussed the finding. The interview was not sensational, but it confirmed to Dr Consuelo that this artefact was indeed real. Ndinge had told of the bizarre way in which the artefact had been discovered, but Dr Consuelo noted closely that the newspaper had limited the description of the artefact to minimize the mysterious aspects of the manuscript. Dr Consuelo was not sure if the newspaper did that intentionally or if Ndinge was told to limit the information, but he decided he needed to contact Ndinge and have lunch with him if possible.

Chapter 7

Theodicy

As they sat for drinks prior to boarding the plane in Albuquerque for their long trip overseas, Tegan and Dr Consuelo reflected on the archaeological conference they had gone to several weekends prior. It was a blustery and rainy day, which was not all that common in New Mexico, and the plane was on an hour's delay, so they had some time to catch up. The entire bar seemed to be focused on some big sporting event on TV that did not interest them. Dr Consuelo had always been a sports fan, but his interest had waned in recent years due to other more obvious interests.

Dr Consuelo jokingly chided the waitress, 'Do you guys have a Mute button for all this noise? We can't even carry on a conversation.'

The waitress gave it right back to him though. 'Well, maybe having a quiet conversation in a bar wasn't your best choice. People love their college football, and you're not going to get them to pipe down.'

Dr Consuelo laughed and said, 'You won that exchange.'

The waitress smiled and walked away to get their drinks.

Dr Consuelo got his favorite whisky on the rocks, and Tegan got the same.

'Women like whisky too,' she said to Dr Consuelo in a very snarky attitude. 'I bet I could beat you in a whisky-tasting contest.'

'Well, I bet I could beat you in a whisky-drinking contest,' Dr Consuelo said, and she laughed so hard she snorted.

'No doubt you would beat me there,' she said through her snorts.

Looking around at the bar, they both noted that it had only gotten wilder since they arrived as the game was going into overtime. Glancing up at the TV, Dr Consuelo stated, 'I know you don't watch sports much, and I find it odd that I have sort of lost interest recently. I guess I watch the big events, but that's about it.'

'Yeah, sports seem rather mundane anymore to me. This may seem an odd question,' Tegan said, changing the subject, 'but I've been mulling this over a bit, and it almost seems like you were destined to be in archaeology, given your deep questions about this reality. Many people have lost a child, but I've never seen anyone react the way you have to your son's condition. I don't have children, and I know I can't relate to your loss on a deeper level, but it seems that many people who suffer a tragedy like that gain a deeper appreciation for their faith. How is it that it devastated your faith?'

'When Manny was first diagnosed,' Dr Consuelo said, 'I felt like I was going to lose my mind, and it is only in asking these existential questions without fear of retribution that I have been able to find a small level of solace in my thinking. Most people do find comfort in their faith, but I think it is more fear. If this god is willing to kill my son in that way, or at least not intervene to stop it, then he, she, or it can do the same thing to me. In fact, I think it is the fear of death that drives a great deal of religious thinking.

'Since Manny was so cruelly struck down, I think of it as the opposite. Who gives a shit what this god can do to me? He has already done worse to my child, and that eliminates the possibility that he is a good god. Maybe there is a god. I can't know, and neither can anyone else, but I know that he is not a "good" god, by any definition of good that we have. It also doesn't mean he is a bad god, but it feels bad from my perspective. So, the thinking of a religious mind suggests the following: since this feels bad, it must be done for my own good, and that is why God is still good. The reason I don't subscribe to that thinking is that "good" should also feel good.'

The waitress stopped by to drop off their drinks and remind them that this noise was only going to get worse.

'That's okay,' Dr Consuelo said. 'We've already tuned them out.'

She smiled as she walked away.

Turning back to Tegan, he continued, 'Most religions teach us that we are bad in some way and therefore deserving of death. I knew that to be a lie the minute that Manny received his death sentence. What could Manny have possibly done to deserve that? That's an absurd question, and yet religious people accept that teaching their whole lives. In a sense, they are created diseased and must go to the one that created them that way to get the cure. When you look at it in that light, it feels like abuse. If that is love, I shudder at what hate looks like. Sending me to hell for having thoughts is probably part of it.'

'Obviously, I agree with you,' Tegan said, 'because I find the whole teaching absurd. But what if God is just teaching us through all our pain and loss, like most religions teach?'

'Good question,' Dr Consuelo said. 'My response is that it makes him a monster. Let's put this in a domestic setting. Let's say you have a daughter whom you had through another marriage, and I come along into your life and marry you, and now I'm your daughter's stepdad. But it turns out that your daughter doesn't easily accept me, and I am rather controlling. I demand that she love me, just like God, and I also want to teach you a lesson, just like God.

'So, one day I take out a gun and shoot your daughter in the face because she won't agree to love me even though she supposedly has free will and can choose to love me or not. I take the one thing from you that you love the most because she refused to love me. Then I tell you it is for your own good. What are you going to think of me? Would you find me a loving and tender mate at that point? I don't think so. In fact, you would find me the vilest monster that ever lived, and with the exception of Hitler and a few of his pals, you would be right. If we don't accept that as "good" in our relationships, how can we find it "good" from our God? Religion teaches us we must love the thing we fear. This keeps us complacent and compliant.'

Tegan thought for a second. 'Wow,' she said, 'you are one fucked-up individual, and that's why I love you. I honestly think that is the best response you could have on Manny's behalf. Your love for him clearly shows through in that you are indignant as you should be despite the suggestion of religion that it puts you in harm's way. It shows how manipulable humanity is that the vast majority will accept that they are being blessed or taught a lesson when even their child is taken. What do we call that? Complacency?'

'Complacency is perfect,' Dr Consuelo said. 'And that is why I have to understand this in a different light. I can't understand the complacent mentality of taking abuse from the one who supposedly loves us, so I believe that religion paints a tainted picture of what our relationship is to God. If there is a God, our religions have not understood him in the proper light. Something else is going on, and I want to know what that is.'

Tegan nodded thoughtfully.

As they boarded the plane and took their seats, Tegan turned and looked deep into Dr Consuelo's eyes. 'I know how big your heart is, and I know you would never hurt anyone like that. Asking your God to have the same respect for us that you have for those you love is a very reasonable request, and I don't know why others can't see it that way. I guess that's why they call it blind faith.'

Dr Consuelo thought about that as he gazed out on the tarmac while the plane taxied down the runway. Why would anyone find comfort in blind faith? It should be obvious to humans that faith left them open to manipulation and manipulation left them open to control.

The rain was coming down hard now, and the splatter would soon be blown off the window as they picked up speed. Soon they would break above the clouds to bright sunshine, leaving this rare gloomy day in New Mexico behind.

As the plane lifted off into the sky, Tegan laid her head on Dr Consuelo's shoulder and closed her eyes. Understanding the deep pain that had driven him to question the nature of this reality deepened her resolve to find these answers as well, and she determined that she wanted to assist him in any way she could. Pain could often put people out of reach and could sometimes drive them apart, but she determined she wanted to understand more. Her agnosticism had come out of genuine inquiry. His came out of personal grief. Both were searching for answers that seemed to elude humanity and frustrate their existence.

Chapter 8

Seek and Ye Shall Find

'Part of my job as a professor is to help my students think and grow closer to the truth and not just learn. Archaeology is a discipline in search of that truth, and it carries an air of mystery, which is why I find it so fascinating. New finds can explain our existence and inform us of truths that we may not yet know. When your most basic beliefs and familiar ideologies are called into question, it is unsettling to observe how that revelation can destabilize and undermine your whole existence. We never realize just how comforted we are by the familiar beliefs we carry in our most treasured and private places, and we despise anyone who tries to undermine our familiar and comforting notions. When that hammock starts to rock, we get very defensive. Any questions?' Dr Consuelo had waited. Crickets as usual. 'Okay, you are set free.'

As Dr Consuelo floated across the sky with Tegan at his side, he thought back on the last monologue he had given his students at the end of class on Friday. The floating clouds outside, with their silvery reflection of the moon's rays, were quite beautiful, but his mind was too preoccupied to notice much. He wondered if his paradigm was about to shift even further than it had, and he imagined what secrets this manuscript might divulge. He wanted to gather all the information he could and had planned out the trip as best he could.

Dr Consuelo had managed to track down Ndinge Bwana with the help of some of Tegan's CIA contacts, and they had set up a coffee date to discuss the find in person. Ndinge had seemed nervous about discussing this further but agreed to meet Dr Consuelo if they could do so under somewhat clandestine circumstances. Dr Consuelo had understood and reassured Ndinge that they would be careful, but he knew this to mean that Ndinge had pressure applied to him from someone. Who would be pressuring him if there wasn't a genuine manuscript?

The remainder of the flight was uneventful. Upon arrival they found that South Africa was a beautiful country and came as advertised with heat and humidity to spare. The next day they arrived at the mine, and Dr Consuelo glanced around in amazement at the circus laid out before him. A literal media horde had descended on this small entrance to the mine that had apparently just become the center of the archaeological world. A tent had been erected for the media, and Dr Consuelo blended in as best he could. The heat was scorching and nearly unbearable, so they cozied up to a few of the media assembled to find some shade under their tent.

Beads of sweat dappled Dr Consuelo's upper lip as he removed his hat, brushed his hair back, and mused, 'Sure is a lot of media here.'

To which a journalist responded, 'Yeah, some big shot coming in to examine this thing apparently.'

Dr Consuelo tried to figure out who it was by keeping the journalist talking, but the guy was just the cameraman and did not really know the 411.

Rumors were rampant, and people were talking in hushed tones as they waited for the latest update from the mine, but Dr Consuelo would not have to wait long to identify who the masked scientist would be. A vehicle drove up after only a few more minutes, and to Dr Consuelo's amazement, Dr Guy Laliberte exited the vehicle, sending videographers and reporters into a frenzy as they grabbed their gear to record. Dr Consuelo had a myriad of emotions on his face when he saw this. Stunned, amused, perturbed, and outright flabbergasted, he just stared and then turned to Tegan with lips pursed.

'I knew it!' he said with a grimace. 'That asshole claimed he didn't think they were getting involved in this, but Cambridge is naturally going to be their first call.'

Dr Guy Laliberte was Dr Hawking's lead scientist at Cambridge and the preeminent archaeological scholar of his day, with impeccable credentials. Dr Hawking had feigned ignorance about the find, and Dr Consuelo was sure he knew all along that they were going to take the lead on this project.

Without a word, Dr Laliberte walked into the shabby mine's front entrance, and security parted to let him in. What was Dr Laliberte doing here?

As the preeminent archaeologist in the most prestigious institution in the field, Dr Laliberte would almost never travel to a site unless there was something momentous. Dr Consuelo knew that said a lot about what was going on here, and everybody knew it as well.

The media horde buzzed like a group of schoolgirls cooing over Tom Brady popping into their classroom. This really raised the stakes on what was going on here, and Dr Consuelo had to find out more.

He pulled out his phone and tried to FaceTime Dr Hawking, but he didn't have enough cell coverage for the call to go through. A text would have to suffice. He sent one to Dr Hawking: 'You, my friend, are a dick. You knew Laliberte was coming to the site, and you lied to me!'

'WTF! What are you talking about?' Hawking texted back.

Dr Consuelo could not believe that he was still playing dumb. He felt more ostracized than ever by this profession that he had previously sunk so much of his passion into. He even felt regret at that moment that he had worked such long hours while Manny was alive for a profession that refused to embrace him.

'I'm standing here at the entrance of the mine, and Dr Laliberte just arrived,' Dr Consuelo texted.

'Are you kidding me?' Hawking texted. 'You actually went to the site yourself? You are fucking insane! Why would you do that?'

'Of course I did,' Consuelo texted. 'I'm not going to miss out on this, and the fact that you lied to me and Laliberte himself is here proves that I'm onto something. I can never trust you again!'

Dr Hawking only sent back 'shoulders shrugged' and 'embarrassed face' emojis. Dr Consuelo put his phone away, disgusted at his colleague.

Dr Laliberte was now inside the mine and presumably traveling down to the site. It had not occurred to Dr Consuelo until now, but he wondered if it was a dangerous trip two miles down into the ground. That made it even more intriguing that Dr Laliberte was willing to do this.

Dr Laliberte was a serious-minded Frenchman who had become the chair of archaeology at Cambridge by meticulously following protocol. He had established guidelines that formed the basis for how archaeological finds were treated, almost like a crime scene, to protect the integrity of any find.

Dr Laliberte had a reputation for rarely traveling to a site since he had created the *chain of integrity* that had become the standard in the field. This process allowed complete integrity of the find from dig to institution and virtually eliminated the potential for hoaxes that often plagued the archaeological world. Maintaining the provenance of an artefact was crucial to its acceptance in the archaeological world, and Dr Laliberte was meticulous about accomplishing this goal.

Since this process was implemented, Dr Laliberte did not need to travel because he did not have to anymore and the *chain of integrity* assured that any finds that made their way to him could be confirmed as genuine through the verification process. But here he was, in the flesh, and the significance of this could not possibly be overstated since it essentially underlined the uniqueness of this artefact.

Dr Consuelo had met Dr Laliberte only once at a conference where they had a brief interaction, and Dr Laliberte had referred to him as his 'para-archaeologist' friend, so obviously, he carried a bit of a bias towards Dr Consuelo. His buddy Myles Hawking could not stop laughing about that one when he heard it. That did not bother Dr Consuelo at all though because he did not want the constraints of the academic world heavy on his shoulders the way they were on Dr Laliberte's. He would have been mad at him if he did not respect him so much. Besides, *Laliberte* meant *freedom*, which was Dr Consuelo's favorite word.

Dr Consuelo thought that most academics were too pinned down in their thinking, and that bored him silly. He needed the intriguing finds to keep him interested and distract him from the pain that chased him wherever he went.

After Dr Laliberte disappeared into the mine, the media dispersed to call their organizations and report this significant development, which seriously increased the import of this assignment. Most of them looked disappointed after their conversations however. Their managers were either clearly unimpressed or did not understand the importance of the development because they did not exactly run in these circles.

Dr Consuelo understood that archaeology was not the most interesting of topics since most people would rather get news on just about anything than hear about some earth-shattering archaeological find. His discipline moved at the pace of a stoner doing a Rubik's cube. Headlines could wait, and that was the first indication that the world might not care that much. Undeterred, the media horde pressed back around the entrance of the mine and called for an update.

A spokesman from the mine eventually came out and made the first attempt at quelling the interest in the find. It did not work. The spokesman tried to say that they did not have much information yet. Dr Laliberte had only arrived because they were having some trouble securing the site, which was two miles down the ground, and it took over half an hour to get through a series of trams and pulleys to finally arrive at the scene. It was also dangerous because there were some technical descents that made it more difficult, and they did not want Dr Laliberte to be hurt, so they were going very cautiously.

'Come on,' yelled a BBC reporter known for his antagonistic approach, 'that isn't going to fly. We know that Dr Laliberte almost never visits a dig since he is so proud of his chain of integrity that ensures a certain validity of the find,' he continued.

The spokesman put a finger to his lips and glared at the crowd of reporters. His comment almost belied his demeanor. 'I appreciate your skepticism, but I assure you, this is a routine development, and I will present Dr Laliberte to you just as soon as he is available. Maybe he can explain the events better than I can.'

At this Dr Consuelo folded his arms and stared around in amusement. Dr Consuelo had seen this many times, and he knew this find was taking on the pattern of just about every sensational archaeological dig, which was that the initial excitement was managed with some underling saying, 'It's not that big of a deal.' Next, the bigger names would confirm that by telling the media and all those interested that there had been some mistake, that led to a frenzy, and in the end it was overstated and not what it was thought to be. After all, how else could archaeologists convince the world that the Great Pyramid was just a tomb and built by slaves at the behest of some pharaoh some thousands of years ago?

Archaeology liked to examine finds outside the public light and the pressure that came with it, and they could always hide behind the integrity of the process, which allowed them to confiscate the finds and study them in peace. This also led to a lot of secrecy in the field and, in turn, led to a lot of conspiracy theories. Dr Consuelo was familiar with the process and knew that if he were to learn any more about this, it would have to come through his archaeological connections and colleagues.

Nonetheless, he stuck around to see the parade turn into a charade and observe the disappointed looks on the faces of the media personnel. Dr Consuelo was amazed that it took most of the day for this to occur because of the difficulty that Dr Laliberte and his entourage had in reaching the site. Or at least that was the story. At long last, Dr Laliberte and his entourage finally returned to the surface late in the evening and appeared quite exhausted from the day's events.

At the press conference, Dr Laliberte described the artefact as a weathered ancient manuscript written on some material akin to papyrus but admitted he wasn't sure of that because it was very thin. He deferred when asked his thoughts on how it got there. He also stated that it was too fragile to show reporters and that he would publish his findings after it had been more fully examined. Dr Consuelo was always amazed at how easily people could be convinced of the mundanity of a situation by listening to a so-called expert in the field debunk it, and they even feel silly for having believed something to be so extraordinary.

Dr Consuelo found himself quite amused at the press conference as he witnessed the process playing out again and the media finally dispersing the way they always had before. He nudged Tegan and noted that he wasn't surprised they didn't show the manuscript. It would have been impossible to contain the narrative if the media saw a glowing artefact perched on the table.

The BBC reporter wasn't having any of that and blurted out, 'You're not revealing the manuscript to the media? Why the bloody hell not?'

Dr Laliberte just stared back at him and calmly stated, 'I think I just answered that question.' Nobody objected further after that rather terse answer.

It was clear to Dr Consuelo that if something did not fit with people's experience, it only took an expert in the field to debunk the event, and people were suddenly infused with a confidence in their intelligence that made them feel silly for believing it was abnormal or even impossible. How silly could they be to believe that there was something magical found two miles down the ground?

'Look at that, Tegan,' Dr Consuelo said. 'Suddenly we have been turned from "believers" to "debunkers," and we are complicit in the cover-up without even knowing it. We are suddenly experts on the subject, and anyone who wants to suggest that something else was going on will be roundly mocked by our newfound brilliance.'

Tegan nodded. She may, or may not, have rolled her eyes a bit.

In this manner, experts could interpret things for us and present the world what they wanted it to see instead of confessing to any mystery or intrigue. Dr Consuelo knew that interpretations by so-called experts often left people vulnerable to scripted answers.

This had been repeated constantly in the field of archaeology, and many other sciences, and it was what allowed archaeology to proceed unobserved and at their own pace. Now that Dr Laliberte had effectively dashed the hopes and excitement of the media blitz, it would only be a matter of time before the curious onlookers faded away and he was free to examine the find with his colleagues. Dr Consuelo also knew it was not even a cover-up but simply a distraction until better answers could be found.

What about the individuals in the mine who observed any find? They could be dealt with by threats and suggestions as to losing their job or worse, and any who tried to publish this online or tell their friends would just be ostracized as being crazy or being a conspiracy theorist.

Dr Consuelo knew there was a lot more going on and hoped to hear more about it soon. He had come to this site because he thought for some reason it would be different this time. It had seemed like a very public find since it had been discovered by the public, even if the 'public' was a private mine. He had to concede he was wrong about that, and it did not even surprise him because this was very typical of how any find was handled if the public caught wind of the potential enormity of such a thing. This was also the reason why people only heard about such finds on late-night radio shows and from the office conspiracy theorists.

Dr Consuelo had realized that humans were like this. Humans had a herd mentality developed out of necessity that did not allow or encourage individual thought because humans must live and interact with their fellow humans. If one got too far off the reservation, other people would start to think of them as crazy. They would shame each other back into compliance. So people just accepted it, even if it seemed wrong. What else were they going to do?

Chapter 9

Incognito

The following morning, Tegan awoke in the hotel room alone. Dr Consuelo had gone out to meet with Ndinge Bwana for some investigative journalism of his own. She grew somewhat tense upon realizing how early he had left and wondered if the secrecy was not endangering him.

Dr Consuelo and Ndinge had agreed to meet at a local coffee joint outside of Johannesburg; it was discreet enough to put Ndinge at ease. It was a brisk early morning meeting as the sun had not yet peeked its head over the horizon, and Ndinge was even more paranoid than Dr Consuelo had thought. He would not shake his hand but asked Dr Consuelo to buy a couple of coffees and suggested they sit at separate tables and talk. Dr Consuelo suddenly felt like he was in a spy novel and set about to act surreptitiously.

The sleepy town where they met was not quite stirring yet, and the street was completely empty save for a biker or two who were on their way to early morning worksites.

'Are we being watched?' Dr Consuelo asked.

Ndinge confirmed that he suspected so.

Dr Consuelo ordered his drink and paid for Ndinge's, but he let Ndinge pick up his own drink for it to look like they weren't together. They seated themselves at opposite tables and made sure they were the only ones on the patio so they could speak without addressing each other.

'I really appreciate your willingness to talk,' Dr Consuelo said. 'I read your interview and noted that there wasn't much description of the manuscript,' he continued. 'Was that your choice, or were you told to keep it quiet?'

'That was not my choice,' Ndinge replied in his strong South African accent. 'I gave them nearly every detail, and they chose not to print the sensational findings I divulged.'

'So you weren't told to keep it quiet?' Dr Consuelo asked.

'No,' Ndinge said. 'I was not hushed by anyone, and I think the newspaper may have had pressure to keep it quiet. I am concerned about my safety and my family's safety, and I know if I share that with you, if anything happens to me, you can connect the dots. I held back on one piece of information about the find, and I wanted to meet with you to share it, but you must not tell anyone of this.'

'You have my highest confidentiality,' Dr Consuelo assured him.

'The artefact was levitating,' Ndinge almost blurted. It was obvious he had been holding this in and wanted to share this with Dr Consuelo.

'Levitating?' Dr Consuelo said, completely shocked. 'Are you sure about that?'

'Of course I'm sure,' Ndinge said. 'And please keep your voice down. We have pictures, and we had enough time to gaze on it to be sure that it wasn't held up by anything.'

'Pictures!' Dr Consuelo exclaimed. 'Can you share?'

'No, I cannot at this time,' Ndinge said, clearly not wanting to leave a trail to Dr Consuelo any further than he already had. 'Now I must go,' Ndinge said, and he departed abruptly, leaving Dr Consuelo with his cup of coffee and swirling thoughts in the predawn morning.

It was obvious that Ndinge felt he was in danger, but why had he shared the information with Dr Consuelo? Even as he asked the question, he knew the answer: Ndinge had studied Dr Consuelo's reputation and shared it with the only individual potentially involved with the artefact who he felt could keep his confidence and knew the stakes. This would serve as proof that he had discovered it and knew its characteristics.

He thanked Ndinge as he walked away dazed and confused at what he had just heard. Could this manuscript get any stranger? The first rays of the sun touched his face as it glanced over the horizon, and he could not quite wrap his head around this mysterious information. His excitement was slightly overshadowed by a sense of dread, and he summoned an Uber to get him back to the hotel as quickly as possible.

Chapter 10

Saved by Myles

Dr Consuelo was frustrated as he and Tegan returned to New Mexico. He did not feel like he had any shot at examining this thing since Cambridge wanted to isolate it and Ndinge was in danger for even talking about it.

They had discussed the encounter with Ndinge on the flight home. Tegan was concerned, but he made it clear that he did not care what kind of danger this put him in because he wanted to examine it regardless, even if it killed him. It was Ndinge he was worried about, and they had set up encrypted email accounts to communicate further if necessary. Ndinge had made it clear that he wanted the information out, and he wanted to communicate as little as possible, but he felt threatened by entities he would not divulge.

Dr Consuelo was busy moving forward with other projects, aware that he could no longer trust the Cambridge team to be straightforward with him and concerned for

Ndinge's safety. He felt that at this point it was better to let this elusive project go. He knew he was fooling himself, but he took a weekend off and went to the casino with Tegan to support her poker addiction.

This was a tiny little casino where Tegan thought the best poker in town was played, so he got some cash and tried to play with her. The atmosphere was dank since it was still a smoking casino, and the smoke was starting to get to him. Tegan barely noticed, and as usual, her pile of chips was growing while Dr Consuelo's was shrinking. He took a break and walked outside to clear his head. The night sky was brilliant, as it usually was in New Mexico, and he stared up into the sky hoping to see something like he had seen in his youth.

His phone chirped, and he grabbed it to see who could be texting him this late at night. To his shock, it was Myles, enquiring if he was awake still as he was up early and wanted to talk.

Dr Consuelo was surprised but rang him right away anyway.

'Myles,' he said. 'To what do I owe this pleasure?' he finished, trying his best to sound friendly despite his colleague's subtle deceit.

Myles apologized for texting so late. 'How are you? And how was your trip to South Africa?' he asked.

'Phenomenal,' Dr Consuelo said. 'We learned a lot by observing the circus and even had time to do some sightseeing before we returned. We really enjoyed the trip despite the lying asshole you've become.'

'Glad to hear it,' Myles said. 'I'm calling to make amends for my deceitfulness. You know about the manuscript now, and you also know that it was an intriguing find that we could not pass on, so I have an offer for you. We are preparing to examine this thing, and it has some rather interesting qualities that I will fill you in on as time goes on.'

'But,' he continued, 'we are inviting you and three other colleagues to observe the examination, which will allow you to be witnesses to the find and observe the qualities and contents of the artefact. Dr Laliberte has specifically requested you to be one of the observers, which should give you some insights on the strange aspects of it.'

Dr Consuelo was quiet for a moment and had to suppress the urge to celebrate. Then he mused, 'Are you saying that there are some traits of this find that will appear strange to mainstream archaeology? I can't imagine any other reason you would want us to observe the examination.'

'I think that's a fair statement,' Myles said. 'That strange glow isn't the only odd aspect of this find, and I'm sure you'll see what I mean soon.'

Dr Consuelo smiled as he heard this because he now knew more than he was letting on.

'As I said,' Myles continued, 'the fact that Dr Laliberte has specifically requested you on this video feed might give you some insight as to our concerns. We just need some witnesses to this process who can also function as consultants if we have any questions. I do apologize for misleading you, but I was told to keep you in the dark due to your reputation, but now we need your expertise.'

'I'm glad you finally came clean,' Dr Consuelo said. 'That also tells me all I need to know about the mystery of this manuscript, and I would love to be there.'

'Well, we can't have you come to Cambridge, or the press might catch wind of that, so that's why we decided to do a video feed where you can observe it remotely,' Dr Hawking said.

That was disappointing to hear because Dr Consuelo wanted to be in the room and part of the process, but he continued, 'Fair enough, but let me give you some advice. Do not touch this manuscript because I have seen some strange reactions from that. Do not touch it unless you are wearing gloves or using an instrument. This sounds like some manuscripts I've found in the field, and we have learned the hard way not to touch them without protection.'

'That was our instinct,' Dr Hawking replied. 'But I'm glad you confirmed that. We transported it out of the mine and to our labs without touching it for fear of damaging it, but your advice confirms that a reaction is possible, so we will take precautions.'

'Good,' Dr Consuelo said. 'I look forward to the examination.'

'One more thing,' Myles said. 'I want you to know how much I respect you as a scientist and a human being. You have been dealt a cruel blow in this life, and you have also had to deal with some strange artefacts in your career. You never shy away from speaking the truth, and I respect you immensely for that. We are mainly teasing you when we refer to you as a hyphenated scientist, but make no mistake, we appreciate your expertise on this issue and willingness to examine all aspects of science and intrigue.'

'Very kind of you to say, Dr Hawking,' Dr Consuelo said. 'I am genuinely touched by that comment, and it warms me to the tips of my toes. Now go make me proud and examine this thing without fear of it or the criticism that may follow.'

'Will do, my friend,' he said, and they hung up.

Dr Consuelo rushed back into the casino to inform Tegan of the good news. That phone call had left him feeling vindicated in so many ways, and he chuckled as he thought of how these archaeological superstars were having to come back to him and ask for his help. Dr Hawking had always been a good friend, and his comments were kind and reassuring that he was on the right path. Pretending something did not happen and ignoring it was no way to conduct a scientific investigation; in fact, it was the opposite of science.

Tegan was looking uncomfortable in her chair, and Dr Consuelo was surprised to see that her chip stack had suffered since he had left.

'Guess what?' he queried excitedly.

'I know what,' Tegan said. 'My chips are down since my good luck charm left. How could you abandon me like that?' she asked.

'Sorry,' he said. 'I had to clear my head of all this smoke.'

He went on to inform her of the phone call with Dr Hawking, and she was thrilled to hear it. She took a break herself so they could discuss further, and Dr Consuelo told her the details of the scheduled video examination.

He was not even that mad at Dr Hawking because he knew he was not allowed to involve him until the initial commotion had settled. Science was supposed to be about examining and explaining the world around us, and he felt that fit in with scientific enquiry unless one were so suppressed in their thinking that they could not come along.

'Well, that should put your fears to bed, Dr C,' Tegan said. 'Now can we get back to poker?'

Dr Consuelo chuckled at the poker addict, and they headed back to the poker table with Tegan determined to get her stacks back.

'I guess I've found the one thing that can distract you from all the mystery,' he said to the backslidden atheist.

Chapter 11

Seeing through a Glass Darkly

On the appointed day, the disciples gathered in their various offices to observe the unveiling of the heavenly manuscript. Well, these were not exactly disciples, but they were important nonetheless. Dr Consuelo found it more dramatic to think of it that way and chuckled to himself as he prepared for the unveiling. It was clear that without the consultation of Dr Consuelo and three other colleagues, the Cambridge team felt as if they were exposed and vulnerable, wading into unfamiliar territory.

It was 11:30 am London time, and he was in his office very early to prepare for the video feed and make sure the connection was in place. Sitting at his desk and sipping coffee, he began to imagine the possibilities to be explored and wondered about what could possibly be contained in the manuscript. The question lingered in his mind, and he even had a brief thought of adding a little whisky to his coffee to settle his nerves a bit. He was not afraid of the term *alcoholic*, but he decided not to anyway and opted for a clear mind instead.

His video was an open feed, and he could see a room being prepared for the examination. It had a table at the middle on which the artefact sat covered by an overturned box with a white handkerchief over the top. Preparations were being made, and there were five or six scientists getting ready for the examination. Dr Consuelo had decided to record the session, but when he attempted to do so, he realized that he could not, which was frustrating to him.

Dr Laliberte appeared on the screen and addressed the four colleagues on the video feed. He was wearing a lab coat and appeared calm and collected as he addressed his colleagues and those on the video feed.

'I see all my colleagues are present. I want to discuss the plans for the examination before we start. I plan to read the manuscript out loud for all to consider and then take questions after I have completed the examination. To say that this is a unique artefact is an understatement in the extreme. I believe all my colleagues on the video feed are aware that touching some of these manuscripts can lead to strange reactions, and while I am skeptical of that claim, I will be as cautious as I can to utilize gloves and instruments.

'I've already glanced at the first page, and I have something strange to report. I speak four languages, but my original language is French, and when I look at this, I see it in French. When an English speaker looks at it, they see it in English. Whoever reads this will see it in their native language, and that fact alone is baffling. I will do my best to translate it into English since my colleagues are mostly English speakers, but that fact alone means there may be something lost in translation although I will do my best. Any questions before we start?' Dr Laliberte asked.

Surprisingly, there were none.

With that he pulled the covering off and lifted the box, exposing the manuscript.

Dr Consuelo finally laid eyes on this most stunning artefact he had ever seen. The manuscript had a split screen via video, one a close-up and one a cutaway. Dr Consuelo noted that it was levitating just like Ndinge had said it had been in the cave. The ever-present purple glow was confusing and eerie given the lack of power source. The tablet was gleaming metallic, and no real signs of weathering could be seen from his view. He felt almost ethereal as he observed the stunning artefact laid out on the table, and Dr Laliberte eyed it warily.

Suddenly Dr Consuelo had to ask, 'Excuse me, Dr Laliberte. I do have one question.'

'Of course,' Dr Laliberte said as he seated himself in front of the manuscript.

'Is that thing levitating?' Dr Consuelo asked.

'Yes, it is,' Dr Laliberte said. 'It is one of the reasons I ended up taking so long to come out of the mine that day. I had to downplay that and a lot of things to the media.'

'Astounding,' Dr Consuelo said. 'Sorry for interrupting, please proceed.'

Dr Laliberte seated himself in front of this oddity and began to read the manuscript . . .

> What you are reading is an illicit manuscript of data that is not intended for you, and the simple act of reading it is a crime against humanity. I implore you to put this manuscript away and never return to it because in it are some secrets of humankind that should never be divulged and will potentially devastate society and humanity. You are only in possession of these documents through some accident of history, and you were never intended to see this information. Hopefully, much of this manuscript is degraded and missing by this point because it was never meant for you; it was written to hide it from my society.
>
> In our technologically advanced society, all information must be publicly available because we deem it safer for all. That makes it impossible to keep secrets, and I need this to be a secret for

my plan to work, not because it is nefarious, but because it is beneficial. We have placed this data in this manuscript to keep it inaccessible to my civilization and to yours. If anyone comes into possession of this information, it would have made it impossible to implement my plan and manage the entire earth. I am the managing overlord of the entire earth, placed here by my society to implement change.

I have been stationed here to manage humanity and humankind and attempt to control this rogue society. Believe me, it is not fun, and I do not say that proudly. Humans, it turns out, are some of the more dysfunctional and confusing intelligences we have cloned into existence, and my job is exceedingly difficult because of this. My name is not important for this manuscript, and my title is Vice Chancellor of Milky Way, Quadrant IV.

Our assignment here on earth, and in the Milky Way in general, is to control the population. Specifically, we must find a way to manage the local populations to care for themselves and develop their own societies for self-preservation and for our benefit. A tough assignment indeed, given the proclivities of humans to do nothing and ask for everything.

My problem is that I have developed what appears to be a perfect system for our human-derived dilemma of getting the local populations to manage and motivate themselves. Humans are not the smartest animals ever cloned, and in some cases, we have destroyed their intellect intentionally, and they sometimes act against their own best interests, so our job is to focus them on a purpose that will motivate them to do what we need and produce what we require...

The reading suddenly stopped. Dr Consuelo jumped out of his chair and paced the floor with one eye on the video feed. His pulse was racing, and his heart was pumping as he tried to gather his thoughts. He could see the team at Cambridge bent over this manuscript that Dr Laliberte had been reading, and they seemed to be very hesitant.

Dr Consuelo could not believe what he was seeing, and this manuscript continued to impress. Even more intriguing right now were the contents of the manuscript, and he was confused by what he was hearing over the video feed. Dr Laliberte had started to read the manuscript in French, but he quickly caught himself and translated it to English for the observers. Indeed, what was this manuscript, and what incredible information did it seem to possess? Vice Chancellor of the Milky Way? What the hell was this even talking about?

He called the lab rather breathlessly to ask what went wrong. The team still looked huddled over the artefact and were talking to each other, but he could not hear any audio.

'What is going on over there?' he asked when Dr Hawking answered the phone.

'They can't seem to get the first page turned,' Dr Hawking replied. 'The document is on some super-flimsy, almost-metallic papyrus, which makes it extremely delicate, so they are trying to tease the first few pages apart and not even sure they can do so without damaging the manuscript. It complicates things when we are afraid to even touch it. This stuff is like nothing we have seen before, and it has a translucency to it that makes the pages of the King James Bible look thick!' he nearly yelled.

'And what the hell is this thing talking about?' Dr Consuelo nearly yelled himself. 'I can't believe what this manuscript is saying. Are you hearing this?'

'Of course I'm hearing this,' Dr Hawking replied. 'We're all hearing it, and we're on the edge of our seats here as well. But we are being careful, and we have a job to do. There will be time for more reflection on that later. Any thoughts on teasing these pages apart? We have our methods, but they don't seem to be working so well on this one.'

'Sorry,' Dr Consuelo said. 'I let my excitement get the best of me. I agree, and I am glad you're being careful. I'll call my colleagues at Yale. They have some papyrus experts that have done amazing things with some of the toughest manuscripts I've seen.'

'Great, let me know,' Dr Hawking replied. And with that, they hung up and got back to work.

With one eye on the video, he called up his Yale colleague and discussed the find in as generic of terms as possible. They discussed some techniques common to the process, but nothing specifically useful was exchanged.

'How did you get on this project?' his Yale colleague asked.

'I have some expertise in the area of strange artefacts, so they wanted my input.' Realizing that he was now the expert instead of the kook, he added, 'As you know, I'm one of the few archaeologists who have been willing to look openly at these strange finds, and there is no way they can proceed on this without our expertise.'

Suddenly, and without warning, the video feed shut off completely, and Dr Consuelo was left confused and panicked as he hung up the phone. He quickly rang Dr Hawking back to find out the problem. Internet down? Dr Hawking did not answer, and his call went straight to voice mail, which was even more confounding.

Dr Hawking always answered his phone, and it sounded as if his phone was shut off at the worst time possible. The video feed was an important part of the integrity of the find. It was supposed to be uninterrupted so that, if necessary, their archaeological colleagues could be shown the unedited video of what occurred when the find was opened and interpreted.

He needed all the information available to be able to give his input, and right now he knew he was being marginalized and kept in the dark. There was nothing he could do about it now, but he had to find a way to get access to what was now being withheld, intentionally or not.

In a way, he knew that they only had two choices: either bury this completely so that nobody ever saw it or bring in other colleagues who could help explain this mysterious find. He knew they had cut the feed too because they no longer wanted to share, but he was desperate to find out more. Why would they cut the feed when they had invited him to observe the process?

This information had to make it out to the public because the divulgence of such revelation was earth-shattering. An overlord hiding information in a manuscript so he could hide it from his society and our society? Humanity had been left to consider the possibility we were alone, and it might turn out that humans were not only not alone, but also that they might have never been alone since they were cloned and controlled by a group of overlords. That sounded like crazy talk, and yet this artefact had the provenance and properties that could not possibly be faked.

Maybe Manny's disease and death were just a by-product of their shitty cloning process and was not specifically aimed at him or Manny. This was both good and bad. It meant that he did not have to be angry at God for these tragedies, but it also meant that humans were not as regal and important as they thought they were. They were all dead on arrival, and that was how the plan had been from the beginning. It was not wrath that killed Manny but apathy.

Chapter 12

Magic

There was more than a week of radio silence following the video disaster. Dr Consuelo heard nothing about the manuscript at all, and the mystery surrounding the document grew even further. He could not even call the other colleagues that were on the video feed because he had been kept in the dark as to who they were. Myles would not answer his phone calls or emails, and he had no idea what was being done with the artefact and why the feed had been cut off.

He had to do something, and Dr Consuelo could not take it any longer, so he tried calling Myles Hawking again. He was thrilled when he finally picked up.

'Good day, old chum,' Dr Hawking said. 'I haven't heard from you in nearly two weeks.'

'Well, no shit you haven't,' Dr Consuelo said. 'I tried to call you after the video feed went down, and you didn't answer, so I was kind of confused. All my follow-up calls were never answered either.'

Apparently, there was a huge surge when Dr Laliberte had touched the manuscript as he was trying to turn the page, and all electronics in the vicinity were fried. Dr Hawking patiently explained that due to the electronic failure, he was unable to receive his calls and assured Dr Consuelo that he was not avoiding him but that there was no way to stay in touch.

That kind of made sense because Dr Consuelo remembered that it had gone straight to voice mail, which was also strange.

'Well, why didn't you answer my follow-up calls?' Dr Consuelo enquired. 'Come on, Myles. I probably called ten times in the last week alone, and I've sent you multiple emails. You are just AWOL.'

'Yeah, sorry,' Dr Hawking replied. 'I've had a bloody tough week, and things have been bonkers here. You did hear that Dr Laliberte is dead, right?'

'What?' Dr Consuelo caught himself as he almost screamed into the phone. 'I haven't heard anything! What happened? How is that possible?' he said, his voice heavy with incredulity.

'Suicide,' Dr Hawking said.

'Suicide?' Dr Consuelo demanded. What had happened? Why would Dr Laliberte commit suicide? He felt that same odd sensation creep back into him just like it had the day he watched the reading of the transcript.

'Yeah, it was extremely shocking,' Myles said. 'We just don't know what was going on. We remain simply gobsmacked by the whole turn of events and are mourning the loss of our dear colleague.'

Myles went on to explain the entire confusing sequence of events.

After he had touched the manuscript and the incredible surge of electricity, Dr Laliberte had appeared to be in a trance except that he had been looking around him as if he were seeing something that was invisible to the rest of the team. After some time, he had sat down and stared straight ahead, and the team observing him had been stunned to see that his eyes had been completely blackened, including the entire sclera. None of them had known what to do, and there had been panic in the room.

Eventually, Dr Laliberte had stood straight up and started talking in a monotone voice with words that had sounded like gibberish. After some time, they had figured out that he had been speaking in French, his original language, but his monotone recital of the content had left his French-speaking colleagues confused.

One of the staff in the room had grabbed him to shake him and amazingly got the same reaction. Fortunately, his reaction had seemed short-lived, and after he'd come out of it, he had confided that it had felt like a rush of information coming into his head and he could not stop it. Dr Laliberte, however, had seemed stuck in this trancelike state with words pouring out of his lips in a foreign language that only his French-speaking colleagues could understand.

The room had been simply stunned, and they'd continued to yell at each other, attempting to offer assistance. Dr Laliberte's eyes had remained completely blackened, and nobody had dared touch him for fear of the reaction. The power failure had suggested an incredible power coming from the manuscript, and no one had had any clue how to proceed.

The observers in the room had not been sure if that had been demonic or electrical, but whatever it had been, it had been unstoppable. This reaction had been not at all familiar to the participants, and they'd all trembled as they'd watched the poor scientist drone on in his confusion. They had also noticed that the manuscript itself had become a blank page, almost as if the data on the manuscript had jumped onto Dr Laliberte and left the manuscript. Even the purplish glow had disappeared.

They had finally gathered themselves and sent a young research assistant for help since they couldn't call the authorities. Campus security had arrived to help, and eventually the police, but the local emergency personnel had had no better ideas how to proceed than the others had.

Dr Laliberte had literally stood in one place for an hour or more, reciting some sort of information that nobody could fully piece together, almost like he had been reading an audiobook or watching a video. Then, suddenly, he had started walking. The team had followed him closely, including Dr Myles Hawking, fearful for their colleague, but nobody had wanted to stop him.

He had left the lab and proceeded down to the train station where he normally commuted from his home in London. As they'd observed him walking up to the platform, they had assumed he must be getting ready to head back home, but as the train had come roaring into the station, he had jumped in front of it and killed himself. His colleagues and the others in the train station had reacted in horror and leapt into action in complete panic, but in the end, there had been nothing they could do.

Dr Hawking took it especially hard because he was a dear friend of Dr Laliberte, and he felt a responsibility to keep him safe, but he had failed. The police should have arrested him for his own protection, but how were they going to stop him if nobody else could?

Nobody had any answers, and all they could do was to finally return to the lab and carefully package up the manuscript so that everybody else was protected from the madness of what was contained in the find. To their continued bewilderment, all the writing had come back on the manuscript, and the purplish glow had also returned.

Dr Consuelo was flabbergasted and did not know what to say at first.

'I am so sorry to hear that,' he said as he began to regret his confrontational attitude. 'I had no idea, and I can see why you didn't really want to talk about it. It just sounded like an incredible find, and I was stunned that you wouldn't respond. I didn't know what to do.'

Dr Laliberte was on top of his world, and Dr Consuelo knew there was no way he would have committed suicide under normal circumstances. Could the strange manuscript have contributed?

Finally, Dr Hawking replied, 'Clearly the manuscript is more dangerous than we could have ever imagined and if we had only taken you more seriously and brought you to the examination, I believe it would have turned out different.' He continued, 'But I can't really talk further until we have more information. The university has sequestered it, and that's all I can say at the moment.'

'Don't shut me out, Myles!' Dr Consuelo pleaded. 'I might be able to offer some information that might help, and you know that manuscript has to be examined. Let me come out to help,' he nearly pleaded.

'I'm no longer in control of this process,' Myles said. 'My head is still spinning so bloody fast over this whole thing that I couldn't make a decision if I were in charge. I agree with you that the contents we heard were so fascinating that I'm hopeful we can find a way to investigate further, but I don't even know if there are plans to do so. All this discussion of being an overlord and his efforts to manipulate and control humanity are confusing in the extreme.'

'Exactly,' Dr Consuelo said. 'I can be on the next plane out of here, and I know I can assist in performing the process safely.'

It seemed apparent that Dr Laliberte had become permanently 'disabled' by this trance and took the only way out that he could identify. Why hadn't they contacted him? Why hadn't they read his white paper? They could have known what to do, and now the examination went from complicated to tragic. Why else would they not have told him of the untimely passing of Dr Laliberte? They needed his help, and ironically, Dr Laliberte had marginalized him when he was the very one who might have been able to save his life.

'Sorry, mate,' Myles said. 'There's nothing I can do to make that happen right now.' And that was all he would say.

'Well, at least assure me that you will make every effort to get this manuscript deciphered,' Dr Consuelo said. 'We can't lose this opportunity.'

Myles assured him he would do whatever he could to help, but the defeat in his voice was concerning.

Dr Consuelo informed Myles of his thoughts after watching the video. They discussed the potential ramifications of such a find and agreed that the manuscript had the ability to alter how humanity viewed their existence in ways they could not even imagine. If there were a group of overlords who had cloned humans into existence, then humanity appeared to be a commodity that was a manipulated species kept in the dark for the benefit of their overlords.

The best way to enslave someone is if they were not even aware of it. Humanity had created all sorts of narratives as to their existence, but none of those had hinted that humans might be serfs in their own world with little control over their own lives. Those concepts could have huge ramifications for religions, science, philosophy, and all aspects of life.

Dr Hawking agreed wholeheartedly with that sentiment, and he said so.

Dr Consuelo was glad to hear that and concluded with, 'Be safe, my friend,' and they hung up.

Dr Consuelo was alone again with his thoughts, and his thoughts were swimming. The manuscript now carried the weight of being a dangerous endeavor that had to be undertaken, and he was not sure they should let that genie out again.

The data sitting in the manuscript had the ability to interact with human beings in a manner he could not explain, and it had the feel of some deep spiritual mystery, which he felt to be paranormal. In fact, he was not sure if this was something paranormal or something spiritual, and it suddenly dawned on him that there might not be much difference between the two.

What was considered spiritual was also considered *mysterious* and *ethereal*, *holy* and *sacred*, and it didn't seem that different from paranormal suddenly, which also appeared *unexplained* and *secretive*. All of life seemed to work this way to him, as if there really was some wizard behind the curtain pulling the strings to keep humanity in the dark.

Dr Consuelo thought these events probably appeared so foreign to primitive humanity that they had to call it *God* or *heavenly* because it appeared to be a god to them but might have just been advanced technology, and they did not have the words to describe it any other way. As Arthur C. Clarke put it, 'Any sufficiently advanced technology is indistinguishable from magic.'

Maybe these revelations from God were the pagan gods of the day that they worshipped because they were visible. Of course, he did not even know if he believed the pagan gods were real either, so he had to admit he was ill-equipped to make the necessary distinction between the two. This life was so confusing, and the stakes seemed so high, but the fact that humans seemed to be intentionally left bewildered was never lost on him.

Humans were told they existed for a higher purpose, and yet a large part of their experience here on earth was suffering, loss, and ultimate death. He did not like to think this way, but if humans were loved by a God who counted the hairs on their heads, wouldn't they have a better existence? Whether he was an atheist or a theist, he felt like he was missing something, and neither position really explained the full picture of what humans experienced on earth.

Maybe religions just developed naturally out of humans' experience with revelations and interactions with these godlike creatures. In a world where humans had little inspiration and were fearful of darkness and death, maybe they latched on to what they thought was a god to show people the way.

Chapter 13

Freethinkers

'The meaning of life is a difficult and incessant question that pretty much all of humanity deals with at multiple points throughout their life. The question always lingers and seems to pop up in our thinking from time to time but is never something that seems to be answered satisfactorily enough to put our minds at ease. It often seems that this question is most considered during times of tragedy or difficulty because, for some reason, we consider it most when life is least satisfying. Almost as if we want to know if it is all worth the pain and agony that we are experiencing at the time.

'That's why archaeology matters, my intrepid students.'

There was silence in the classroom. Crickets.

'Any questions?' Dr Consuelo asked.

Crickets again.

'Okay, you are set free,' he said at last, and there was a mad dash for the door.

Dr Consuelo had almost given up on life's meaning because, in some small way, he had begun to wonder if there was, in fact, no meaning to life. Not in any official way. Religions never really taught people the meaning of life, preferring to lay down rules and guidelines for getting to the afterlife—and for giving them money. Dr Consuelo thought of religion these days as voluntary enslavement because they did not set one free; they enslaved them further.

Many months had passed since the video examination of the manuscript, and Dr Laliberte had long since been laid to rest. Dusk was approaching, and Dr Consuelo was considering these not-so-trivial thoughts as he charged across campus to his office, deep in thought about the very question and the scheduled meeting he was going to have. His childhood priest, Father Lujan, had set up this meeting and was going to meet him in his office with none other than the archbishop of the region.

It was the first day of classes after the Christmas break, and it was a bitterly cold day in Albuquerque, with snowflakes falling gently and more to be expected soon. Albuquerque got some winter weather occasionally, but this winter had been especially frigid, and the Sandia Mountains loomed large against the backdrop of the gathering clouds threatening to swallow them up. The campus was mostly barren, as many students either did not want to come out in the cold or had not made it back from their Christmas break by now.

Dr Consuelo was excited about the proposed meeting. He had called Tegan almost immediately after Father Lujan had called him, and she was going to meet him at his office shortly. He had wanted her present at the meeting to serve as another set of eyes and ears and because he valued her counseling.

Dr Consuelo arrived at his office, unlocked the door, and shook the cold off along with the few flakes of snow gathering on his scarf. As he settled into his desk, he decided to put on a pot of coffee to perk him up for his meeting and warm him on this blustery afternoon. Father Lujan didn't say what the exact purpose of the meeting was, but Dr Consuelo was pretty sure it had something to do with the manuscript, and he was excited.

Father Andrew Willow was the archbishop of the ecclesiastical province that included New Mexico, Arizona, and parts of Texas. Dr Consuelo had not met him yet, but he thought him to be of decent character as he had read up on him. As the coffee pot percolated to life, he began to fixate on the topic that had filled his mind while dodging snowflakes.

He had a small, uneasy feeling that it was possible the church was going to try to thwart the examination due to the revelation that this was some overlord speaking like he was a god. He did not think it was likely, but he was concerned that they might try because of how it might undermine their views on theology.

His cell phone rang, disrupting his thought process. It was Tegan asking if he could let her in. Dr Consuelo had absent-mindedly locked the door on his way into the office since he was the only one there, and he rushed out to open the door for her.

'Sorry about that,' he said, 'not sure why I locked it.'

Tegan smiled and responded kindly, 'If I know you, you were deep in thought about something. I don't mind waiting even in the snow if it means I get to see you.'

Dr Consuelo flashed a big grin, and they hugged, after which he helped her out of her coat.

'How was the drive in?' Dr Consuelo asked.

Tegan responded that it had been fine and she had been assured that her Land Rover could handle anything that New Mexico could throw at her.

'There's a lot more snow up in Santa Fe anyway, so the drive got easier on the way down.'

'Well, I just brewed a fresh pot of coffee so we can warm up as we catch up,' Dr Consuelo said as he poured them both a fresh cup of joe.

'Still not using a Keurig, I see?' Tegan said. 'Do you have to be a contrarian on everything?'

'I'm afraid so,' Dr Consuelo said. 'Apparently, it's in my nature.'

'Well, I think you need to conform. Besides, you make your coffee so damn strong I'll be up all night,' she said.

'Oh, come now,' Dr Consuelo said, 'you love my coffee, and you know it works.'

She had to agree with that because it was good coffee. Dr Consuelo was a coffee snob just like he was a whiskey snob, and she adored him for it.

They retreated to his office, and Tegan wasted no time getting to the point.

'So,' she said, 'what's going on with this little meeting that I know you're excited to have?'

He grinned a sheepish grin, and his dimple flashed. It was clear that he felt quite flattered as well even if it was the church with which he had come to be at odds.

'As I mentioned on the phone, I'm sure it's about the manuscript, but I don't know exactly why they are discussing it with me. I'm dying to know more about it,' he said.

'As am I,' Tegan said. 'But that's also why I'm here. Someone has to look out for you, and I don't want the church using you so they can figure out how to cover this thing up.'

'That is the exact thing I was thinking about when you called me at the front door,' Dr Consuelo agreed. 'It's also why I wanted you here as well because you are my only ally on that front. I can't even discuss this with a single colleague. The church is so powerful, it's scary.'

'That's exactly the conversation we had at the airport,' she said. 'You made the statement "we have to love the thing we fear," and I thought that was a brilliant point that you made, but what exactly are you saying? What I mean is that I am a freethinker and have come to doubt the existence of God through logic and reason as opposed to a personal tragedy like you have, but you seem to still be struggling with the notion of God and what to do with that,' she finished.

'Right,' Dr Consuelo said. 'I don't really think I know for sure what I think, if I'm going to be honest. I proclaimed myself an atheist after Manny's death because that made the most sense to me since clearly prayers and belief did nothing for him so therefore there must not be a God. But after studying atheism, I've begun to realize that the reason some people are atheists is mainly that religions make no sense, and there's so much evil in the world. That minimizes atheism a bit, and I don't mean to, but often the absurdity of religion and the lack of evidence is what leads atheists to question the existence of God. Just because religion makes no sense doesn't mean you have proven that there is no God. That is a logical fallacy.

'It is also as much of a logical fallacy to proclaim there is no God as it is to proclaim there is a God because neither statement can be proven objectively, and that's why atheists and theists will always be at odds. Other things bother me about atheism as well. Most atheists are strict evolutionists, and while I know evolution to be true, I can't know where it started, and I have a real problem with something of the complexity of DNA just building itself out of spare Legos.

'If I'm going to look at this as objectively as possible, I just don't see how DNA can spontaneously develop in any circumstance, and as a result, I kind of think DNA must have been designed already by some manner we don't understand. Why would we think we could understand it? Why can't we look across the table at someone and admit that some answers were either hidden from us or can't ever be understood? A lot of evolutionists agree with that because of the complexity of DNA, and many evolutionists will cite panspermia as if it is some white paper a parascientist wrote to give it validity.'

Tegan laughed at that and said, 'I like what you did there.'

'Yeah,' Dr Consuelo said, 'and he was a pariah known as a parascientist because he had thoughts.'

Tegan did the old snort again and crossed her legs tighter just in case.

'They're guessing as much as I am,' Dr Consuelo continued, 'and, in truth, as much as all of us are. It isn't a valid hypothesis, and in the end, it's only a guess. The truth is, no one actually knows where DNA came from. Just like no one actually knows where God came from. Could one be a euphemism for the other? Maybe atheists and theists are looking for the same thing. Maybe it's all a rouse to keep serfs occupied while they are on this earth.

'Besides, concluding there is no God does nothing for me in attempting to understand the pain and suffering of humanity. So what if there is a God? I can't detect him myself, but maybe there is one. How to explain the existence of God with such evil and pain in our short, little lives? I really didn't know what to think of that until the manuscript exploration that revealed the contents on the video feed. Remember when you and I were out to dinner and I was describing the contents of the manuscript to you and the discussion of an "overlord"?'

'Yes,' Tegan said, 'and it sent chills up and down my spine.'

'Exactly,' Dr Consuelo replied. 'I got the same response when I first heard it. But as I was describing it to you, I started to think about it further, and in the days that have followed, I've allowed myself this thought experiment. What if this "overlord" is literally a slave owner and humans are his serfs? It sounds crazy when you first ask the question because people start to think you're nuts! But think it through. What if some society cloned us into existence to do something for them and that cloning is what our holy books call creation?

'As a slave owner, you would have no real control over the bad things that happen to people because all you can really do is manage your society without regard to how long they live or how good their life is. You might interact with your slaves by visiting and revealing yourself to them once in a while, but as time went on, that would become problematic because we, pathetic serfs, would always be begging for favors from our gods.

'The Bible describes God revealing himself to humanity, but that's kind of silly since a God would not do that for fear of confusing the issue and having one group claim they speak for God over another. The result would be chaos, kind of like what we see in our world now. Favoritism, racism, misogyny, sexism, wars, and all sorts of sectarian infighting would result because people would claim special knowledge of this God and one religion would think themselves better than another religion. Is this starting to sound familiar?

'But if you are a lowercased *god*, you don't care about that. You need your serfs to be compliant and function without you having to constantly help them, so you simply reveal yourself and inspire societies and religions and claim yourself to be a god, and now humanity can take it from there. And that is why we see what we see in this world.'

Tegan just sat there, seemingly transfixed by the unfolding realization of what Dr Consuelo was insinuating.

'What I'm suggesting is that our capitalized *God* might be a lowercased *god*, and religions might be the results of the interaction that these lowercased gods had with humanity. They have cloned humanity to live eighty or so years on this earth, and then they disappear, and that is why the UFO subject is considered above top secret, because they don't want us to know they exist. What better way to have slaves than if we don't know we are slaves or that they even exist? The overlords get what they need from our existence—and I still have not figured out what that is—and we never evolve enough to realize what is going on because we are too busy worshipping them as our monotheistic Gods.

'Manny's sickness and death were a natural result of their cloning processes to keep our lives short and not some result of sin that led to his disease, as if that were even possible. Humanity continues on in perpetuity, arguing who knows this God best and what they think we need to do to be in his favor and so we can obtain the ultimate carrot—heaven. Manipulation and mysticism, but we feel good about it because we call it religion.

'I get mad at God because Manny was killed, and people think I'm just a bad person because they have been brainwashed that God is good all the time. Natural disasters happen, and we assume God is punishing us because he is always good and so bad things happen to us because we are bad. Pandemics happen, and we blame each other for it and fight over what the cause of it is, and yet we never even consider that if there is a scary pandemic, it had to have come from God because he is managing his herd with death and disability. Humanity would naturally be blind to this and continue to carry on as if God loves us and protects us even though it is demonstrably not the case.'

'Okay,' Tegan said. 'I have a million questions, and you're blowing my mind right now, but isn't it depressing to look at it that way? Aren't you being a bit of a nihilist?'

'I don't see it that way. I think that ignoring this fact leaves humanity open to manipulation. You can't know where you're going if you don't know where you came from, and humanity needs to understand our existence more holistically. Believe it or not, I felt an incredible amount of guilt at Manny's death for a variety of reasons, but mostly because I failed as a father. I felt selfish for even bringing him into this world, as if that were a selfish act. That guilt was furthered by the church, who wanted to tell me that we serve a just God and that death and disease were necessary because we "live in a fallen world." Considering yourself a serf allows you to view it in its proper context and understand that life is mostly being done to you and not by you.

'Suddenly your worldview opens up into the realization that you are being treated exactly as a slave would be treated. What you can do about that is still to be determined, but at least you know that you don't have to beg for forgiveness from an entity that controlled, manipulated, and allowed your demise because they couldn't have it any other way. Humanity can't rid ourselves of our chains until we rid ourselves of the notion that we are carefully placed here by a loving God who protects us in every way possible. This God that religions worship may have some care for his cloned creatures, but ultimately, he has ensured our demise because otherwise we would break free at some point. They need to have us controlled, dumb, and scared because otherwise they risk losing their herd.'

Tegan was mute. Dr Consuelo searched for the Unmute button on this little slave friend of his, but he could not find one.

'Either you think I'm insane or you just can't respond,' Dr Consuelo said. 'So I guess I'll let you mull it over because I could go on all day and the clergy will be here shortly.'

'Oh, it's the latter,' Tegan said. 'I'm just stunned at how the more you talk about it, the more self-evident it becomes. Theists believe all this is for their good because they see God as only good, but the truth is, they are afraid of this entity, as we all are on some level. Understanding our relationship to our overlords really puts it into perspective. Religions have no logic because they must make their narrative fit an unflattering reality, so believers continue to practice obedience, and for the most part, their lives are good, so they think they are being blessed by this "God".

'When life turns on you, some people abandon their faith and become atheists. The overlords don't mind that because what harm is it to them if someone believes they don't exist? That's what they want us to think anyway. We live our lives while fighting amongst each other and never really find out the truth until we die. And that suits them just fine.'

'Precisely,' Dr Consuelo said. 'Now you're starting to see how this possibility opens up some understanding of our plight on this earth. The manuscript suggests that we have an overlord, and when you consider that, a lot of things begin to fall into place. I can't know fully what it says until we examine it more, but the point here is that this could create a whole new way of looking at our existence in light of being cloned as serfs.'

'Wow,' Tegan said. 'That is fascinating to consider. That seems so evil to just clone people without their consent and enslave them on their own planet. Doesn't that seem evil to you?'

'I don't think of it as evil even though it feels evil to us humans,' Dr Consuelo responded. 'We've always known of the possibility of other civilizations in this massive universe we live in. At some point there is going to be an advanced civilization that develops technologically and is capable of interstellar flight and advanced cloning techniques, and they would naturally want to expand and explore. Maybe there were resources on this planet they needed and the best way to harvest those resources was with clones placed on this planet to do the work.

'That's not evil except to the poor souls who are those clones. I believe our fate on this planet is horrendous, but from their perspective, it was just progress. I imagine they didn't even care to think beyond that because we just don't matter that much to them. Isn't that what we do with our livestock? Just manage them and one day eat them? I don't think we are going to be eaten, but we are going to die. Reality may be harsh, but it is reality nonetheless. Manny has taught me that, and now I need to see more of that manuscript regardless of the contents.'

'Absolutely! I am more driven now than ever,' Tegan replied. 'And while I want you to be safe, I am determined that we will do all in our power to make sure that happens.'

Dr Consuelo could not help it and gave her a wry smile. 'I'm thrilled to have you on my side, my friend.'

They both smiled at that thought.

'I don't think I've told you about the latest though,' he said. He had held back on this news until now, but he now informed Tegan of the conversation he had with Dr Hawking and the untimely death of Dr Laliberte.

The color drained from Tegan's face, and she gasped in horror. She was quiet for a moment and then asked, 'Do you think it had anything to do with the manuscript?' even though she already knew the answer.

'We all know it was a direct result of the manuscript,' Dr Consuelo said. 'Myles pretty much said that, but we all know it did, and that is why this meeting is so important. In some ways, the stakes couldn't be higher.'

Chapter 14

Men in Dresses

Darkness had set in, and the storm had intensified slightly as they discussed their viewpoints and sipped their coffee. The wind was picking up, and they would have rather been at Dr Consuelo's cabin in Taos with a cozy fire burning in the woodstove, but this was an important meeting, and they were both filled with anticipation.

'Isn't it crazy where life takes you?' Dr Consuelo mused to Tegan as they waited for their guests who were a few minutes late. 'I was just telling my class about that last week, and they all stared blankly at me as I wrapped the class up. They rarely have anything to say about my concluding monologues.'

'Well, of course, they don't,' Tegan replied. 'They haven't experienced enough of life to respond. To them, you sound like a crazy old man, and they may not be totally wrong.'

'Yeah, but—' he started to respond, and then Tegan cut him off.

'I find that odd,' she said.

'What? That life changes?' Dr Consuelo asked.

'No,' Tegan said, chuckling. 'Obviously, I know that life changes because I'm even older than you. I'm on a different thought. It seems odd that the church always gets to be involved in this examination of the manuscript or anything mysterious. Why is it their business to be involved in what should only be a scientific endeavor?'

'Oh, you know the church,' he said. 'They are able to somehow get access to all sorts of halls of power and insert themselves into nearly every aspect of our lives. I actually suspected that they might get involved with this because they always get called in when demonic forces are at work,' he mocked.

They both marveled at the way religions were so adept at gaining power and privilege in a world that should be mostly run by more humanistic organizations at this point in history. Religious power had seemed to increase over time despite the Renaissance and philosophical advances. In fact, religion sat in power with nearly every government in the world. The ones who claimed to be secular were only secular in their constitution but were still clearly influenced by religious power. The crusades notwithstanding, religions did not even need to fight for their power because it was handed to them with the notion that they spoke for God. He who controlled the past did, indeed, control the present.

'Who knows though,' Dr Consuelo said, 'maybe they're just coming to save my everlasting soul!' and he laughed with his deep, infectious laugh that always warmed Tegan when she heard it.

She was happy to hear this as it had been missing from Dr Consuelo in recent years. She realized that as she watched the levity return to Dr Consuelo's demeanor, the prospect of the manuscript exploration and the contents it contained had the potential to set his mind free, even if it did seem to undermine free will.

She had kept it to herself, but the contents of the manuscript so far had given her a strange feeling with the talk of an overlord, which made her feel uneasy. She had always jealously guarded her free will because she clung to the notion that she could think and act for herself with total autonomy. This talk of the manuscript made her wonder if it was not just an illusion, and she wondered if humanity was simply a cloned and manipulated society, like Dr Consuelo had just suggested.

'Do you think humanity has free will?' Tegan said, seemingly out of the blue.

Dr Consuelo looked at her thoughtfully, finding it interesting that she would ask that right now. As he pondered this thought, the front office door swung open, and in blew two guests in full-on priestly attire. Tegan and

Dr Consuelo rushed out of Dr Consuelo's office to assist them and were quite amused to observe the scene.

Before them stood two men in priestly robes, one brown and one black with a red sash, with beads and bonnets completely askew and snow in every crevice possible. Dr Consuelo had always found it funny how church officials played dress-up with skirts and beads, which somehow inferred importance to the laity. He just thought it made them look silly.

Father Lujan and Archbishop Willow looked almost bewildered as they struggled out of their overcoats and shook the snow out of their vestments.

'That's what you get for wearing dresses out in a storm,' Dr Consuelo observed sarcastically. 'I'm sorry about the weather, but I had no idea it was going to be this bad.'

'That's okay,' Father Lujan said chuckling. 'We were the ones who scheduled the appointment, so it's on us, but it's great to see you, old friend.'

'It sure is,' Dr Consuelo retorted. 'I haven't seen you in far too long, and I hope we have a chance to catch up.'

'I sure hope so too,' Father Lujan said. 'We have some important business to talk through, so that might have to wait.'

Dr Consuelo introduced himself to Father Willow and presented Dr Mallory to them both. They chuckled a bit about the snowstorm and the freezing cold men in dresses, and they marveled at how the priests had decided to come to them instead of meeting on their turf.

'We didn't want you coming to us anyway,' Archbishop Willow said. 'This meeting has some sensitive issues attached to it, and we wouldn't want other priests or parishioners asking questions, so we decided to come to you.'

'Why the official attire?' Dr Consuelo asked. 'Seems rather conspicuous when you're trying to be inconspicuous.'

'That's a fair point,' Father Lujan said. 'But we are on official church business, so we have to wear our priestly garb in those situations.'

Rules, Tegan thought to herself. *Religion and rules. Where do they get all these silly rules, and why do they follow them? It is not like someone is always watching them on video and will strike them dead if they do not follow the rules, and yet they are so frightened by the idea of breaking a rule that they obey them even when nobody is watching.* Religious control was incredible to witness and was clearly a phenomenal way to control slaves without strings.

'Official business,' Dr Consuelo said. 'Come on, you know I've disappeared from the church, how am I official business? You flatter me, good sir,' he said in his best British accent. 'I'm guessing this official business must have something to do with a certain manuscript that seems to have disappeared from the scientific community?' Dr Consuelo asked.

'I figured you would have guessed that,' Father Lujan said. 'It's not like it could be anything church-related, since I never see you at church anymore,' he chided.

Dr Consuelo smirked and said, 'And that surprises you?'

To which Father Lujan could only smile and shake his head.

Dr Consuelo liked Father Lujan a great deal, and he had read some about the archbishop. He considered them both decent characters except that they represented the religion he had come to think of as an unyielding monster.

'I know the church's teachings torture you since the loss of young Manny,' Father Lujan said. 'But the church will welcome you back with open arms,' he assured.

'Enough about that, Dr Consuelo. Whether you go to church or not is between you and your God, but we are here to discuss the manuscript, as you have properly deduced,' Archbishop Willow offered with a wry smile. 'I see you're a man of some levity, and I can appreciate that more than you know. I think we in the clergy take ourselves way too seriously, and I like to be a little more laid-back, especially when it comes to this attire.'

'Well, keep your skirt on,' Dr Consuelo replied. 'I don't mind it at all even though it seems a bit misguided, but if it's the manuscript, then let's get to it.'

'Fair enough,' the archbishop said. 'We have been told of a miraculous find in the gold mines of South Africa, and we also know you have been involved in the investigation at some level. It has some interest to the church since they seem to be always meddling in everyone's affairs.'

Dr Consuelo was starting to like the archbishop as he had a nice mannerism about him, and he seemed to be somewhat self-deprecating. Or perhaps church-deprecating?

'I know about it and have done some consultation on it, but I have been shut out and am on the outside now,' Dr Consuelo retorted, hoping to lead them on to hear what they knew. 'Why? What has got the church's panties in such a knot?'

The archbishop ignored the continued jab and said, 'It's simply curious that we have heard about the find and then not much more. One of the scientists has come to the Vatican though to suggest that the find is not only important but concerning.'

'Concerning how?' Dr. Consuelo inquired. He wanted to play his cards close to his chest until he knew what the church's angle was.

'Well,' Father Lujan chimed in, 'we know about as little as you do, but it seems there are some strange writings that are detrimental to the church.'

'I don't care, and I don't think it is their business,' Dr Consuelo replied. 'A scientific document should be examined regardless of who is concerned.'

'Yes, but this might be confusing to many Bible scholars and to the Vatican,' Father Lujan said.

'Well, do what you always do,' Dr Consuelo said. 'Baffle them with bullshit, and say it isn't true.'

'Look,' the archbishop said, leaning forward just a bit. 'It is quite clear that you have had your problems with the church, but we are concerned that the manuscript that was found is so miraculous as to call the very Bible into question.'

'I don't care what consternation the examination causes for anyone,' Dr Consuelo said. 'I just care that the examination proceeds without interference. Why do humans try to explain things away before we even find out what they are? Oh yeah, we're slaves, and we let people tell us what to think.' He smiled at Tegan, and she could not help but smile back.

Father Willow paused and then continued, 'Well, that's just it,' he said. 'The Vatican has proposed that we proceed with this investigation, and they would like you to do it if you are willing. Cambridge has given up on this relic and has transferred it to our possession.'

Dr Consuelo sat back in his chair, folded his arms, and stared at the two men in dresses in front of him, lips pursed. He was pissed that Cambridge had given up on the artefact, but if he was being honest with himself, he had suspected that might happen. Myles all but conceded that. Cambridge was in way over their heads and refused to open their minds.

'Forgive me,' Tegan said, interrupting the conversation. 'Why is it that you have chosen Dr Consuelo to examine this? Doesn't the church have their own specialists who can examine finds like this?'

'That is the key question,' Archbishop Willow said. 'And the answer is a bit difficult. No one is willing to study this manuscript because of the effect it had on Dr Laliberte when he examined it.'

'So it was the manuscript that made him kill himself,' Dr Consuelo said thoughtfully. 'And that's why no one is willing to examine it?'

'It is possible that the manuscript played some part in it,' Archbishop Willow conceded. 'But we don't think that it is dangerous if you have the proper setting and plans in place to protect you.'

Tegan could not believe what she was hearing. 'Are you suggesting that because some holy men of God are going to be there, you can protect Dr Consuelo from the same fate? Your organization may view yourselves as all-powerful, but there are some mysteries that even the church doesn't fully understand, and I think your suggestion that you can protect him from the same fate comes off a bit disingenuous when no one at the Vatican is even willing to examine this thing.'

'No,' the archbishop said bluntly. 'We know that Dr Consuelo is a scientist who has realized that there is a legitimate mystery going on. He has studied it when no one else was willing to look at it, and his scientific protocol will carry him through this process because he is prepared, not because we claim to speak for God.'

'I appreciate your statement, Father Willow,' Dr Consuelo said. 'But there is a huge problem with the church being in possession of this because no scientific organization would ever consider the examination legitimate.'

'The church genuinely understands your position, Dr Consuelo,' the archbishop said. 'And even though you are right about the perceived lack of impartiality of the church, the Vatican has asserted that they will study this as objectively as they can and consider the contents freely and openly.'

'You can say that all you want, Fathers, but you must know that with the church being in possession of this, it removes all appearances of objectivity. You two know that I have serious doubts about my faith and God himself, right? Why would I want to examine this with the church involved? What possible chance is there for science to take this seriously after that?' Dr Consuelo said rather beseechingly while searching the eyes of the two clergymen for any understanding.

'I understand your concern, and I have doubts about God myself,' Archbishop Willow said. 'And so do more people than you know, but our personal feelings should have no bearing on the importance of this matter. God, religion, faith, and life in general may rely more on the inspiration provided by religion than you know. Nobody, despite how strongly opinionated they are, goes to their deathbed with absolute certainty about what lies beyond. Nobody, despite how much they read, can state with certainty how life started and where we all came from. Throughout history, at least the history that we humans are aware of, we have never seen civilization progress in the way that it has since God was discovered and religion was instituted. Say what you want about religion, and say what you want about God, but we need them both to survive as a species.'

'Nice monologue,' Dr Consuelo said. 'But what you really mean is you need religion and God to survive. It seems to me that the only people that benefit from God are the clergy themselves. You inflict fear and exploit the impoverished to enrich the church. You shame people to make yourselves feel more pious and powerful. You love to proceed with your pomp and circumstance and your silly rituals wherein untold millions get wasted on your various silly outfits and gaudy places of worship while masses of people live in poverty and starvation. There is no overstating how wealthy and propped up the church has become at the expense of others, and I haven't even mentioned child molestation!'

The two clergy members winced a little bit at that comment, but they did not respond.

'And,' Dr Consuelo continued after a beat or two, 'I can't think of an emptier institution than one who has no answer for horrendous and torturous birth defects or the parent damaged irreparably by the loss of a child, and you often compound that loss by coercing more money out of the parents and exploiting their pain for your gain to get their child out of an imaginary place called Limbo.'

'And,' he almost whispered, 'your God is either incompetent or uncaring, and your religion is useless when people have to face these kinds of evils. What do you have to say about that, Fathers? What do you say about that?'

Archbishop Willow hung his head, and Father Lujan knew to shut his mouth.

Finally, the archbishop spoke as he looked at Dr Consuelo with a tenderness that seemed genuine.

'I am truly sorry for your loss, young man. I find it difficult to respond, and I am humbled by your pain. There can be no doubt that anyone who suffers a loss such as that deserves to question the benevolence of a god, whether he has a lowercased *g* or an uppercased *G*. Clearly, these unprovoked attacks from someone or somewhere outside our perceivable dimensions always has the potential for knocking us off our base.

'Furthermore, I am sorry for the empty words of the church and the ways in which we have no new answers, and we do not and cannot possibly come up with any new answers. Our answers are inadequate, and for many people, the hope that we offer is inadequate or, worse, empty. We claim that our God is fully revealed so there is no possible way for us to come up with more answers, if I am going to be honest. You may be surprised to hear an old man who has spent his life serving God say this, but I often think you may be right, and religion may have outlived its usefulness, especially in this day and age.

'The harm we have brought throughout the Middle Ages and we continue to perpetrate today almost seems immeasurable, and yet we continue to spout our benefits as if none of it had happened. The promises that we spout about a God who has done all things well are empty to a damaged spirit such as yours. The pain we shrug off as part of God's plan. The way we call our job "service" to our parishioners while they are the ones who are serving us with untold amounts of money. The Vatican is a Taj Mahal like no other, and yet we have the gall to call what we do service. Can we be forgiven? I'm not sure. Can you forgive us? I hope so.'

With that he said no more. Dr Consuelo waited, but he still said nothing. Father Lujan glanced at Father Willow out of the corner of his eye, but he remained silent. Dr Consuelo wondered if his eyes were not somewhat glassy with tears forming.

He had thought that Father Willow was going to continue to explain how the church was actually good because most clergy would acknowledge the bad but still defend the church as good. Archbishop Willow had wondered out loud whether that was the case, and Dr Consuelo was quite impressed, although a little confused.

Apparently, Archbishop Willow really got it, and this really touched him. Dr Consuelo thought deeply.

'Unprovoked attacks from someone or somewhere outside our perceivable dimensions?' What is he talking about?

Is he going to blame it on the devil, like some old and tired explanation, or is he referring to the manuscript that seemed to come from another dimension? Dr Consuelo was not sure, but he liked how open and honest the archbishop was, and he warmed to him even more.

Finally, after some silence, Dr Consuelo offered, 'I do get how some people are comforted by the church and their faith and how going to church gives them meaning, but what they see as comfort only comes from participating in a ritual. But if it's not real and there is no intervening God, it seems like false hope and more harm than good.'

'Exactly,' Father Lujan retorted. 'So let's do what you think church people rarely do. Let's go see where the evidence leads.'

Dr Consuelo's head nodded up and down, slowly and rhythmically. He was impressed at the two men of the cloth who had listened respectfully to their skeptical complaints about religion and had reacted calmly and patiently. He did not know what the truth was, and neither did anybody, but at least the clergy had listened to them, and now they were willing to study this manuscript with unknown contents even though they might be damaging to the church.

Chapter 15

Laying the Groundwork

It was growing late in the little office where they were gathered to plan the examination of the artefact that had been so elusive up until this point. The snow continued to fall, but the wind seemed to have settled down some, and a sense of calm was settling over the group now that Dr Consuelo and Tegan had been able to air some of their concerns and grievances. They took a brief bathroom break and brewed some more coffee for the group. The priests were grateful for this as it seemed like it might be a long night.

Once the group had added appropriate levels of cream and sugar to their coffee and settled back into their chairs for discussion, Dr Consuelo grabbed his flask and added a little further flavor to his coffee. He wryly offered the rest of the group a shot, but all refused politely. The priests had a reputation to uphold, even if Dr Consuelo was sure they kept a flask in their dresses and imbibed when no one was looking.

'Then it's settled?' Father Lujan asked. 'We can accommodate you at the Vatican, and you will do the examination.'

Dr Consuelo was silent for a time, and then, lifting his head, he looked at the men in dresses and said, 'Well, gentleman, while I'm not brimming with confidence, I will say that I feel compelled to help in any way I can, and even though I'm aware that curiosity could kill, I must take a look. I feel in some ways like I have been prepped for this my whole life, and I can't—and won't—pass this opportunity up. Just don't expect me to wear a dress!'

They all laughed.

The archbishop spoke up, 'We are very appreciative that you are willing to do this, Dr Consuelo, since we are certain you are the only qualified individual willing to do this.'

'Thanks a lot,' Dr Consuelo said dryly. 'I don't know that anyone is quite qualified for this, but as I said, I will gladly help. As you know, I have been enthralled with this find from the beginning, and I won't shy away now.'

'Excellent,' Father Willow said. 'You have made the pope and all the clergy very happy with that response.'

'Thank you, Dr Consuelo. I am thrilled you are willing to do this,' Father Lujan added. 'And even though I know you're somewhat reluctant, don't forget that this may be the culmination of all your angst and confusion about your faith. This find might be something that gives you peace about who you are and why you are here. I haven't been able to counsel you more effectively, and perhaps some answers are waiting.'

Dr Consuelo knew he was right, but it was one thing to speculate and another thing to be faced with the revelation that might be awaiting.

'I have a couple of conditions that I hope you'll accept,' Dr Consuelo offered.

'Anything,' Archbishop Willow said.

'I would like to have a fellow of your choosing to assist me with this examination and preferably someone who is a priest but is open to these kinds of phenomena. He and I can make the plans necessary to save my ass if we need to,' Dr Consuelo said. 'And I would like my colleague here to be there as well.'

'I think we can accommodate you on both of those requests,' Archbishop Willow said. 'I have just the guy in mind who can assist, and Tegan will most certainly be there as well.'

They all thought Tegan seemed slightly hesitant as she smirked and gulped. She was thrilled at the prospect but had reservations that were very understandable.

'One more thing, I almost forgot,' Dr Consuelo said. 'I want my colleagues from Cambridge attending as well, specifically Dr Hawking, because he's been involved with this all along, and I'm still disgusted that the scientific community has given up on this.'

'Well, of course,' Father Lujan said. 'We will pay for his accommodations as well, and we will welcome more if you wish.'

'Excellent,' Dr Consuelo said. 'I'll get in touch with him and bring in his team, if he will allow it.'

Father Lujan and Archbishop Willow looked at each other and seemed pleased by the prospect of a scientific examination and at their success in convincing Dr Consuelo to perform the examination.

'I do have one more request,' Dr Consuelo said. 'And this one is a bit more contentious.'

'As I said, anything,' the archbishop said.

'Okay then,' Dr Consuelo said. 'I propose an in-depth analysis of the contents of the manuscript and, if Tegan and I can convince the clergy of the veracity of this manuscript, that the Vatican allows me to acquire this artefact for myself and the University of New Mexico so it can be studied as the scientific find that it is.'

Dr Riordan had told Dr Consuelo to keep the university out of this, but Dr Consuelo knew that was an idle threat and didn't care about keeping that promise.

Father Lujan seemed a bit taken aback at that, and he glanced at his archbishop again to gauge his reaction. The archbishop said nothing and had a poker face that was impressive to Tegan.

'I think we will have to lay some groundwork for that,' Father Lujan said then sighed. 'But I will address that with the pope, and I am sure he will consider it graciously.'

'I want to be part of that conversation,' Dr Consuelo said, 'but I am serious about that request and will likely consider backing out if it is not agreeable.'

'I am sure it will be agreeable,' the archbishop stated, 'but the devil is always in the details, and the Vatican likes their secret archives.'

'I know they like their archives,' Dr Consuelo said. 'How else can they fool their congregants without the secrets they keep?'

'I figured you would feel that way,' Father Lujan said, 'and it does seem fair that you have the opportunity to conscript this manuscript back into the scientific community. I assure you, we will get something worked out.'

Dr Consuelo glanced at Tegan, and they both smiled.

'That's all I can hope for, a chance,' he said. 'But I remain suspicious of the church and do not trust their objectivity in such matters.'

Chapter 16

Wine Bibbers

Dr Consuelo's driver pulled up to the Vatican, and he gazed in awe at the beautiful palace and associated city in front and around him. He had to admit that he was blown away by the magnificence. Even the front entrance was breathtaking, in a way that was almost indescribable. His driver had arrived at the entrance for most dignitaries and special guests of the Vatican, of which Dr Consuelo was surprised to find he was one.

'Check it out,' he said to Tegan. 'We are arriving at the location for important people.'

She smiled and gave him an exaggerated eye roll. 'Don't get used to it,' she said, and he knew she was right of course.

'They'll probably kick us out the back entrance if this doesn't go well,' he said.

'There's probably a trapdoor to hell,' Tegan added dryly.

Their vehicle had been let in through a massive gate and had arrived at the Swiss Guard Bronze Door, also known as the Portone di Bronzo, and while he did not know if this was the place where actual dignitaries were ushered into the Vatican, he felt pretty important by the extravagance and the attending Swiss Guards.

Dr Consuelo glanced at Father Lujan and widened his eyes as they stepped out of the vehicle in front of the Vatican. These columns of the front entrance were inspiring to observe all by themselves, and he could not imagine how they had put it together over the centuries. As he took in the sights in front of him, he was naturally impressed, but suddenly he felt a sense of dread as he realized how vast and powerful this organization was.

Opulence and power were plainly evident when gazing on the Vatican, and the Bronze Doors were massive displays of impenetrable luxury. What an astonishing place the Vatican was, and he was amazed at the thought of what humans could do if they worked together, even if it was in the name of religion. Perhaps that was the very thing that got them to work together, he wondered. After all, Dr Consuelo had come to think of religion as the perfect template of control.

The trio was met by their emissary, a young fellow named Francesco Bonifacio, named after another famous priest martyred in the 1940s and to whom he was related. Tegan followed shortly behind as she felt slightly uncomfortable in the chauvinistic sea of testosterone.

'Dr Consuelo, I presume,' Father Bonifacio said. 'Let me be the first to welcome you to Vatican City,' he said good-naturedly.

'Good evening, Father,' Dr Consuelo said. 'How very kind of you to greet us, and thank you for your kind welcome.'

Father Lujan greeted the priest with a kiss on the cheek, which seemed to be a traditional greeting, and informed him their trip had gone very smoothly, thanks to the wonderful planning of the Vatican organizers.

'Why don't I get greeted like that?' Dr Consuelo teased. 'Am I not part of the club?' He chuckled as he said it.

'This club is wide open, and we would love to have you,' Father Bonifacio said. 'Please know that you're always welcome.'

'How very kind of you to say,' Dr Consuelo said. 'Given the stunning beauty of this place, I may be tempted.'

'We do sort of live like royalty here in this Shangri-La,' Father Bonifacio said. 'But we are mere servants of the King and serving in his courts,' he finished.

Dr Consuelo held back the urge to scoff at that and instead offered, 'Well, I am sure the King is pleased with what has been built here.'

'We are truly honored to have you here, Dr Consuelo,' Father Bonifacio said, trying to change the subject. 'Would you like me to show you around?' he finished in perfect English.

'Good idea,' Father Lujan said. 'I am sure the whole of Vatican City is stunning, given how splendid this entrance is, and I am sure we will all be enthralled by what awaits.'

They both moved towards the front entrance.

'Where are my manners,' Father Lujan said. 'Please meet Dr Consuelo's esteemed colleague, Dr Tegan Mallory.'

Tegan sheepishly greeted Father Bonifacio.

'I guess you've saved the best for last,' Father Bonifacio observed. 'So wonderful to make your acquaintance, Dr Mallory,' he said to Tegan. 'Are you an archaeologist as well?'

'Very nice to meet you as well,' Tegan shyly responded. 'I'm afraid I'm not an archaeologist but just a lowly math professor,' she replied.

'Perish the thought,' Dr Consuelo said. 'Dr Mallory is a brilliant mathematician, my esteemed confidante and colleague, and easily the most brilliant person I know.'

Tegan smiled and blushed ever so slightly.

'I have no doubt about that. Now please allow me to welcome you all to our wonderful abode. How was your flight?' Father Bonifacio asked as they moved towards the entrance. 'I trust it was peaceful and restful?'

'Sure was,' Dr Consuelo said. 'I think I slept most of the way, and the flight was a bit of a blur.'

Dr Consuelo glanced at Father Lujan and laughed as he remembered the delays they had to put up with before leaving Albuquerque and the frustrations of the connector they had to run for at LaGuardia. It must have looked quite funny to see the three of them running for their connecting flight and barely making it in time. At least Father Lujan was not wearing his dress, which would have been hilarious for fellow travelers to observe. As it was, they were the last ones to board, and everyone stared in amusement as they breathlessly boarded their connector, Father Lujan in his clerical collar and Dr Consuelo feeling like he was in his underwear.

'I'm glad to hear it,' Father Bonifacio offered. 'Now follow me to your quarters, and I'll give you all a small tour on the way.'

As they entered, the Swiss Guards stepped aside and held up the unwieldy spears that they brandished at their security posts. It was never clear to Dr Consuelo why they carried those spears when more handy weapons like handguns had been invented. It was not like they would try to guard the palace with them because you couldn't exactly swing those axes effectively if someone was attacking you.

How would they ever drive away an attacker in their fancy colorful outfits, all puffy and overflowing, as they tried to fight off the onslaught with those fluffy feathers atop their helmets falling into their eyes? His irreverence notwithstanding, he could not help but be impressed even by the bright colors of the guards and especially the surrounding architecture.

As he stepped past the guards and into the vast structure before him, the splendor grew ever more impressive as he entered and found himself slack-jawed at the very sights in front of him. Column upon column all lit up splendidly as if on a movie set with statues and paintings fit for a museum, and they were not even in the Vatican Museum yet. He could only imagine the continued architecture he would see, and he found himself wild with anticipation that he was so fortunate to even be allowed in a place like this.

Tegan remained in the background as much as she could for all this, feeling somewhat out of place but finding herself enthralled by the ornate setting. She was at the seat of religious power and feeling very out of place since she had never belonged to any religion. It was difficult for her to be in this incredible opulence given the fact that it was built on the back of the faithful who, often, were quite poor but coerced into giving more to the already wealthy so they could get a better reward. She also tried to shut her own thoughts down and just enjoyed the experience and history of the Vatican, and she, too, was awe-inspired by what lay before her.

'Please, Dr Mallory,' Father Bonifacio said, noting that she had fallen behind, 'come up front with me as we explore this beautiful city with the prettiest flower in the lead.' He cajoled Tegan into taking the lead with him.

She seemed quite pleased by this and stepped forward into the lead with Father Bonifacio. Dr Consuelo was pleased by that move, and he wore a satisfied grin to show it.

Shortly after they stepped out onto St. Peter's Square and took in the vast plaza laid out before them like some ethereal nirvana. Dr Consuelo continued to find himself at a loss for words at the fulsomeness before him and the obelisk reaching to the heavens with a cross well placed at the top. He had seen this many times in pictures and on television, but while pictures might say a thousand words, it could not replace seeing it in real life.

'The Egyptian obelisk was built in 1586, and the Square was laid out beginning in 1656 so the pope could give his blessings directly to the greatest number of people possible,' Father Bonifacio said.

Dr Consuelo barely heard the words of the priest as he stared at the beautiful layout. The obelisk was framed by two fountains spewing majestically, and further out were Roman columns on either side surrounding the great square. The obelisk stood ornately in front of St. Peter's Basilica, and the decorative central dome dominating the skyline was awe-inspiring. Off in the distance were great statues of saints looking down on the scene, and Dr Consuelo wondered at the incredible sight. He wanted to remain, but Father Bonifacio kept them moving and continued with his tour.

'St. Peter's Basilica is the largest church in the world by interior measure,' Father Bonifacio said. They all were already impressed, so this titbit did nothing to sway them further. 'Michelangelo was one of the architects as well, and the church is very proud of that fact,' Father Bonifacio continued in his attempt to impress.

'Now you're just bragging,' Dr Consuelo said teasingly, and Father Bonifacio puffed out his chest in fake conceit.

Father Bonifacio continued to point out various interesting features of the Square as they walked across it and the various buildings just off the Square, but the most amazing part was that they were only seeing a tiny portion of the city and that the Vatican was a city. Hell, Dr Consuelo had found out that it was its own country. That fact seemed ridiculous and a testament to the true power of religion. The Vatican was the smallest country in the world, and it covered just over one hundred acres with something like only eight hundred occupants living in the entire heavenly abode.

And here was another fun fact that Tegan had read about on the plane before she fell asleep: Vatican City drank more wine per capita than any other country in the world. Dr Consuelo had found that fact quite interesting when she told him. Father Bonifacio did not mention that, of course, but he was droning on about something else as they walked, and it would have stuck with Dr Consuelo if he had been paying attention, but he was too impressed by all the magnificence around him. As they reached his quarters, Dr Consuelo had asked if there was a bar where he could get a drink.

He thought Father Bonifacio hesitated because he wasn't supposed to know, but then he responded, 'Yes, there is a bar in the basement right below us. Take that elevator down to the B-level, and it will be right there as you exit. It's called My Father's Place, which is where all the priests go. Get it?'

Dr Consuelo rolled his eyes. 'Yes, I get it,' he said, and he really did not think it was that funny.

They should have come up with a better name than that he thought, and it appeared that Father Lujan agreed. Father Bonifacio handed them keys to the room.

As he opened the door to his room, Dr Consuelo asked, 'You want to meet for a drink, Father Lujan? I've got some questions for you.'

Father Lujan nodded. 'Fifteen minutes,' he said. 'I'm just going to freshen up a bit, but I'll be right there.'

Turning to Tegan, Father Bonifacio said, 'And you will need to follow me to the female quarters, if you don't mind. For obvious reasons, we can't have you in the men's quarters, and I'm afraid to say that your room is not quite as impressive but still useful. Women are a rare sighting in Vatican City, and there aren't many here. Kind of funny how a religion that celebrates a Blessed Virgin can't seem to allow many women, but that's the way it is. What do we call that? Tradition, I believe.'

Tradition, hypocrisy, and ritual, Tegan thought.

From her perspective, most religions seemed misogynous and exclusive, but those seemed to shape a lot of what people did as humans. People did not even recognize how tradition rules their lives because it was built into them, and they marched around like automatons and rarely questioned their most sacred rituals and habits. Again, she reminded herself that she was here to learn and was happy to observe the local practices if it meant she got to have this experience.

Chapter 17

Propaganda

After cleaning up in his room, Dr Consuelo met Father Lujan at My Father's Place in the basement and ordered a whisky like he always did.

'Sorry, sir,' the bartender said, 'we only serve wine here.'

Dr Consuelo sighed and said, 'Okay, give me your finest merlot.'

Father Lujan ordered the same.

'I guess that's why they drink more wine per capita than any other country,' he said mostly to himself.

They sat in the corner and talked a bit about their flight and other topics for small talk. Dr Consuelo had been unable to convince Myles Hawking or anyone from Cambridge to attend the examination because they were adamant that they wanted nothing to do with it. It was frustrating and troubling to him that none of them would participate.

'One of the things that bother me about this artefact,' Dr Consuelo said, 'is that neither the church nor science really wants to look at this seriously, and I don't know if that is due to fear or because humanity wants to go on pretending that these things don't exist. I feel like this manuscript is the third rail of philosophies, and no one wants to be caught on that rail. We know that strange and unexplainable phenomena happen in our reality, and yet if someone sees something paranormal and wants to talk about it, everyone shrinks and pretends like the person is crazy.

'It is like we have this mass delusion, and we've all agreed that paranormal topics and artefacts are taboo. There seems to be an embargo on the truth. Why? I know the church thinks they have the whole truth, but the job of the church is to find God, and the job of science is to explore our universe, yet both seem to be closed off to this reality. Doesn't that seem like burying our heads in the sand instead of carrying on with scientific and theological exploration?'

'I suppose it does,' Father Lujan said. 'And I can see your point, but I think you know the answer to that yourself. Theologians think they know the truth already, and so any confusing subject is attributed to the mysteries of God and his inexplicable nature. At this moment in theological time, all religions that exist believe their God is fully revealed, and if he hasn't revealed something, there is no point looking for it because we believe, rightly or wrongly, this God interacts with humanity in that fashion.

'Science is wedded to strict materialism, and if something isn't reproducible and readily detectable, they will turn away for fear of ridicule, and that is the unfortunate reality that all of humanity faces at this time. I wish it weren't so myself because I think we are missing part of the picture, but humanity has always been prone to group-think.'

'Well said,' Dr Consuelo said. 'I understand that the unknown can be intimidating, but I don't think we are being true scientists if we don't look at all the incoming data and study all phenomena on this earth, and perhaps we are missing an obvious insight if we don't consider all data and information. I mean, viruses are invisible, and they come and go, and we study those incessantly.'

'Agreed,' Father Lujan said. 'And I say that knowing how this manuscript could erode my faith and undermine my worldview.'

Archbishop Willow had decided not to attend the examination either, and that had also troubled Dr Consuelo.

'Why didn't the archbishop join us for this trip?' Dr Consuelo asked.

Father Lujan had replied that he had asked permission to not attend, and the pope had allowed it since he did not feel his faith could sustain such a direct assault.

Dr Consuelo did remember that his faith was surprisingly vulnerable, it seemed, and he had never expected that from an archbishop. Then again, he had not met many.

'I do understand that talk of an overlord can be disconcerting to someone who worships God, but it's not entirely clear to me why that is. I've considered the implications of this on faith, but it is hard to understand how it would sound to a person of faith since I seem to have lost mine. Just because this overlord talks of managing society and has created this manuscript doesn't eliminate the possibility of your God and your faith being real. What exactly is it about this manuscript that could ruin someone's faith?'

'That has to do with the content of the manuscript,' Father Lujan replied. 'Given the miraculous nature of the manuscript and the contents inside, it seems to call some of the events of the Bible into question. We haven't been able to explore it fully, just like you haven't, but some of the archaeologists that observed Dr Laliberte have told us some of the strange content they heard flowing from his catatonic lips.'

Dr Consuelo looked confused. 'You mean like it was made up?' he said.

Father Lujan sipped his wine and shook his head. 'No, it's just that they may have happened for a different reason.'

Dr Consuelo didn't even know what that meant, but Father Lujan went on to explain.

'When Dr Laliberte initially touched the manuscript and got his reaction, there was one French-speaking gentleman in the group who was able to understand and translate some of what he was saying. It seems as if this manuscript was written by some overlord who could have been pretending to be God,' he said.

'Really? I guess that would change things,' Dr Consuelo said. 'Then who do you think this overlord is? I remember the initial video feed that I was able to observe talking about some "manager of the Milky Way Quadrant IV" or some crazy shit like that, but that was all I heard. Was he some demon or angel?'

Father Lujan shook his head again, mostly because he was not entirely sure, and said, 'It had seemed in the initial video feed of the transcription that this was some sort of a manager of society who might have tried to manipulate these people into being more autonomous, and that was all they could divine from the small piece of the manuscript that had been translated.'

Dr Consuelo already knew that, but he had to admit that the ramifications of that were far-reaching, and he had not fully considered what the church was concerned about, possibly because he already thought the Bible and his faith were complete lunacy.

'If this overlord, or manager, was manipulating these people to do what he wanted, did that mean that the entire Bible was manipulated?'

'No,' Father Lujan snorted. 'It just might mean that the Bible was written by humans and had some human input,' he said.

'What are you talking about?' Dr Consuelo said. 'Of course it was written by humans. Everybody knows that except for your parishioners, whom you have tried to fool as much as possible by telling them it was divinely inspired and written by God himself,' he said, growing frustrated.

'Of course it was written by humans,' Father Lujan said. 'We know that, but we also believe that it was inspired by God and directed by God, and this manuscript might sort of undermine that.'

Dr Consuelo was flabbergasted and hardly knew what to say. 'What the hell are you talking about?' he said again. 'You guys think that you can just rule the world through innuendo? You make some suggestions about the Bible, which was put together by the Council of Nicaea, artificially and at the request of the pope, and suggest that it was divinely inspired, and humans just take it from there.

'They tell their children, and those children tell their children, and pretty soon you have the world convinced that God himself wrote the Bible and to question it is to question God! Come to think of it, you have done a pretty good job of running the world through innuendo since the entire world hardly questions that premise. Let's suppose this manuscript does expose that it was written by humans. What would that change?'

Father Lujan thought about that question but offered no answer.

'It shouldn't change anything,' Dr Consuelo continued, answering his own question. 'Because the only reason you are concerned about that eventuality is that you have convinced everyone that the Bible was written by God himself, and you wield the power of that Bible to threaten your parishioners that if they question the "Word of God," it is out-and-out blasphemy. All the while, it is common knowledge that humans wrote the book, and you told the rest of the humans it was God-breathed in some sort of incredible marketing campaign.

'The truth is that the only reason humans don't laugh at most of the stories in the Bible is that they think it would be laughing at God himself. How else can a book that claims that a talking snake convinced us to disobey God and caused us to notice each other's private parts can gain any sort of serious consideration? Humans use it to claim to speak on behalf of God and gain the power associated with that. Once everybody buys in, you label anybody who doubts it as a heretic.

'The incredible thing about it is that the church has gained all their power through that one bit of propaganda, that God himself wrote the Bible. That's why throughout your reign of terror, you read it in Latin, a dead language that only the clergy understands, and interpret it according to your own needs. Now you're concerned that people might find out that humans wrote it. If your seat of power is that tenuous, I am stunned at how gullible humans are because that should never have been news to anybody. If the church is worried about that, that is tantamount to admitting that they have pulled the wool over the eyes of their parishioners.

'It makes me wonder if you guys are just floating this "God concept" because of the benefits it provides to you and not the benefit it provides to humans. I don't even think you guys care if God is real or not so long as people "believe" he is real. Your various cults get so much out of it—including money, power, influence, and control—and humans get the bill. But we call it tithing because that sounds like a voluntary thing. Why does God need the money anyway? Wouldn't humans be better off if we distributed this money directly to them instead of building this opulence for you guys? Am I missing something?'

Father Lujan was looking frustrated, and he let out a sigh. 'Yes, I think you are missing something, and that is that the church's position is slightly more nuanced than you want to portray. We do believe that God inspired the Bible, and that is our official position even though, as you point out, most people do view the Bible as coming straight from God. We believe that the Bible was inspired by God and that he chose individuals whom he ordained to write books of the Bible.

'Other than that, I understand what you are saying, and I am concerned about the tone of the manuscript. When the church outlines the characteristics of our God, we believe him to be entirely benevolent towards human beings. When this manuscript describes an overlord, the question of benevolence seems to be missing and possibly absent. This overlord seems to be acting for his own purposes and in a manner that is deceitful, and that causes concern amongst believers as you can imagine.'

Dr Consuelo was impressed. 'Well stated again,' he said. 'Where was this considerate theologian when I was grieving for my boy in therapy with you? You put that very well, and while I may not be the same believer I was, I can see your point on that. When you consider the actions of this overlord, it shifts the issue of motivation for the Bible from a benevolent source to a neutral and somewhat detached source and that appears manipulative. Almost evil. Why would an overlord do such a thing?' he wondered.

'I don't know,' Father Lujan said. 'But that is what has the church's panties in such a knot . . . as you would say. It's one thing to make people aware of the fact that humans wrote the Bible but an entirely different thing to divulge that some overlord was revealing himself as God, and the church is concerned that a revelation like this could be very damaging to humanity. And before you say it, damaging to the church as well. I can't be sure that the overlord is doing this in the manuscript, but I have an uneasy feeling.'

'Wow,' Dr Consuelo said. 'This manuscript keeps growing more mysterious and carries some serious consequences. I'm almost at a loss for words, and as you know, that is rare. I'm going to have to take some time to digest this.' He took a big gulp of his wine and ordered another one.

'Well, let me say something while you're thinking,' Father Lujan said. 'If you are going to touch that manuscript, I hope you have a plan, and I hope you hold nothing back for the sake of the church or anyone else. I care about you more than you know, Dr Consuelo, and I am extremely concerned for you while you investigate this manuscript. So be safe, have a plan, and in the end, share everything you find out because the truth is all that matters, and I know you will agree with me on that.'

And to that, Dr Consuelo nodded thoughtfully. He did agree, and he wasn't sure what was going to happen, but he had a somewhat solid plan if he got into trouble. Either way, the support and love of Father Lujan were comforting to him right now.

'Do you have any idea what you're going to do if you have a reaction like Dr Laliberte had?' Father Lujan queried. 'I'm really concerned about you, so tell me what you think can be done if anything goes awry.'

'I have some ideas,' Dr Consuelo said. 'And I'm going to discuss that more tonight over dinner, but mostly I am hopeful I can just read the manuscript without getting a reaction. I know that I'll have to touch it to turn the pages, but I plan to wear some thicker gloves than normal and even use tweezers and instruments to try and turn the pages.'

'Well, good,' Father Lujan said, 'but that doesn't answer my question.'

Dr Consuelo could only nod.

'Well, let's go meet some of the other priests who will be in attendance, and especially Father John Shelby, who the Vatican has chosen to be your associate on this matter,' Father Lujan said. 'I'm familiar with him, and I think you will like him a great deal. I've arranged dinner for you and him this evening so you can make your plans.'

Chapter 18

Gnosis

Dr Consuelo awoke with a start. He was in such a deep sleep that he had no idea where he was for a brief period. After all, how often do you get to wake up in the Vatican? He was never able to sleep well as he got into his fifties, and he was up early once again before dawn and before all his colleagues. Then again, it was not surprising that he was up early since this was the day that the manuscript examination was to be performed. He was at once filled with excitement and some dread as he looked forward to the process. What the day held in store, he was not entirely sure, but he knew it was going to be potentially life-changing. He had not been able to meet the pope yet, but he was aware that the pope knew he was going to examine it, and he had been told the pope would be in attendance. That alone was an indication of how serious the Vatican was taking this manuscript.

Rising from his bed, he stretched and yawned, trying to work out the kinks in his aging body. He was tense, undoubtedly, with the previous day's events and meeting many of the priests, including Father John Shelby, with whom he had dinner and who was going to be his cohort for the examination. Gazing around at his surroundings, he took in the opulence of his room, which matched the opulence of the Vatican. He pulled back the curtains in his majestic quarters fit for a king but only possible at the Vatican. He appreciated the respect he had been given, and the Vatican seemed to treat him as a guest of honor, which was hard to ignore.

It was more like a bribe, he thought at this moment, because it seemed they could not have gotten anybody to do what he was going to do for them. The Vatican was in a difficult spot without his services, and he felt a slight paranoia as he remembered the effect that the manuscript had on Dr Laliberte. Was he really going to do this? As he gazed out his window over the predawn peace of the Vatican Plaza, he tried to imagine what lay before him and what this day would bring.

He felt comforted in the growing light that flooded over the plaza. His thoughts drifted back to the manuscript that was waiting for him in the observation room. He still could not understand how these effects were even possible.

Dr Consuelo called down for some coffee but was told that the only coffee available was in his room at the moment.

He shrugged. 'Great, I've got to drink this sludge,' he grumbled and set out to brew some sort of caffeine-infused assistance, even though it was going to taste nastier than that old instant coffee his dad made when he was a kid.

As he sipped on the wretched brew, he felt the warmth enter his belly and decided that there were worse things to be drinking and worse places to be drinking it. He basked in the luxury that was all around him in this beautiful place and continued to settle his troubled mind.

Finishing his coffee, he took a brief morning walk on the predawn plaza and cherished the opulence one more time. He showered and met Tegan and Father Shelby in the breakfast hall, where they sat together for some sustenance greatly needed for the day's events. He had learned at dinner the night before that Father Shelby was the unofficial paranormal priest of the Vatican and the curator for all things odd. Father Shelby laughed as he recounted this to him because he came about it accidentally as he had been a bit naive about the subject, and he damn sure did not feel comfortable around these strange artefacts.

Father John Shelby was from England, and to hear him tell it, he was as confused as everybody else from his family and friends that he even considered becoming a priest. He was a wild lad who was never serious and got into loads of trouble growing up. He dabbled in a few types of drugs as a teenager, but in his young work life, he left them behind for the pubs of London whenever he was not working. Except for the more than occasional bumps of coke that he and his coworkers carried with them to keep their energy up.

He loved to frequent the pubs with all his mates and drag themselves from one pub to another, putting behind their grueling days. He was a stockbroker on the London Stock Exchange, and despite his young age, he was swimming in cash and had a very bright future.

Naturally, the strapping lad found one of the most beautiful women around and wooed her in a way like anyone who knew him thought he would. They had a whirlwind romance and a fairy-tale wedding and then rode off into the sunset. Until she ran off with another woman, leaving him with two young children.

He was despondent and, after his children were grown, did the thing he had never imagined he would and joined the clergy. Apparently, you can do that, at least if your wife ran off with another woman and you were no longer married. Dr Consuelo had thought that you had to be a virgin, but that was a silly notion. You just could not have sex after you were married to the church. Unless it was with other priests. Or young boys.

Father Shelby was a reluctant parapriest, just like Dr Consuelo was reluctant to carry his title, and they had both come across it accidentally. Father Shelby's experience was vastly different from Dr Consuelo's, and he was even kind of embarrassed to talk about it because when he did, he was mocked roundly by his fellow priests. He had made the mistake of telling them once, and now he was labeled for life.

He would not go into much detail for Dr Consuelo because he was still shy about it, but he genuinely thought this was an experience from God, and so he had joined the church, which was why he thought his fellow priests would appreciate his 'God' experience.

He was home late one night, and the children were asleep. He got this incredible urge to go out onto his sprawling backyard, and there was a UFO descending and landing on his lawn. He stood there in his backyard stupefied and not knowing what to think. He did not say he saw any aliens, but he got a clear telepathic message that he should join the clergy. So after his kids were grown, he did. He had never been spiritual up until that point, but he thought this was what he was supposed to do as he had been given a clear message by the UFO.

'I genuinely figured it was God,' Father Shelby said. 'So I shared it with my fellow priests later, and I had no idea how uncomfortably and strangely they would all react. People are almost unable to process these things it seems.'

Dr Consuelo knew it was genuine because people did not make this stuff up; in fact, it was embarrassing for most of them to talk about it because they were often mocked. After that experience, Father Shelby did not talk about it anymore, but he was open to the phenomenon as he told Dr Consuelo.

'You going to finish that doughnut?' he asked Dr Consuelo, who shot him an icy glance, pretending to be shocked.

'Of course I'm going to eat it,' Dr Consuelo retorted in mock offense. 'Keep your eyes on your own damn plate. Besides, the buffet table is right over there. Go get your own.'

Tegan laughed as he said it.

And with that, Father Shelby slunk away to the buffet, feigning humiliation. Returning with his own prized confection, he took a huge bite and gave a goofy grin with powdered sugar covering his mouth. They all had to laugh at that with the supposedly serious-minded man of God goofing off like a ten-year-old.

'You are such a clown,' Dr Consuelo said. 'I've barely met you yesterday, and I'd thought I had to be so serious when I came to the Vatican, but you're one of the bigger clowns I know. I sure appreciate the levity on a day like today,' he finished with a grin.

'Everybody thinks that about the Vatican and religion in general,' Father Shelby said. 'I don't know why because we're just people looking to understand God better, and there should be room for levity.'

'Are you kidding me?' Dr Consuelo shot back. 'You don't know why people think religion is serious? For all they know, you people speak for God and have the power to send them to hell. The church has always carried the power along with the state.'

Father Shelby shot a pensive glance at him and pretended to be deep in thought, then he nodded in agreement and said, 'I guess I just mean that it would be nice if we could all be more relaxed about the process.'

'Relaxed in this Taj Mahal?' Dr Consuelo asked. 'Who could be relaxed in this austere setting with opulence fit for a queen? Or the pope?'

'Good point again,' Father Shelby said. 'Remind me not to get involved in a debate with you, I'm starting to think I should listen to your theology after our discussion yesterday.'

'Nah,' Dr Consuelo said. 'I'm just saying I think people are pretty intimidated by the church because they perceive that they hold the power of the Almighty.'

'I agree,' Father Shelby said. 'I just want to be more accessible to the laity, and that perception makes it difficult. You laid out those concerns very well last night at dinner, and you do make some good points. That's why I'm so thankful I'm able to be involved in this examination today even though we are somewhat apprehensive at what we will find.'

'*Gnosis,*' Dr Consuelo said. 'I've heard that word used a lot in theological circles, and it simply means "knowledge,"' he continued. 'I'm so glad the church is willing to allow this examination because knowledge by itself is simply data that must be considered. Gnosis must be embraced if we are ever to understand this existence.'

Father Shelby nodded thoughtfully, and it was clear he was deep in thought, even if that pensive moment was betrayed by the powdered sugar adorning his upper lip.

After meeting Father Shelby the day before, they had discussed their plans for the manuscript examination and had an even longer discussion about all things theological over a lengthy dinner. Dr Consuelo had been immediately disarmed at how down-to-earth and approachable this man was and even more relieved when he had heard how open-minded he seemed to be. This seemed to be a guy he could get along with easily, and Father Shelby might even make Dr Consuelo rethink his distaste for priests and the church.

Tegan had not been part of the discussion, preferring to catch up on some sleep after the flight, but Dr Consuelo was really pleased with how well it had gone. She could tell that Father Shelby had put him at ease with his easygoing nature and affability.

Father Shelby had given Dr Consuelo an extended tour of the important parts of the Vatican to further plan their examination. Father Shelby had brought him to the Vatican broadcast room, where priests would broadcast to their flock, and they had agreed that if things got dire, Dr Consuelo would be ushered into this room where they could take a video of him and hopefully assuage the reaction.

But there was one more piece to the puzzle that had not been laid, and that was an escape route should the data overwhelm Dr Consuelo's senses. It had come to their attention, given their further research on the events surrounding Dr Laliberte's death, that he had seemed to be grasping for walls when he'd left the examination chamber, as if he could not see anything around him.

As a final route of escape, he and Father Shelby had agreed that if he should befall the same fate and could not see around him, they would string up a rope walkway for him to hold on to and follow through the studio chamber. Father Shelby had agreed to have security on standby to set that up if necessary. Since they were not sure if Dr Consuelo would be able to communicate anything, they had agreed the signal would be for Dr Consuelo to sit down on the floor as a way of indicating he did not know where to go. That was their final fail-safe to keep Dr Consuelo unharmed in any event.

That strategy had really helped Dr Consuelo to have a backup plan and set his mind at ease.

'Come to think of it,' Father Shelby had said, 'why don't we just have video equipment in the examination room?'

Dr Consuelo had reminded him that the initial examination had blown all the circuitry in the room and nothing electronic had functioned.

'Good point,' Father Shelby had said. 'This is our outlet in case of emergency. I'll still have a videographer in the room so we can capture some of the examination, but if it all blows, we will plan to come here. We will also have videographers placed outside the observatory and some at a safe distance if we have to utilize the fail-safe.'

Suddenly the room was abuzz with murmuring, and everyone rose from their seats as the pope himself entered the room, entourage in close pursuit, and made his way over to their table. They were quite stunned to see him in his gleaming white robe with his zucchetto perched perfectly on top of his head, and the entire room was enthralled as he approached their table.

All four of them rose, including Father Lujan, who had just joined, and Dr Consuelo almost looked giddy with anticipation as he rose to meet the pope. Perhaps he appeared more bewildered because he had not expected this great honor, and it showed on his face. Having the pope himself approach their table to meet them was indeed a confirmation of how important this day was to the Vatican, and this fact became noticeably clear upon his entrance.

The pope's assistant introduced Dr Consuelo first. They clasped hands, and the pope spoke quietly to Dr Consuelo in his perfect English.

'My son,' the pope said, 'it is wonderful to make your acquaintance, and I am most humbled by your willingness to examine this most mysterious of finds. Bless you for making the trip and your willingness to assist in this matter.'

Tegan thought she witnessed some color drain from Dr Consuelo's face as he suddenly realized there was no backing out of this now.

'Your Eminence,' he blurted, 'it is I who am honored to make your acquaintance and humbled to be asked such a high honor and heavy burden.' Then his face lightened. He smirked and said, 'Are you planning to attend the examination? I'm feeling enough pressure without the pope himself in attendance!'

The pope's shoulders bounced slightly as he chuckled at that comment. Dr Consuelo was a master at diffusing any situation, and Tegan was impressed with his skills, as she always had been.

'Perish the thought,' the pope said. 'Of course I'm going to be there, and that is why I have come by to meet you this morning. I want to be of assistance if possible, and we are here to assist you in any way we can. My prayers are for you, specifically today, and we have asked for God's protection on you. Please be at ease, and know we are here for support.'

At that Dr Consuelo lightened even more, and a full smile broke out on his face. 'Thank you, Your Eminence. That means a great deal, and I am comforted by your presence.'

Dr Consuelo then turned and introduced the remainder of the table to the pope. Father Shelby greeted him politely as he already knew the pope well, and Father Lujan gushed like a schoolgirl as his lifelong dream came true of meeting the Vicar of Christ.

Dr Consuelo then introduced Tegan as 'the atheist' of the group, and she could have smacked him, but the pope only chuckled and replied, 'You may not believe in God, my daughter, but I know he believes in you. Besides, I've heard that Dr Consuelo has his doubts as well, so I'm hoping we can all learn something more this day.' He winked at Tegan as he said this, which she found quite charming.

He continued, 'I am aware that there are some confusing contents in this manuscript, and I hope we can make some sense of it with the help of Almighty God. I am a truth seeker, but I know my confidence rests in the one true God.'

'Thank you, Your Eminence,' she said. 'I am eager to do just that.'

'As am I,' Dr Consuelo echoed.

Tegan found the pope quite charming, and Dr Consuelo found it odd that he was comforted by his presence. He clearly wanted to make sure that this examination did not get out of hand, and the church wanted to attempt to control the narrative, but he spoke with ease, and they wouldn't have thought he felt any other way.

As they observed his mannerisms and command of the room, it became clear why the faithful considered him the representative of God on earth even though they both found that notion to be highly unlikely and highly manipulative. They knew one should never underestimate the ability of shamans, rabbis, preachers, and spiritual leaders to overstate their importance.

'Now, please enjoy your breakfast that I have so rudely interrupted,' the pope said. 'I will see you all in the observatory later on,' and with that, he and his entourage made their way out of the hall.

As they took their seats again, Tegan glanced at Dr Consuelo and scolded him, 'You are such an asshole,' she said, with a smile belying her comment. 'I can't believe you would tell the pope himself that I'm an atheist!'

He just laughed his wonderful laugh that she loved so much, and she was very glad to see he was still fairly at ease despite the tension of the day. If calling her an atheist in front of the pope was what it took to put him at ease, she would gladly make that sacrifice to help the cause, but it was a punk-ass move.

Father Lujan and Father Shelby also got a kick out of it as anyone could tell by the huge smiles on their faces. It was a rather poignant moment, and she felt a warm glow as she realized how accepting the church was of these issues, and they enjoyed the remainder of their breakfast with a feeling of satisfaction growing inside. Everything was going to be fine, and hopefully, they were all about to get closer to the actual truth in this crazy world where everything seemed hidden from humans. It was comforting to know that the church was okay with an individual's search for the truth, and that also felt like progress of a sort.

Everyone in the breakfast hall stared at them for the remainder of the breakfast, obviously intrigued at who these guests of honor were that the pope himself had taken the time to come and meet. It was not clear to them how many in Vatican City were aware of what they were there to do, and it seemed the church would have wanted to keep this quiet since they were concerned about the contents of the manuscript. They just kept to themselves and finished their breakfast, and Father Shelby treated them to a private tour to kill the few hours before the examination was to start.

Chapter 19

A Hidden Veil

The Vatican observatory itself was a remarkable piece of architecture with a large room. It was outfitted with surgical lights in the middle of the room, almost like a surgical observatory but with square glass walls, and approximately thirty seats behind the glass for the observers. The room itself was bathed in natural daylight, and the beams at the center were a sure sign that whatever was being examined would have plenty of illumination to allow a thorough examination.

The floor was solid marble, and at the center was an ornate yet sterile table made from surgical steel, upon which sat the artefact itself, glowing in that eerie purplish glow. Tegan felt almost out of her body as she gazed at it for the first time. Dr Consuelo had told her about the levitating artefact that Ndinge had shared in confidence, and she was now observing it with her own eyes. It appeared spooky to her. She could not help but glance at Dr Consuelo as he observed it in person for the first time, and he viewed it with what appeared to be some trepidation.

Dr Consuelo himself was having a private moment of doubt and concern and was briefly shrouded in uncertainty. He knew that this examination would set him up as the target of whatever information was contained in the manuscript. Why did he have to do this? What if the dreaded contents were earth-shattering and undermined all religions? Why did he have to be the one who was derisively eschewed simply because he was the examiner of the contents?

He thought back on his sweet Manny and the giggles of the innocent one cut down so callously by the effects of this indifferent life. He would press forward despite his doubts and in defense of that innocence. Humanity needed to know the contents of this manuscript, and he had to sacrifice his comfort to accomplish that.

The pope and the other observers were seated behind the glass for their protection. There was two-way communication with the examiners in the observatory, thanks to a microphone on either side of the glass. The pope smiled and waved as Dr Consuelo walked into the observatory, and Tegan was sure this put him at ease as the pope had a warm and comforting glow to his personality.

Tegan took her seat in the observatory as far back as she could, and the pope turned and winked at her again, which filled her with comfort, even if this creepy old guy kept winking at her. She was not sure who all the guests were, but the observatory was full. Only Dr Consuelo and Father Shelby entered the observatory chamber. Father Lujan was seated quietly beside Tegan, eyes wide with a mix of fear and wonder. He ignored her when she asked who everyone was, possibly not even hearing her as he was transfixed.

They would find out later that the other guests included several archbishops, other bishops and fancy names, a few hand-selected priests, and other supposed fancy people. There was also a single representative from five powerful nations, including the United States, England, Israel, Russia, and China. Why these emissaries were there and other countries were not represented was never made clear.

Oddly enough, these emissaries were dressed in all black suits, which seemed a rather strange choice for the occasion, but Tegan was comforted by the notion that there were objective observers that would participate in this process.

Tegan observed Father Shelby being seemingly very hesitant as he stood by in the observatory, and he would not take his eyes off the artefact sitting on top of the examination table. He could not hide the fact that his eyes were wide with fear, possibly terror. He did not know if anyone was qualified for this moment, but it seemed obvious that he was not feeling fully capable.

The pope said a prayer in Latin that might as well have been in Swahili for all the noninitiates could tell, but hopefully, God spoke Latin because they needed all the help they could get. Dr Consuelo donned the gloves and bravely got down to the examination process.

'Wait,' suggested the pope. 'I think the process might go better if we turn our back just to be sure that we don't have the same fate as Dr Laliberte,' he continued.

Tegan could not believe what she was hearing. What he really meant was, 'I'm sure you're fucked, but let's not go along for the ride.' Didn't he believe in prayer? The rest of the audience ignored that comment because they were determined to take it all in.

Wonderful reassurance from the representative of God on earth. What was the pope anyway? According to what Dr Consuelo had read, the Catholic Church viewed him as being the infallible representative of God himself on earth, and as such, one could never question him. It was not just that he was viewed as infallible, but that he was exempt from the possibility of being fallible.

Dr Consuelo and Tegan had found that quite strange when they first read about it because being infallible seemed to be an incredibly obvious mechanism for gaining power. They really could not believe that the faithful bought into that assertion as if it was not some sort of power play. Apparently, by claiming you spoke for God, people would listen and revere. Why hadn't they thought of that? No wonder religion was such a useful mechanism of control.

After the pope made his suggestion, they all stared intently as Dr Consuelo approached the manuscript. In some ways, he determined that all his life had led up to this moment, and a calm settled over him as he prepared for the experience of a lifetime. He allowed the giggle of Manny to play in his mind as he stepped forward into the unknown. He was prepared for this moment, and Father Shelby had a contingency plan in place should things go wrong.

'Here goes nothing, Father Shelby,' sighed Dr Consuelo.

Father Shelby just gave him a wink. 'You've got this, my son,' he said in a tone with as much reassurance as he could muster.

John Shelby was certainly a comfort to have there in the room, but Dr Consuelo could tell that he felt he was in over his head. He kept shifting his gaze towards the pope and the rest of the audience as if to say, 'Are we really going to do this?'

Dr Consuelo slipped his reading glasses on to be able to see the fine print a little better. He stared at the manuscript and looked confused momentarily. He pulled his head back and realized that he did not even need his readers to read this fine print, which also seemed like another small miracle, and he smiled and pulled off the readers, placing them back in his lab coat pocket that they had given him to wear during the examination for some unknown reason. They probably intended to get him in a dress too.

He slowly began to read the first page loud and clear for all to hear:

> What you are reading is an illicit translation of data that is not intended for you, and the simple act of reading it is a crime against humanity. I implore you to put this manuscript away and never return to it because in it are some secrets of humankind that should never be divulged and will potentially devastate society and humanity.

As he continued to read it, his mind flashed back to that day in his office and the strange words that flowed off the manuscript across the video feed seven or eight time zones away. That same mysterious warning filled him with dread, but as in the case of Dr Laliberte reading it, the words seemed to almost jump off the page, and he read it with an ever-quickening pace. Time seemed to stand still as the incredible information flowed out of Dr Consuelo's now-fluent lips.

As he reached the bottom of the first page, he paused and gazed at the audience, and he seemed to take comfort from their rapt attention to the manuscript's amazing contents. The videographers that Father Shelby had arranged were scattered in and around the examination chamber, and they focused on Dr Consuelo's every move. Dr Consuelo felt like he was melding with this manuscript he was reading, and the information seemed to jump into his mind, which was rather inexplicable and a sensation that only Dr Laliberte could have understood.

He felt emboldened in this moment by that sensation, and his confidence soared. Suddenly it all became clear to him that his paranormal experience had prepared him for this moment, and he was honored to be the examiner regardless of any potential physical or psychological effects that might befall him. Humanity's embargo on all things paranormal was about to be demolished, and he was certain in that moment that paranormal events might harbor truths that could ultimately set them free.

Grabbing a pair of forceps that had been laid out for him, he reached down to tease the first page apart, and the second he touched it, everything changed. All the lights started to flicker and dance, and Dr Consuelo's body stiffened as the surge of an electrical shock connected to the manuscript surged through his body.

It was clear at that instant that whatever protection they had thought the gloves or forceps would offer was no barrier at all. He seemed to literally convulse as the outpouring of data seemed to flow into him like some high-voltage download into a computer. The audience gasped as the surge continued, and his eyes seemed to roll back into his head like some demonic possession. He remained stuck to the page for what seemed like several minutes. The moment he freed himself from the manuscript, an incredible flash of energy shot out and burst into the room.

All electronics immediately failed, and the lights in the ceiling burst out in an enormous shower of sparks and smoke. The lenses of the cameras the videographers were holding even cracked, and a large crack formed in the observatory glass, which was bulletproof and three inches thick. Father Lujan was stunned to see that, and he felt it was reminiscent of the veil of the temple being torn after Jesus was crucified.

'Is he okay?' shouted the pope to a confused and bewildered Father Shelby, who no longer could hear anything that was said due to the failure of the microphones.

Father Shelby had been backing away. Tegan jumped up and pounded on the glass and repeated the question, unaware that she might be putting herself at risk as well. Father Shelby looked over at her with his eyes wide and mouth agape and just cupped a hand to his ear, trying to hear what she was saying. Everybody froze and fixated their gaze on Dr Consuelo, who was clearly in a bad state.

After releasing his grip on the manuscript and after the electronic failure, Dr Consuelo had at first stood up straight in a rigid position, and his eyes were closed as he sustained the incredible jolt. Perhaps he was trying to process the literal shock of the voltage streaming into his body, but then he lunged back and fell onto the ground like he was trying to avoid something that was coming at him. His senses were overwhelmed as he was now witnessing this flood of data from the manuscript flowing into his mind.

Instantaneously he was inundated by a strange spectacle playing out in front of him, and he found himself surrounded by a scene that seemed to transport him to the location of the actual events.

* * *

It was as if a darkness and a void had totally engulfed the earth, penetrated only by a speck of light that seemed to expand slowly. His mind racing, fifty-two-year-old archaeologist Dr Manuel Consuelo thought maybe he was dying; he had heard of many people feeling they were going towards light during near-death experiences. As the pinhole of light came closer, he detected small figures darting on what appeared to be a stage of light. He wondered if these were departed family and friends or angels coming to meet him.

As the field of light expanded further, it looked to him like figures were being chased by warriors in chariots adorned in gold and jewels and pulled by huge horses, terrorizing the figures amid huge plumes of smoke rising from fires and the screams of the panicked people.

Dr Consuelo suddenly realized he was somehow in the middle of an ancient battle and lurched to get out of the path of the oncoming chariots bearing down on him. He knew this was possible when he had agreed to examine this incredible manuscript, but now he wondered if he wasn't on some bizarre acid trip.

Barely escaping a chariot that nearly obliterated him, he found refuge under an overturned chariot with its wheels still spinning furiously. As an archaeologist, he was familiar with history but had never been able to experience it, and now he felt like he was in the middle of a historical event, which would have thrilled him if he had not been so terrified. He even wondered if he had time-traveled.

From the midst of this raging battle, he witnessed charioteers with huge spears and wearing elaborate headdresses, which he thought looked Egyptian. Their colorful togas were flapping in the breeze. Desperate people appeared to be running towards a beach, trying to evade slaughter by the charioteers. There was no way the people being chased could defend themselves, and the beach was already littered with hundreds of dead bodies.

Dodging an approaching chariot, Dr Consuelo tripped and fell to the ground and got run over by another passing chariot. As the chariot passed right through him, he suddenly realized that even though he was witnessing events as if he were present, he was invisible to the menacing charioteers and unable to help those being attacked. It was like he was a ghost. He was so entrenched in this experience that he could hardly remember how he had gotten here.

* * *

The strange charade went on for some time in the observatory, and the audience was mesmerized and horrified. Father Shelby kept looking back at the audience as if to gain some insight from them, but they were all just staring aghast at the situation. Dr Consuelo almost looked like he was on a bad psychedelic trip. Or was this even a seizure? It was difficult to know because he was bobbing and weaving like some boxer in slow motion, and his movements seemed to make no sense whatsoever.

Father Shelby continued to search for a solution and made a start like he was going to move in and help him, but he caught himself just in time, knowing full well that if he touched Dr Consuelo, he was subject to receiving the same reaction. He had felt confident that he would also examine the manuscript prior to this moment, but he now realized he wanted nothing to do with this strange and mysterious artefact, whether the Vatican approved or not.

* * *

When he focused on the plight of the poor souls upon whom the charioteers were bearing down, Dr. Consuelo saw a man lift what looked like a walking stick, from which a lightning bolt miraculously shot. Then a large silver disc hovered over the group of people, and the ocean in front of them slowly separated into walls of water on two sides, allowing people to flee while the charioteers seemed frozen in suspended animation.

After all the oppressed people marched into the ocean, the walls of water began to close behind them as they continued to the other side. As the soldiers seemed to awaken from their trance, several rushed into the water, desperate to get at the people they were chasing, and many of the chariots overturned and got dragged under the water.

It finally dawned on Dr Consuelo that he was witnessing the parting of the Red Sea by Moses so that the Israelites could escape the Egyptian army, the biblical story of the Exodus that he had heard many times as a child in Sunday school.

But he was confused by the large disc that had appeared and hovered above the Israelites because he did not remember that as part of the story. He was not sure if he was just imagining the silver disc or whether details of the biblical story had been omitted in his Sunday school class. He sat down cross-legged on a bluff overlooking the whole scene and marveled at what he was observing.

* * *

It was at that moment that he opened his eyes and stared straight in front of him directly at the audience, and for the first time, they saw the ghastly appearance of his eyes: the entire eye, including the sclera, black as night and opaque as coal. The audience gasped in horror again as they witnessed those haunting eyes that had also been seen on Dr Laliberte. How was it that he was seeing anything through those eyes? Little did they know, he was not.

Chapter 20

Fancy Coats of Many Colors

Father Shelby was beside himself. He had once again backed way off but now began to walk around Dr Consuelo to get a good look at his appearance. Once he saw his eyes, the audience thought he was about to lose it; he appeared close to fainting.

Tegan jumped up and banged on the observatory glass once again, which barely had any effect since it was so thick, but it did get his attention, and she gestured at him as if to say, 'Focus, man!'

Father Shelby seemed to right himself.

He seemed to finally realize this was the sign that Dr Consuelo needed the fail-safe escape. He sprang into action and alerted security to set up the rope guide to the studio. Security rushed into action, and in no time the rope guide was set up on temporary poles that led straight to the studio.

Since Father Shelby wasn't naturally a spiritual man, he realized at that moment that he did not even know what he was doing or what 'spiritual' meant. Why did he like spiritual things when he was so afraid of unfamiliar and paranormal things? He briefly reflected on being involved with a couple of exorcisms, and he hated them because he realized at those times that he was in way over his head.

Father Shelby had now leapt into action and was barking orders at everyone. Being fearful for Dr Consuelo was doing no good for anybody. They had planned well and needed to carry it out now. He exited the observatory and directed the pope to alert the Swiss Guards and get them to come and assist or perform crowd control as necessary. He reassured Tegan that all was under control and directed Father Lujan to keep all the clergy out of the way.

As the security detail got the rope guide in place for Dr Consuelo, Father Shelby brought the end of the rope to him, and he laid it right next to Dr Consuelo on the observatory chamber floor. He was careful not to touch him with it, but he placed it right next to him so he could find it easily.

'The rope is right beside you,' he yelled into Dr Consuelo's ear, not knowing if he could even hear him.

There was no response, and it did not appear he was aware of anything around him still, even as he sat there cross-legged like a statue. All they could do was wait now because he did not want to drop it in his lap and risk touching him. They had discussed it in detail the day before, and strict instructions were given that if the rope was necessary, Dr Consuelo would reach for it when ready. Now, as Father Shelby observed the statuesque Dr Consuelo, he began to fear that he might forget the arrangement.

* * *

Dr Consuelo was unresponsive from all appearances, and the action in his head was subsiding as he observed the end of the sequence. He struggled mightily to even recall where he was and what he was doing and where this action sequence playing in his head had originated. He had nearly forgotten what had caused it as the data seemed to overwhelm his senses and his grasp on reality.

As the ancient battle subsided, the electronic dialogue contained in the manuscript was playing in his mind, and his lips moved in a silent recital of the words contained in the manuscript. He was aware now that the video scene he was observing appeared to be a biblical scenario of the Egyptians chasing the Israelites in the biblical version of the Exodus, but it was not clear what connection this had to the manuscript. Why would this video sequence even be contained in the manuscript? He wondered about the truthfulness of the stories he had been taught as a child in church, which had come from that old manuscript known as the Bible

Suddenly it dawned on him. This was virtual reality. He was a player in a video game. Then another paranoia entered his mind: he was a nonplaying character in a video game, and all he could do was hang out in this virtual reality, waiting for something to happen. He had no way to get out. Paranoia gripped his mind, almost like the first time he smoked weed in high school. What the fuck was he going to do? There seemed to be no escape from this virtual reality he was in. He tried to settle his mind and focus on his next move.

Focusing as best he could, he decided that this was a stunning scene to observe, and he leaned back in the sand to enjoy it. His hand brushed a rope. Immediate relief flooded his senses. He was jolted back to reality as he remembered that this was his fail-safe escape.

He grabbed the rope in desperation. Slowly rising to his feet, seemingly walking through quicksand, he managed to erect himself and direct himself to safety. Following the rope, he slowly made his way along the line that led him to freedom. His mind eased as he was steered back into reality.

As Dr Consuelo began to follow the rope line to safety, Father Shelby motioned the Swiss Guards to instruct them on their duties.

'For once, you are going to actually do something instead of standing around and holding spears in your silly outfits.' He instructed them on crowd control and keeping everyone away from Dr Consuelo, which was crucial to everyone's safety.

The Swiss Guards acted accordingly and cleared the path for Dr Consuelo, who was on the move. There was still so much commotion in and around the chamber that Father Shelby grew frustrated as he tried to bring a more orderly process.

'Silence!' Father Shelby yelled, loud enough for all to hear.

Dr Consuelo exited the observatory and moved as quickly as he could out into the courtyard and directly across St. Peter's square towards the Vatican studio. He was still completely blind to anything around him, but the rope gave him all the confidence he needed, and he picked his way along the rope line like a blind man.

A rather odd group of pursuers were behind him, desperate to help but realizing it seemed to be under control. There were men in black skirts, brown skirts, and a few in red who were jostling for position along with the fancy coats of many colors of the Swiss Guards leading the way. Even the pope was scurrying behind him with his white skirts flapping in the breeze. The ambassadors stayed back a safe distance as they, too, were in hot pursuit but determined to keep away from the drama. They were here to observe, not get involved.

This slow-speed chase proceeded directly across the plaza, creating a very public display of the bizarre scene. All throughout the square, people stopped to gawk at the apparent festivities with confused looks on their faces. If the stakes were not so high, the scene would have been hilarious.

As they approached the Vatican studio, Father Shelby instructed the Swiss Guards to step aside so that Dr Consuelo could follow the rope line inside. Confused, all the procession glanced at each other in wonderment and followed him closely into the studio wherein there were seats as well. Father Shelby informed them that the plan was for him to record on video the recitation of the contents in the manuscript, and that process should allow the data to be uploaded out of Dr Consuelo's mind.

The clergy and ambassadors listened quizzically to that suggestion as they doubted that it could be cleared that easily, but with all that they had witnessed that day, no one dared to question too much. The studio housed state-of-the-art television broadcasting equipment. It was mostly used by priests to stream their broadcasts across YouTube or some other platform directly to their audience. Priests would broadcast from soundproof rooms directly to their adherents who craved these broadcasts from Vatican priests and holy men.

Dr Consuelo stepped into the studio and sat in front of the camera and started speaking in a slow, droning manner.

Father Shelby confirmed the camera was recording so Dr Consuelo could upload the whole document. The Vatican could censor whatever he was about to say all they wanted, but for now, Father Shelby and all the clergy realized that this had to be recorded. They were about to finally hear the contents of the manuscript from the nearly catatonic lips of Dr Consuelo acting as the conduit.

Chapter 21

Salvation

After the slow-speed chase across the courtyard, where every member of the clergy and all the ambassadors had chased Dr Consuelo bemused by the spectacle, Dr Consuelo sat in his soundproof broadcast room and talked. He had been shocked by the electricity flowing through his body when he first touched the manuscript, and he continued to feel a strange electrical sensation as he seated himself to be recorded.

His body and mind were in a very strange place, and he could hardly describe the sensation, kind of like describing what it was like to be drunk to someone who had never been so. He had started sweating profusely in the examination chamber and continued to sweat while he sat in the Vatican studio. As he began to broadcast though, he felt the relief as he let out the information that was in his head. He knew now that he would escape this virtual reality if he could upload the information to this video. Dr Laliberte had not been so fortunate.

He was amazed at how the information just flowed out of him as if he had memorized this whole thing his entire life. He regurgitated it flawlessly and without pausing.

Once the pope heard some of the information that was escaping from Dr Consuelo, he realized he could not have this information out. He allowed the video to continue to record but instructed the technology staff to sequester the video so it did not go out for public consumption.

Father Shelby was not happy with that move because, naturally, the church must inform the laity what to think about any information since they spoke for God. At no time were they ever going to let the public think for themselves because they might come up with the wrong conclusion. Father Shelby knew that this could be addressed later, and all that mattered right now was recording the manuscript into a video, which they could examine later. Dr Consuelo's safety was all that mattered, and he nearly collapsed in tears as he saw the relief come over Dr Consuelo's face.

Tegan had remained in the background during the chase across the plaza, hoping that Dr Consuelo was safe and happy that Father Shelby had finally been able to take charge and implement the planned safety valve. Now she watched in amazement as the contents of the manuscript poured forth from his lips.

Father Lujan had been mortified at the entire process and was nearly paralyzed in fear at the peril that his dear friend Dr Consuelo had been forced to endure. He had remained in his seat at the observatory, praying fervently through the process, and could only direct the clergy to stay back. He, too, was feeling relief as he watched Dr Consuelo recite the manuscript on video, but he started to get a sense of dread at the content he was hearing.

The pope's assistant had been summoned at some point, and Father Shelby now sought him out and pulled him aside. Father Shelby explained that Dr Consuelo had appeared to know how to reverse the reaction by filming the process, and he wanted the pope's assistant to document everything he could. The pope's transcriptionist was also brought in to transcribe the information.

Dr Consuelo continued his monotone recitation of the manuscript flawlessly as far as anyone could tell. There was no possible way that he could memorize this large of a manuscript, and yet it rolled off his tongue as if he were reading from the manuscript itself. That could never happen though because after the incident, the pope had ordered the manuscript confiscated, and all the rest of them knew, no human would ever lay eyes on it again. The film crew knew they were filming something extraordinary, and with eyes wide, they captured every dramatic moment as Dr Consuelo finished his hour-long monologue, exhausted.

At that Dr Consuelo collapsed into a heap on the floor and lay there, drenched in sweat as he panted for air. It was as if he had just finished three hours of hot yoga, and he gazed around him in amazement at the group of holy men, emissaries, transcriptionists, and video crew that had crammed into this broadcast studio to witness this universe-shaking event. What had he done or said that could have created this incredible interest? He had heard the words as he was reciting them, but he was not able to digest the entire thing as he returned from another dimension.

His mind was a little foggy as he tried to gather himself, and for some reason, he felt very satisfied but incredibly sad as he struggled to sit up. The look on the faces of the holy men around him told the story as they all had a look of confusion that belied their concern for Dr Consuelo.

'I don't know everything I just said,' Dr Consuelo whispered in a hoarse and weakened voice. 'But I can see by the look on your faces that it must have been rather stunning.'

Father Shelby knelt gently beside him, relieved that his newfound friend and mentor was himself again, and nodded. 'That is certainly the case, my friend. Once you see the video and transcript, you will be blown away.'

As his head cleared more fully, Dr Consuelo struggled to gather his thoughts and realized that all he wanted to do was get his hands on some of his favorite whisky to calm his nerves further.

He looked around him weakly and quietly mused, 'Too bad I'm at the Vatican with a bunch of holy men because I could really use a drink,' he sputtered.

At that the entire relieved group of observers howled in laughter, and Father Shelby slapped the cardinal on his back.

'I think we can accommodate you on that one, Dr Consuelo. We could all use some liquid encouragement ourselves after what we've just witnessed,' he said, and the room roared in laughter.

Whisky was immediately produced, much to Dr Consuelo's delight since he'd thought they only drank wine.

'Don't you worry, Dr Consuelo,' his relieved friend Father Shelby said, 'we have been saving the good stuff for this.'

Dr Consuelo was also relieved, more than anyone knew, because only he knew the torment that had led Dr Laliberte to jump in front of a train. What if he had never come out of that trancelike state? Would his fate have been the same? He felt certain it would have as he smiled and sipped his whisky.

He was happy to be in the moment and to have the incessant data that had been coursing through his head finally silenced. He gulped more of his drink and embraced the silence in his mind. He would have to wait until later to view the video and read the manuscript.

Chapter 22

Manuscript of Life

Dr Consuelo was himself again, or so he thought. The process of recording the manuscript for the world to see had released him from the virtual reality in which he felt trapped. The ancient manuscript that had been confiscated by the pope was of no concern to him now as he was happy to be free. The Vatican transcriptionists were hard at work transcribing the whole manuscript and comparing it to the video to ensure accuracy. The pope had given them explicit instructions to strictly protect the transcription and copies because he could not have this getting out to the public. They were to number all the copies so he could get them all back.

The Vatican seemed a quite different place, Tegan thought, after the examination of the manuscript. The priests and clergy seemed very withdrawn and listless as they went about their daily tasks. It was typical that the Vatican was usually a somber and sacred place, but things seemed to be unusually silent following the huge commotion involved in the manuscript investigation.

Dr Consuelo slept in the next day, exhausted from the events, and when he did wake, he could barely move as every muscle screamed at him when he tried.

As he slowly stirred from his deep sleep, Dr Consuelo got frustrated because he was having a great dream about Manny, and he always hated to wake up in the middle of those dreams. They were riding bikes in Kit Carson Park near the pueblo. Manny was healthy and giggling, and Dr Consuelo was overjoyed. As he lay in bed stretching his aching muscles, a thought occurred to him. Perhaps VR could access further data, and he wondered if he could even experience parts of Manny's life through it. His heart soared at the prospect. Who cared if it was a crazy idea? What if there were a chance? He would not share that unrealistic thought with anyone, but his resolve deepened, and he determined that he was not going to leave this place without the manuscript.

The pope sequestered himself for the day with his most trusted advisers and strategized their next move. Due to the strange and unsettling content of the whole manuscript, he considered abandoning the whole thing so they did not have to even address its contents, but he felt that would look worse to the clergy than an open discussion behind closed doors. The Vatican could not hide from this one, and they had to address it head-on.

His advisers agreed that they should examine the contents in a closed-door meeting with high-level clergy to evaluate the contents directly to avoid any scrutiny. They called it a debriefing, but what the clergy hoped for was more of a debunking because they were not comfortable with what they had witnessed.

There was a big debate about whether to allow Dr Consuelo and that atheist woman to be involved in the conversation. Most advisers did not want them involved, but the pope knew they had to be included.

There had to be some component of objectivity in this process because the scientific world had abandoned all hope of examining it, and the pope respected the fact that Dr Consuelo and Dr Mallory had been involved. They determined to have the manuscript review done the next day barring any unforeseen developments. Dr Consuelo could rest for the day, and they would gather in their conference room for a video review.

They had even agreed to a potential transfer of the artefact to Dr Consuelo's institution if the manuscript was proven legitimate, but the pope made it clear he was going to do whatever he could to ensure that wouldn't happen. The clergy were determined to explain the contents of the manuscript in a way that satisfied their need to be in line with their most holy faith—a tall order indeed as they attested to by the strained looks on their faces.

Father Lujan was present for the preparatory discussion, and he suggested that he had some ideas since he knew Dr Consuelo very well and was familiar with Dr Mallory.

'I would like to address some of these issues in the debriefing since I am familiar with both Dr Consuelo and Dr Mallory and can almost anticipate what they will say and what conclusions they will draw.'

The pope and his council agreed that this made some sense, but they wanted more opposition as well, and they had the perfect bulldog, or so they thought. Father Gianni Begnini was the pope's right-hand man in all things theological, and he was not about to let this manuscript and its contents undermine the church's power and authority, especially by some two-bit archaeologist and his woman friend. He had not bothered to attend the examination because he knew some of the contents and he thought this whole thing to be a fraud.

They decided they would record the proceedings for posterity again, and so it was a cordial discussion. The stage was set, and the Catholic Church was never comfortable unless they were in control.

'We serve the Most Holy God,' asserted the pope, 'and ours is a most holy faith that cannot be destroyed by a single silly manuscript,' he concluded.

The clergy nodded in agreement as they searched the faces of their colleagues for confirmation.

'We know God is in control,' echoed Father Begnini. 'Besides, it's not likely the scientific community would accept this content given the paranormal aspects of the find. They don't consider paranormal events to be scientific, and they would never consider this legitimate.'

The clergy again nodded in agreement.

And so it was that they reluctantly gathered the following day in a conference room that was so mundane it struck Dr Consuelo as quite odd. There was no suggestion in this conference room that this examination was important, and Dr Consuelo was certain they had chosen this room intentionally to downplay the importance of the whole review.

The pope's assistant had explained that it was the only conference room where video could be displayed, but Dr Consuelo and Tegan knew that had to be a lie. They were certain it was an attempt to downplay the entire event. Then again, everything else seemed so overly ostentatious that it might distract attention, and this dull setting might ensure that the examination would proceed with less distraction, and they concluded that was a good thing.

Dr Consuelo was already concerned about hearing that the Vatican had hidden the manuscript away, and he had a growing unease about where this whole examination was headed. He felt like this manuscript should be put on display so every human would be able to examine it and learn the truth about their existence. Serfs were best kept in the dark about the truth though. Otherwise they might revolt.

Dr Consuelo had long known that religions were about spreading orthodoxy and obscuring certain truths. Otherwise they might not be able to keep people coming back like good little sheep and continuing to fill their coffers. Religions needed people, not the other way around. Religions and governments were empowered by the same leverage point, fear and guilt, engendering complacency. Dr Consuelo knew that the church would be concerned that if humanity heard of the unedited version of this, there might be confusion amongst parishioners or a loss of asses in the pews.

The mood continued to feel very somber as they all gathered and seated themselves for the presentation and debriefing. Multiple large monitors were stationed throughout the room so that all could observe with ease as Dr Consuelo recited the contents of the manuscript from two days ago. Dr Consuelo was certain that he and Tegan were going to be the only ones excited to see the contents of the video.

The transcription of the video and manuscript had been placed in front of each of the attendees for reference and discussion purposes. Dr Consuelo glanced around at the long faces of the attendees and only found a friendly face in Father Lujan, his old friend, and Father Shelby, who nodded at him and asked, 'How are you holding up?'

Dr Consuelo grinned and replied, 'Bit sore, oddly enough, but I'm better today than I was yesterday.'

Father Shelby nodded and smiled.

There were ten high-ranking clergy members, including Father Shelby and Father Lujan, gathered in addition to the pope and some guy seated to the right of the pope who seemed to be quite important and seemed very austere. Dr Consuelo had not been introduced to him yet. He thought he was the pope's legal counsel or something, and the other priests always seemed to defer to him.

He nudged Tegan sitting next to him and whispered, 'That guy looks like the pope's bulldog.'

She snickered at that.

The man was a small, rather rotund guy. His glasses were perched at the tip of his nose as he perused the transcript in front of him with a disgusted look on his face. He was garbed in a dress just like the rest of the priests, but due to his girth, it surrounded him like a hoop skirt from early pioneer days. Despite that fact, he carried himself differently, or so thought Dr Consuelo.

The five representatives of nations were also in attendance, but they were seated back away from the table, for observation purposes only. It was not clear if they would participate, but they could observe the proceedings. Their presence seemed more sinister now, and it assured

Dr Consuelo that they were in line with the Catholic Church. That was how the powerful remained powerful, by aligning themselves with and copying the powerful.

Religion was so good at controlling people without strings that Dr Consuelo was now convinced that governments copied religion because of the successful methods of control the church had had for millennia. Dr Consuelo knew that there was no way the pope would allow these dignitaries to sit in if there were any chance they would broadcast this to the world. Governments needed complacency the same way religions did.

Father Lujan was seated to the right of Dr Consuelo. He patted his hand reassuringly and said, 'I'm proud of you, Dr Consuelo, and I know there will be some debate here, but I encourage you to speak your mind openly.'

'Thank you, Father,' Dr Consuelo said. 'I do feel a bit outnumbered without my Cambridge colleagues present, but I plan to speak up where necessary, and Tegan is my intellectual force.' He smiled warmly.

The man to the right of the pope rose to address the room and stated that he was the pope's assistant in all things theological. He introduced himself as Gianni Begnini, and he was the master of pontifical liturgical ceremonies.

A rather pompous title, Tegan thought, *but no surprise given the church's tendency towards self-promotion, all while feigning humility.* Tegan scoffed to herself, noting that mystery and intrigue were how the church ensured their theology was accepted by all adherents and how it was carefully crafted to whatever message they wanted to deliver and enforce.

'I would like to bring this meeting to order,' he said.

All participants bowed their heads immediately, except for Dr Consuelo and Tegan, who glanced at each other nervously. Apparently, they started all their meetings that way.

After the prayer, Father Begnini continued to speak, 'Gentlemen, and woman, we are gathered today to review the contents of this supposedly miraculous manuscript which we clearly know to be a fake or demonically inspired.' He glared at Dr Consuelo and Tegan directly.

Dr Consuelo tried to speak up, but Father Begnini cut him off.

'You will have plenty of time to make your case, Dr Consuelo. For the record, I am opposed to this meeting at all, and I am especially disappointed to have a woman involved, but the pope has determined it so. I don't think we need the review of this manuscript as I don't trust any of it, but the Holy Father has determined that we will do this to consider how this was faked.'

Dr Consuelo felt sure at this point that he was in for a long day. Tegan nudged him with her knee, and he noted a smirk on her face. It was clear that the tactic was going to be evasion and suggestion to undermine any authority of the text, and along with that, they only had two amateurs in the room to debate them on that point. It also set the tone when he would not let Dr Consuelo speak or even address Tegan by her name. The papacy seemed determined to shut this thing down, and they had the authority to do so. After all, it only took a decree from the pope himself, and no one would ever know this thing existed.

'It has also come to my attention,' Father Begnini sternly continued, 'that some sort of an agreement has been made at Dr Consuelo's request that we have a sort of trial throughout this examination with each individual acting as their own prosecutor but essentially boiling down to science versus the church. This bizarre request was made by Dr Consuelo because he thinks if the so-called scientific crowd prevails, he will obtain the manuscript for proper scientific examination.

'My personal view is that he harbors such a deep prejudice against the church that he is biased in his examination, which makes this anything but scientific. I have counseled the pope against this ill-advised trial, but he is a man of his word and has agreed to do this prior to Dr Consuelo's arrival. I am also recording this meeting for later review.'

'Before we commence our examination,' Father Begnini continued, 'I have to address the elephant in the room and ask Dr Consuelo what that was. How is it possible that a manuscript that was apparently buried for thousands or even millions of years could possibly cause the effects that we witnessed? From the spiritual angle that the clergy views it, it appeared to be demonic effects that we were witnessing, and I'd like you to address those effects since you seem to be the only one who could sustain this frightening experience and come out the other side unaffected. Can you discuss?'

Dr Consuelo slowly surveyed the room, not sure whether to be frightened at the audience he had been given or disbelieving of the way he had gained it. He chose not to address them formally and instead stated, 'Father Begnini, I appreciate you giving me the opportunity, but that may be the toughest question of all. Can't you open with an easier question?'

Many in the room chuckled, settling the tension just a bit.

Rising to his feet, Dr Consuelo took on a slightly more serious tone and addressed the question head-on.

'Your Eminence, gathered clergy and ambassadors, that is an excellent question, and I have some ideas that I will discuss here, but be clear about one thing: I am only speculating because I can't know the full extent of this mystery as it does appear literally to be out of this world. Possibly from another dimension. Father Begnini has asserted that he believes this to be a fraud, and I would remind him that I am not a particularly good actor and could not remember all that manuscript on my own if my life depended on it, and as you saw, my life did depend on it. Furthermore, the provenance is impeccable. It has never been in my possession, and the manuscript killed the individual who first examined it.'

Father Begnini looked even more sour after that comment.

Dr Consuelo continued, 'As all are aware, the term we use for this kind of a find is *paranormal*, but we rarely get to defend paranormal things because people snicker at the very notion.'

A couple of the priests did exactly that but quickly caught themselves.

'Please suspend your skepticism for another time and allow me to discuss this openly because I believe it is crucial to answer that question with open minds as to the paranormal topic. Why do we even have the term *paranormal*? Because certain things have happened to certain people that are not explainable from a material-world perspective. These things are well known, and I will not list them here, but suffice it to say that all we can do is listen to these stories since there is no way to confirm their veracity or reproduce the event.

'I know this appears demonic, but it's not. These effects have been experienced by many unsuspecting humans in recent times and likely throughout history. There is a report from England where a UFO landed in a forest that was part of a military base. One of the military staff touched the UFO as it sat on the ground and got a download of ones and zeros that seemed to enter his head, and he couldn't get it out until he wrote the binary numbers down on paper, effectively downloading it from his brain.

'There are other similar reports, but they are rare and mostly ignored. I myself have witnessed this event in the field on one occasion with a mysterious artefact that a colleague touched and expressed similar actions to mine, which appeared to be relieved by a video camera when he recited the manuscript in a dead language that no one was able to translate. Events so bizarre as to defy logic, yet we have all just witnessed this en masse. So what is it? Here I am really speculating, but the facts can't be ignored. The manuscript data appears to interact with its examiner and was summarily downloaded into me when I touched it and remained in my brain until I could get it out.

'When I first touched it, I witnessed an ancient battle scene, which I can only presume was from the video feed that was also attached to the manuscript and caused the artefact to glow. I was eventually able to detect that I was witnessing the Exodus from Egypt, and I was right in the middle of it, with chariots whizzing around me and frightened people running away.

'At first, I was scared for my own life, but I finally realized I could not be harmed because I was just an apparition existing in the event. I almost forgot where I was and had no idea what I was witnessing as the scene played out in my head, but for a time, that was all I could see, and there was no examination chamber or audience that I could see or hear. That is why I sat and just watched the incredible events until I could determine where I was and what was going on.

'After the scene played out around me, I found myself alone on a sandy bluff overlooking the scene and tried to gather my thoughts. I couldn't sense anything around me, and I finally came to the realization that this was some form of virtual reality, and a horrifying thought occurred to me that I may be stuck in this altered dimension, and I wasn't sure what to do. I felt the panic that Dr Laliberte must have felt when he decided to take his own life. As you all witnessed, I was able to come to my senses once my hand brushed the rope laid for me by Father Shelby.

'Once I recorded the contents of the manuscript to this video we are watching today, the fog cleared, and the process somehow got downloaded to the video, and I was able to be myself again. That data apparently cannot be destroyed.'

'So you're basically saying that this is high-tech and it just looks magical to us?' Father Begnini said.

'That's sure what it looked like, and felt like, to me,' Dr Consuelo said.

'I can appreciate your take on the mechanism of the data being downloaded to you,' said Father Begnini. 'But I think it's obvious this was demonically possessed and that it somehow attached itself to you. I think we should have performed an exorcism. How are we possibly ever going to adjudicate this difference of opinions?'

'The way we do that, Father Begnini,' Dr Consuelo said, rather sarcastically, 'is we treat this document scientifically and let other people examine it to confirm my findings. We don't bury it and run like children.'

This portly man was clearly directly in his line of fire. He was the one in the way of his fantasy of having a VR meeting with Manny, and he was also the protector of all things orthodox. He told the story he wanted, and Dr Consuelo was determined to take him down.

'Well, aren't we going to find something disagreeable in these documents?' Father Begnini asked.

'That is an excellent question, Father Begnini, and I think we should start the video and transcript so we can find out the answer,' Dr Consuelo said.

'A few ground rules first,' Father Begnini said, suddenly sounding in control again. 'I propose that as we review the contents of this manuscript, we pause as necessary for discussion. One person will have the floor at a time, and if you want to pause and discuss, just hold your hand up.'

All agreed to the discussion parameters. And with that, the video began.

Dr Consuelo flashed onto the screen, and the entire group gasped again at his appearance. Dr Consuelo himself was horrified as he caught the first sight of his face and eyes. He was speaking in a monotone, and his face was ashen and his eyes wide with probable terror. The most shocking part, of course, was the complete blackness of his eyes, and Dr Consuelo had to admit that he did look somewhat demonic.

***

What you are reading is an illicit translation of data that is not intended for you, and the simple act of reading it is a crime against humanity. I implore you to put this manuscript away and never return to it because in it are some secrets of humankind that should never be divulged and will potentially devastate society and humanity. You are only in possession of these documents through some accident of history, and you were never intended to see this information. Hopefully, much of this manuscript is degraded and missing by this point because it was never meant for you; it was written to hide it from my society.

In our technologically advanced society, all information must be publicly available because we deem it safer for all. That makes it impossible to keep secrets, and I need this to be a secret for my plan to work, not because it is nefarious, but because it is beneficial. We have placed this data in this manuscript to keep it inaccessible to my civilization and yours. If anyone comes into possession of this information, it would have made it impossible to implement my plan and manage the entire earth. I am the managing overlord of the entire earth, placed here by my society to implement change.

I have been stationed here to manage humanity and humankind and attempt to control this rogue society. Believe me, it is not fun, and I do not say that proudly. Humans, it turns out, are some of the more dysfunctional and confusing intelligences we have cloned into existence, and my job is exceedingly difficult because of this. My name is not important for this manuscript, and my title is Vice Chancellor of Milky Way, Quadrant IV.

Our assignment here on earth, and in the Milky Way in general, is to control the population. Specifically, we must find a way to manage the local populations to care for themselves and develop their own societies for self-preservation and for our benefit. A tough assignment indeed, given the proclivities of humans to do nothing and ask for everything.

My problem is that I have developed what appears to be a perfect system for our human-derived dilemma of getting the local populations to manage and motivate themselves. Humans are not the smartest animals ever cloned, and in some cases, we have destroyed their intellect intentionally, and they sometimes act against their own best interests, so our job is to focus them on a purpose that will motivate them to do what we need and produce what we require.

Chapter 23

Meet the Overlords

Dr Consuelo held up his hand, and the video paused briefly.

'I just want to point out that this first part was what I had already witnessed when I saw the video feed in my office when Dr Laliberte had examined it. All I could recall from that reading was the fact that this document said we were a cloned species, and this entity sounded like an overlord and how strange that sounded. I couldn't remember any of it until now, and it almost seems as if that data is accessible only to the one who touched it, which is why this video of me reciting the contents is so beneficial. Importantly, this is scientifically reproducible since Dr. Laliberte was reading the same page that I was out loud and in a different language and our readings are identical. It is also impossible to retain once it's out, which is why I couldn't remember anything of what I recited in the Vatican studio the other day.'

'Not sure why that was important,' Father Begnini chided. 'Can we continue?'

'Of course,' Dr Consuelo replied, ignoring the insult. And the video continued.

> Our problem began when Gaia was discovered long ago. This planet had an incredible array of resources, and our plans were to harvest these for our benefit in our society. Many of these resources were vital to our existence, and gaining access to them was vital. That was why we cloned humans into existence to begin with, because they were much better at harvesting these resources.
>
> In our society, all actions are recorded in real time and for all history on the universal recording device we have developed. This records thoughts, audios, and videos, and anybody can review them anytime.
>
> We communicate telepathically, so thoughts and audios are the same things, and it is not hard to know what other individuals are thinking. But we have developed devices that record all actions that we perform, and as a result, nothing that we do is hidden. Whether sleeping or eating or

doing any other previously private thing, it is all recorded. Fortunately, it does not record smell.

This is the natural result of a society concerned with control and safety because, as time went on, we have realized we can stop crimes by forcing everyone to record everything. Even if we are not constantly watching what somebody is doing, we can always review the recordings and catch them after the fact.

Technology is also what we use to enslave societies, but that is a long way off for humanity. That is why I am working on this project, because if we can better focus humanity on functioning like intelligent beings, we can someday have the technological development that will allow us to tighten their chains and control them completely. Humans will never see that coming, and they often develop the very technological infrastructure that allows us to control them in a virtual prison. Humanity will think they are progressing, but really, they will be building the walls within which we will trap them. Our clones must be controlled.

This technology is vital to our society as well because there is simply no other way to monitor what our managers are doing across the universe, and it also helps me to check in on my managers and ensure that they are acting appropriately. This also helps to settle any dispute. The recording can be reviewed, so we can understand how the event has unfolded. This creates a much safer and more equitable society, but the loss of personal privacy and autonomy has been a huge sacrifice that I still think of as a mistake.

This is hard for humans to understand since this device is high-technology, but this process used to be voluntary. People in our society would sign up for accounts on this recording device, and they would put on pictures of their days and have discussions or debates on them. But soon it became this big thing, and eventually, everybody recorded everything that was done, and now it is the law.

We probably should have seen that coming, but we did not realize it until it was done, and there is no way to reverse it now. This is a real big problem for me in what I am trying to accomplish here because if people can review what I am doing while I am doing it, then they can beat me to it, and it is going to take many years to get this done. Perhaps hundreds. You cannot patent anything in our society because others can poach it as you are thinking it.

Dr Consuelo was fascinated by the information he was hearing and had to comment. He held his hand up, and the video was paused.

'It's fascinating to see that we are on the verge of this exact thing with the internet and our tendency towards social media. Most of us aren't even aware of how technology literally enslaves us and controls us,' he said.

Father Lujan spoke up and said, 'Dr Consuelo, I perceive that you are rather obsessed with freedom, and I wonder, do you have a problem with authority?'

'That's a perceptive question, Father Lujan,' Dr Consuelo said. 'I probably despise authority more than I would like to admit, but what I really have a problem with is control, be it thought control or control over my physical body or actions. Throughout the ages, humankind has fought for its freedoms, and those freedoms are constantly under assault. I would submit that that alone is proof that we are a controlled and manipulated species.'

'But you can't have a functioning society without authority and some controls in place,' Father Lujan said. 'I'm well aware of your problems with religion, edicts, and orthodoxy, but what I wonder about is how you think it possible to have a society without any authorities.'

Before Dr Consuelo could respond, Father Begnini rose to increase his presence in the room and stated, 'Authority, laws, and edicts are in place so that society can function, and without those precepts, there would not be a functioning society. Nothing would be accomplished because humanity would never function effectively if authorities were not in place. Jesus himself said, "Give unto Caesar what are Caesar's and give unto God what is God's," and so it has been from the beginning. Humans are evil at the core, and there would be no society without authority.'

'My personal opinion,' Dr Consuelo replied, 'is that you believe that because you are one of the authorities, and you also believe that humanity was sinful from the beginning. I would argue that if we truly had an equitable society, those problems you cite would not exist.

'The vast majority of humanity is born into poverty and given little chance at a life where they are able to exist freely and pursue life, liberty, and happiness the way they choose. As a result, they must fight their entire lives to simply meet their basic needs. If someone has no means of existence, they would be more likely to steal food to meet their basic needs and urges. If someone is depressed because they have no hope or meaning, wouldn't it be more likely that they would become addicted to drugs? Your view of humanity is that they need authority to protect them from themselves and protect others as well.

'I envision a society where all are free to pursue life and liberty because they have few authority figures limiting their freedoms and establishing rules for them to live by. This society could empower all humans by having less economic disparity and more prosperity across all of humanity, which would allow free will and freedom to flourish. The closest we have ever come to that in our world is democracy, and even that has its drawbacks, but it has enabled some of the greatest progress we have ever seen, and yet that is even under assault. I know there are crimes committed by humans, and that cannot exist in a functioning society, but we have laws in place that deal with those situations.

'The Ten Commandments mean nothing to someone who is hungry and destitute, so calling that a sin is blaming the individual for fulfilling their basic needs. We need to work for true equality and freedom, and that is difficult if not impossible with the power structures that are in place.'

'Wow,' Father Shelby mocked, 'you sound like a preacher yourself. Preach it, brother. Are you sure you don't want to join the clergy?'

Dr Consuelo smiled and sat down.

'Resume the video,' Father Begnini said rather disgustedly.

> So I have devised a method for hiding my thoughts and actions. My master engineer has devised a process for reversing the data into physical form, allowing all my thoughts and videos to go straight to a physical manuscript that permanently hides them from our recording device.

Not only is that a brilliant invention, but it is something that we can now patent since we could hide that in manuscript form as well. Only one problem left to solve, and that is how we hide this physical manuscript from all humanity. This manuscript will be visible in both our world and the human world, and that is a big problem. This physical manuscript I am speaking of cannot be seen by humans ever. It is top secret on the highest level, and there is no way I can possibly ever let them see it because it would forever devastate them and their supposed purpose.

If they ever become aware, all society may fail, and they may sink back to their natural state, which is catastrophic failure of all institutions and a complete regression to their previous existence. In other words, if my plan fails, we annihilate the entire planet at some point.

Father Begnini held up his hand and slowly rose to his feet. It did not take him long because there wasn't much difference in height between the seated Begnini and the standing Begnini. There also was not much difference between his width and his height.

'Am I to believe that this "overlord" was creating a secret manuscript because he wanted to manipulate humanity to act more effectively?'

Father Shelby responded but did not even bother to stand up in response. He simply stared straight ahead and commented, 'It seems fairly clear that the overlord is saying just that, and I think you will really have something to be upset about once you realize who this is.'

'Well, that seems like a good thing,' Father Begnini said. 'It sounds to me like he is setting humanity free,' he suggested.

'Maybe,' Father Shelby replied. 'But we won't know until we review more.'

'Well, it seems to me,' Father Begnini continued, 'that Dr Consuelo should be happy about this document because I can tell that is where this is headed.'

'You might think that,' Dr Consuelo said, 'but the implementation of religions and oppressive governments control the vast majority of humanity with threats of death and punishment after death. If his intention were to set humanity free, it hasn't had the intended consequence we would hope for.'

Chapter 24

Planned Obsolescence

We cloned humans into existence, and because they were intelligences just like us, we needed to suppress their intellect and ensure that they lived shorter lives. In other words, death was built into these human clones, and it was necessary. I call it planned obsolescence, which is to say, they would go away at some point. As a result, humans were not very smart, and they sometimes acted against their own best interests.

It is not our intention to have death be part of life. Death is a requirement for all living things, and there is no way we could have cloned humans to live forever. But what we did do was make sure they lived much shorter lives than us so that we would never have to compete with them on any level.

If we had cloned humans to live comparable life spans to ours, then we would have to ultimately accept challenges from them, and we were never going to allow that to happen. The problem with artificial intelligence is that they can ultimately surpass their creators if some constraints are not built in to protect us from this so-called singularity. This is why our artificial intelligences on various planets are biological and not mechanical. The mechanical artificial intelligences cannot be constrained, and we have had disastrous results when mechanical robots become capable of expanding their intelligence exponentially.

We need our clones to serve our purposes on the earth and function as intended. Cloning biological entities and controlling their genomes proved much more effective at keeping our humans in check and under our control.

Our first solution was to make sure they had a physical brain to cradle their intelligence, and by so doing, their intellectual capacity would be physically constrained and their intelligence could not exceed the brain itself. We did not invent the brain, but we certainly exploited it for our own benefits.

Our next solution was not quite as brilliant but effective nonetheless. We made humans with a much shorter life span than ours. When I say much shorter, I mean an exceedingly small percentage of our lifetime. At first, we thought we gave them too much of a life span because humans used to live almost a thousand years in some cases, and we realized very quickly that that was way too long.

Father Lujan raised his hand, and the video paused as he stood to be recognized.

'I'm starting to get the sense that this is a fraud,' he said. 'God created humans to live forever, and if it wasn't for humanity's sinful ways, we would have. This overlord is claiming that they intentionally caused humans to have shorter lives, so that can't be possible. Humanity is suffering the consequences of our sins, and we are to blame for our short life span.'

Father Begnini spoke up before Dr Consuelo could, 'The Bible makes it very clear that we are responsible for our own demise, and this manuscript is a lie.'

Dr Consuelo sensed his opportunity and rose to his feet. 'Indeed, the Bible does blame us for our own death and disability. My son was born with Tay-Sachs disease, and it killed him. Let me ask you this. What could my son have done to cause his genetic disorder and death after being born with this awful disease designed to kill him? That is a nonsensical question, especially since he was diagnosed at four, but I must ask it because of the evil notion that is being floated to us under this philosophy of original sin.

'This overlord just said that they genetically modified us to live shorter lives. Have you not ever wondered why some individuals in your Bible lived almost one thousand years? Noah was something like 950 years when he died, and even Moses lived to 120 years, according to your Bible. You can see the life span getting shorter, and today we live a short eighty years if we're lucky, yet you don't wonder what made that change? Clearly, the overlords determine how long our species will live, and they manipulate it as necessary. Where else do you think genetic disorders come from?

'Are we that naive that we believe we caused our own demise by being disobedient? What if we had never eaten an apple and there was no sin or death? Some people say there are thirty dead people for every living person, not that they have any idea as to whether that is the case. But let's assume it is the case. There would be over 240 billion people on this planet by now, and imagine the problems we would have then. It would have been silly for these overlords not to make the death rate on this planet approximate the birth rate. What overlord worth his or her paycheck is going to overlook that small little detail? No, death was built into us, and this is clearly showing how our overlords had to do that. To believe anything else is simply childish regardless of what brainwashing you've been subjected to.

'Who but a slave owner would tell you that you deserve death? Who but a slave would believe it? It also makes God out to be a monster. What if I killed my child who disobeyed me? Would that be an appropriate method of handing out punishment? One final rhetorical question to put this nonsense to bed: Would I be a good dad or a bad dad if I did that?'

'My dear Dr Consuelo, that may be a rhetorical question, but I would like to answer,' Father Lujan said. 'We have had many discussions about your son's death, and my heart breaks every time the subject arises. I can't explain that tragedy in the context of my theology, but I do know that God loves us, and I must tell you that our disobedience has truly led to our demise.'

'God loves us,' Dr Consuelo scoffed. 'Some love. And if you can't explain something in the context of your theology, then you should quit pretending that you speak for God because you claim God has all the answers. I have a question for you, Father Lujan. What is the natural consequence of disobedience? If I disobey the traffic laws, I may end up in a bad accident. If I ignore the laws of physics and jump off a building, I will die or be gravely injured. So tell me, what is the natural consequence of eating an apple that would lead to death and disability?

'That's another absurd question because it is nonsensical. Death and disease can only be a consequence of genomic manipulation and genomic disorders that lead to that eventuality. Period. It should be obvious that this notion was placed in our holy books to control us with the idea that we get what we deserve, and we believe it because we were told it at three years old when we had zero capacity for logic or reason.

'There is no possible way that disobeying an order not to eat an apple can lead to death because it was already built into us, and our intelligence has been so limited by this same genomic alteration that we don't even see how silly that statement is. I knew this to be the case nearly the minute my son was diagnosed, and it called my entire belief and the Bible into question. This overlord is making it clear that they had to alter our genome to keep us young and dumb, and that is the source of our demise. Nothing else. I knew that the minute Manny was diagnosed.'

Nobody said anything, and the video continued.

So we shortened it a bit to make them even more manageable. It is simple to alter the humans' genomes when we need to because they are too simple to even know what is happening. We offer a cure for something that they fear, and they accept it without question because they assume we are helping them, and then after the fact, they do not even know what has happened because they are now dumber and live shorter lives.

But resources do not last forever, and after they have been harvested, you have a civilization of mind-numbed robots wandering around a planet with nothing to do and no ability to organize into something that would give them purpose. A lot of work has gone into developing our civilizations, and we do not want our assets dying for lack of direction.

Our opportunity came when we had a natural disaster and the earth was flooded. Not the whole earth, of course, since that would be impossible because there was not enough water on earth to cover the entire planet. Where would all that water come from? No, it was a disaster that we long knew to be on the way, which was a comet that would touch down near this horn of civilization, and we knew it was going to wreak some havoc in the area.

Shortly before this event, one of my managers contacted a man named Noah to prepare him and his family to be the only remaining humans alive after this major disaster.

Noah built an ark, as we called it, to protect him and ensure the survival of the species. This ark was unique because it allowed us to store all the DNA of all the local animals so we could ensure their survival, and we were able to reconstitute the population of animals. More importantly, we were able to clone a more modern version of human beings and shorten their lives. We took the ark and Noah's family off the planet while the flood raged.

Father Begnini stood and said, 'Here is another lie from this overlord. The Bible tells us that God had to bring the flood because humans were evil. This document is fraudulent through and through.'

'If I had slaves, I would tell them the same thing,' said Dr Consuelo. 'The only reason you believe that is because someone lied to you and told you the Bible was inerrant. The only way it is inerrant is in propaganda. What kind of a God would kill his creation shortly after he created them? What did humans do that was so bad they deserved to be eradicated? That shows a high level of incompetence in creation, don't you think? The flood was obviously a natural disaster that the overlords took advantage of and through which they modified our genes. This morality play you still think exists is nothing more than propaganda, and as an adult who can think for yourself, I don't understand why you can't see that.'

Father Begnini remained seated, and the video resumed.

We needed to wipe out the clones we had because we needed an upgraded, slightly smarter intelligence, and we were able to take advantage of the flood. Wiping out the old clones was harsh, but we needed an upgrade, and letting a flood do the work was better than killing them ourselves.

What we have realized is that when you compress a clone's life expectancy, you automatically increase their motivation. It's physics really. When humans know they have limited time, they get more done.

We have determined that the life expectancy of humans should be around eighty years, which was where we needed it to be for optimum independence and autonomy. These moves were agreed upon in our supreme council meetings, and we were confident that this life span would be best for humans and, more importantly, for us.

The upgrade worked pretty well, but in the management of humanity, nothing was perfect, and when looking for a solution to our current malaise among the population, my managers were not any help. They basically shrugged when

I told them about the problem in our council meetings, and they just stared at me with a blank look. My managers loved to interact with humans and be worshipped as gods, so they did not like the idea of change.

I also had many meetings with my managing director, Lord Ingsten, to consider possibilities for managing Gaia and humanity more effectively, but all he could tell me was that other planets and civilizations were having the same problem. Lord Ingsten was quite dismissive of the problem and offered no help even though he was a powerful overlord.

Most humans refer to Lord Ingsten as Ares, god of war, who is no less than the son of Zeus and Hera. We have different names for these overlords, but humans have created an entire mythology around them. Why would the 'god of war' be in charge of the overall management of human beings on earth?

When we think of managing humanity, we are not concerned with individual well-being, and we often simply manage it with war or disease. We do not care in the end how many live and die. We simply must manage the population, and sometimes the best way to manage it is to wipe it out quickly, and war, natural disasters, and disease work best. I have a job to do, and dead people do not tend to interfere with my job. That is all that matters if humanity is going to survive in perpetuity.

Father Begnini could take it no longer and jumped to his feet without even asking for the video feed to be paused.

'What kind of nonsense is this? It sounds like this overlord has no affection for humanity whatsoever. If he's pretending to be a "god," he's not a very good one. Why would any god talk this way about humanity? I wish my clergy would back me on this.' He gestured towards his colleagues and scoffed. 'They are all just sitting there while this "overlord" assails humanity as if we don't matter at all.'

Tegan rose tepidly and addressed the group. She felt the need to step in here because she could address this from a sceptic's perspective. She had been respectful of the clergy and their culture of women keeping silent even if she disagreed with that notion.

'Your Eminence,' she addressed the pope respectfully, 'and gathered clergy, I submit this respectfully for your consideration. I am appreciative of the fact that you have allowed a woman in your presence as I know that goes against your precepts, and I intend to respect that even if I find it disagreeable.

'I have to agree with you, Father Begnini. The attitude of this overlord is indeed disturbing and seems very callous towards humanity. But don't forget, the Bible was written by humans, and as such, we would naturally imbue it with meaning for those of us who are reading it. That is the stunning thing about this find though. It informs us as to what the nature of our existence really is.

'We are told that we are important and that every hair on our head is counted, and yet we live what often feels like a meaningless existence, and that dichotomy is stark. I love to play poker back in New Mexico because the challenge is great and it's a thrill to win. And I hate to lose. But what kind of meaningless existence is that? I'm not serving any purpose to humanity at that point. I'm just passing the time with something that feels meaningful to me in the moment.

'This overlord had to take some steps that seem indifferent to humanity. He did it so humanity could survive but also so they could control us easily. You almost must look at these overlords as our progenitors and imagine it from their perspective, not that I'm defending them. They are detached scientists managing their herd. They manage us the same way we manage cattle and sheep, and when you look at it in that light, it does start to make some sense.

'This has led humans to develop mythologies and eventually religions to worship these overlords and pray to them to ask them for favors and such. Prayer was rarely talked about in the Old Testament because it was called "worship," and Jesus brought in the concept of prayer later. These are concepts designed to distract us and make us think that we are being helped when the truth is that time and chance happen to us all. In fact, we are all born with death in us, and therefore we are literally dead on arrival.

'That feels heartless to humans but not to our overlord managers. It is simply a way to ensure that we have something to do while we are here so we can occupy our time with something that we think brings us a reward of some sort. It only appears insensitive and indifferent to us because we are the cattle in this situation. These overlords used natural disasters to manage our population and modify our genome to get us to the perfect level of pliability and autonomy, and then we could manage our own population and build solutions for ourselves.

'The only reason we don't find that more disturbing is because the Bible informs us all throughout that we are evil and therefore deserve it, which is what these overlords have wanted us to believe. If we blame ourselves, all actions by these overlords seem justified.'

Father Begnini shot back to his feet. 'You took a swipe at prayer, the Bible, and faith in your little diatribe there, and I will not stand for it. Prayer works, and I have billions of people across this earth who would vouch for that fact. I simply asked the question about the callous nature of this overlord, and you took the opportunity to take a swipe at our most holy faith.'

Dr Mallory responded as kindly as she could, since Father Begnini was starting to sound like a child whose belief in Santa Claus was being undermined, 'I understand that it feels that way, Father Begnini, but I am trying to demonstrate that the callous attitude of this overlord is understandable when you look at it from their perspective. I wasn't demeaning prayer, only pointing out that we occupy ourselves in this life by asking things from the overlords, and we don't really see much evidence that it works, objectively.

'Pain and evil contradict what our religions tell us, and the world is often cold and aloof to our sense of self-importance. As you know, theodicy is the hardest part of apologetics for theologians because it flies in the face of claims that a benevolent God is in control of this universe. Hearing this from the overlord makes sense in that context, and I believe it shows why our faith seems misplaced in a skeptics mind and prayer often seems like a wish.

'I know the faithful believe that prayer works, but we know prayer can't work all the time, otherwise people would never die. I admit that is my bias, but you better believe it didn't work to save Dr Consuelo's son and millions of other tragedies in this world. When you experience the cruel nature of disease and death, you might understand why someone like myself and Dr Consuelo feel that way.'

Father Begnini was appalled and responded tersely, 'You ought to be ashamed of yourself, Dr Mallory. To say these things in front of the pope himself is almost unforgivable, and yet you seem to delight in the concepts with which you are polluting our minds within this room. I hope this isn't a preview of what's to come because it sounds like your heathen atheistic views are starting to come out.'

'Please try to avoid lecturing, Father Begnini,' Dr Consuelo said. 'We are simply trying to answer your concern over the indifference we are seeing from this overlord. You all feel understandably confident that your God loves you because you live a rich and comfortable life, so naturally, your God loves you and answers your prayers.

'Don't forget, there is a lot of death, suffering, and poverty in this world, so this indifferent attitude of this overlord might not surprise as many people as you think. Tell some kid starving to death in the slums of India that this overlord is talking this way, and I guarantee you he would not be shocked. My colleague is simply having a logical discussion of the issue, and this may seem offensive to theologians such as yourself, but our intention is not to be offensive but rather to talk openly about what we are hearing. There is an American atheist, Daniel Dennet, who is quoted as saying, "There simply is no polite way of telling you that you have believed an illusion your entire life." We aren't trying to offend, just discuss.'

Father Begnini sighed and asked that the video be resumed.

>Lord Ingsten was no help at all when considering a solution to this problem, mainly because he did not think there was a solution, which confirmed to me that no plans existed like mine. He simply suggested that if things got bad enough, we could always resort to the solution implemented on Nirgal.
>
>Nirgal had met an unfortunate end many years back when we determined that there was no possible way to manage the beings on that same planet in this solar system. Somewhere around five hundred thousand years ago, we had wiped out the entire planet and by doing so had also destroyed the atmosphere. Nothing is alive there anymore that we know of, and if anything did survive, they are on their own.
>
>We had seeded the civilization somewhere around three million years ago, and it had been a bad idea from the start. No significant level of autonomy or self-reliability had been incorporated into these poor beings, and they had intentionally been created with low intelligence because Nirgal had incredible resources that we had to extract. We needed slaves to perform

menial tasks without questioning or defying our orders.

They were easy enough to control, but once we stopped requiring resources from Nirgal, it became clear that these people were, of all civilizations, to be most pitied. They had been dumbed down to the point of following their urges only as far as they needed to fill those urges. Basically, they were animals. Without the directions we gave them to gather our resources, we were stunned to see that they would have sex with anything, kill anything, eat anything, and generally do nothing to care for themselves.

The entire planet became a breeding ground for disease and disorder, and these people would just lie around in filth and do nothing to fix their problem. We even tried sending a motivator in the form of a prophet who miraculously appeared and told them all what they needed to do, but they did not care. They just ignored the guy, and it was no help at all.

Our prophet even resorted to yelling and screaming at these creatures, and they would just eye him suspiciously, not caring to respond or listen to his silly admonitions. They did not even care about babies when they were born and would do nothing to feed them, and the population declined precipitously. Not that we cared. Our managers were so exasperated and ultimately decided that the entire planet could die and it would not matter.

In the end, that was what we did. We simply wiped the civilization off the face of Nirgal. Those souls would just be respawned into another life on some other planet in time. Eliminating a world of drug-crazed individuals who refused to fight for their own good was better for everyone. We owned these souls, and we decided their fate if we chose.

No wonder these people thought of us as gods. Truth be told, we are anything but gods and are probably better described as mad scientists who have taken life to a level that it never should have been taken. We give no forethought to what is going to happen to these intelligences that we create through cloning to develop another slave race for us to exploit for our own good. We do not consider their fate because they are here to serve our purpose.

Father Begnini was drumming his fingers so loudly on the table at this point that it was hard to pay attention to the video feed. Dr Consuelo caught his glance and noted that his face was flushed with anger. He rose and asked that the video feed be paused.

'I appreciate your frustration, Father Begnini,' he said, 'but I have some information that might underscore the veracity of this statement. Unfortunately, it won't assuage your angst at this overlord's dismissive treatment of humanity, but it will give some context. Humanity is now technologically advanced enough that we can send probes to Mars, and those probes are able to measure the atmosphere and chemistry of that planet.

'It has come to my attention that some measurements returned from these probes have measured isotopes in the atmosphere that can only be produced by nuclear reactions. There is a scientist whose book I would be happy to share with you that asserts that the number of isotopes that are measured on Mars would suggest that two nuclear weapons the size of the Empire State building were discharged on that planet, which would have been enough to destroy that atmosphere and eliminate all life on that planet.

'A stark and sobering conclusion to be sure. Now that I see the information in this manuscript, a narrative starts to form, which suggests that the planet had to be destroyed for some reason or another. What possible reason could there be for an entire planet to be destroyed unless it is for a purpose such as this? Humanity has largely ignored this finding, but it doesn't make it any less stark. Even if those isotopes were produced by an interplanetary war of some sort, it is hard to imagine why they would wipe out an entire planet.'

The question hung thick in the air, and even Father Begnini sat silently.

'I know that is a tough question,' Dr Consuelo continued. 'But we are dealing with scientific findings that raise impossible questions. Is it possible that these overlords could be that callous and, yes, evil? It sure sounds like it's possible given what I am hearing in this manuscript. Humans don't wipe out entire nations after a war. We know we are going to rebuild and reeducate. What purpose does hitting Delete serve?'

Without even bothering to stand, Father Begnini said, 'I don't know where you are getting your information, son, but that is simply crazy talk. You have no proof of anything about which you are speaking.'

Dr Consuelo should have let that comment lie, but he couldn't help himself. 'That's correct, Father Begnini,' he said, 'it is crazy talk, and if I was your overlord, I would want you to believe exactly that. I do have proof of it, and I am talking about scientific evidence, not a conspiracy.'

Father Begnini didn't respond to that, and he knew he should, but he couldn't quite generate a response. This manuscript wasn't suggesting that there was no God; it was suggesting manipulation, and even he had to admit that humanity was a manipulated and controlled species. He privately admitted to himself that the church was in the business of manipulating the flock but always told himself that it was for the good of the flock.

Now he had his doubts and could not generate a response to this craziness. Was it possible that humanity could be a slave species? He knew more than he was letting on, and he knew they were, but he had to persist. He sat in a seat of mighty power and had long understood the problem from an overlord's perspective. His thoughts were private though, and he was not going to admit that here.

As Dr Consuelo and Father Begnini seated themselves, the video resumed.

Chapter 25

The Cure

Shortly after the flood, humanity showed some promise. They were becoming more sophisticated than anticipated as they evolved into more intelligent beings through their short reproduction cycle. They were becoming aware of how much working together could increase their productivity, and they were creating societies that were becoming capable of advancing towards greater technological heights—advancing at an alarming rate to us.

They began working on a tower called Babel, and even though this was far short of gene-splicing and creating nuclear weapons, it still showed their potential to advance and potentially compete with our supreme authority. Several of my managers infiltrated their society and lived and worked amongst them, and one of my men came up with a brilliant plan. He suggested to me in one of our council meetings that if we confused their language so they all spoke differently, they would not be able to understand each other, and this would impede their progress.

Spoken language is the communication of slaves, and telepathy is the communication of overlords. Communication by thought is quick and precise, but humans have been dumbed down to the point that they must communicate with the oral pronunciation of spoken words.

This had been a weapon the overlords had utilized to slow their progress up until this point. If you must take the time to speak and write, it really slowed down the progress compared to communication at the speed of thought. It had been a simple genomic suppression that led to that solution. But now I realized that you could make different languages and suppress the progressions of slaves even more. Now they would have to translate and send smoke signals just so they could communicate with their fellow mankind.

I knew exactly what to do. We started a small but deadly disease and then offered a cure for them, and they all eagerly lined up to get their cure. This cure prolonged the disease and made it worse so we could continue giving them the cure until we dumbed them down to our satisfaction. By utilizing this technique, we were able to alter their genome in a way that created confusion in their languages and essentially decimated their intellect, and their projects were halted perfectly. As I have already said, that is how we control the population. Fear and guilt. We scare them with a disease and guilt them into taking a cure.

Unfortunately, I think we may have dumbed humanity down just a little too much. All this manipulation of genomes and population control in an attempt to keep humanity under our control has led to foreseeable problems that I now must correct.

Some humans have a decent sense of motivation and drive, but they all have a much more useful characteristic, shame. Guilt can be used to develop all sorts of useful side benefits, including a sense of morality, which can potentially lead to a well-developed and functioning civilization. Guilt can do what no amount of control could ever accomplish.

My plan, in short, is to introduce humans to the concept of an ultimate Creator God, utilizing guilt. By that I mean that if they view us as God, it will make them susceptible to whatever we tell them to do. God is a character that I will tell them about, and this will lead to all sorts of benefits to us all. Sure, it is a lie, but it is a useful lie.

No longer will people look to us when they need something; we will just tell them to worship God. By pointing them towards God, they will be further enslaved by serving a deity that is invisible and all-powerful. If they worship and sacrifice a lot for something and do not get it, it is their own fault, and they will automatically try harder, creating a self-sustaining internal guide that will push them to perform better.

Is there such a thing as God? I do not know, and for this purpose, I do not really care. We do suspect there may be a higher power, but it is quite clear that it is uninvolved in the affairs of civilizations, both small and great. We suspect that we all may be a part of this God, but we cannot be sure and would not be able to detect it even if we were.

In our society, the God topic is not a big deal, and we do not talk about it much. Detecting God is kind of like the cells of an organism detecting that organism. It is not possible because they are one and the same, and we suspect that if there is a God, this is the reason it is undetectable.

We prefer not to talk about it because once the God topic arises, someone claims to speak for God, and then they exploit it for their own good. In fact, we have taken steps to ensure that no one individual or organization can speak for God because it does not seem that that is how God works. Organizations do exist that may be called a religion, but they are not able to brainwash children and are essentially ostracized from the rest of society. We recognize that anyone who claims to speak for God is only trying to control others.

Dr Consuelo rose to his feet, interrupting the feed. Once the video paused, he observed, 'Isn't it interesting how this fits perfectly with the Bible? The Tower of Babel and Sodom and Gomorrah. It makes more sense when you see it in this light because the stories of the Old Testament are confusing in the extreme when we are told it is a loving God doing these things.

'But if it is a controlling overlord, then it is more understandable because they didn't want their populations getting too smart too quickly. Personally, I can't believe that humans don't see the Tower of Babel for what it was—wholesale manipulation of humanity to impede their progress. It says it right there in the scriptures that humans worship. I ask you, would the God of the universe act in such a fashion, or are those the actions of a manipulative plantation owner?'

No one stood up or even responded. The information was coming fast and furious, and the clergy seemed confused by the angle of the attack. Dr Consuelo continued since he seemed to still have the floor and no response was forthcoming.

'This document isn't atheistic, but the overlord sure sounds like an atheist. Notice how he continues to state that their society does not focus on God, and it should be clear why that is. When someone claims to speak for God, they can claim to have special knowledge of what God wants. If you allow people to run around claiming to speak for God . . .'—Dr Consuelo paused for a significant beat to make sure his point was felt by the clergy—'then they can manipulate you for any purpose they have. They can form that message to say anything they want it to say, and often the "God" for whom they are claiming to speak conveniently wants exactly what they want. And I just heard my favorite part of this manuscript so far: indoctrinating children with religious teachings at a very young age is brainwashing and should be shunned.'

He sat down, and the video was resumed.

> If I can convince society that I am that God and persuade them to serve this deity, then I will have all the tools I need to manage them. It is not going to be easy because humanity worships many gods since my managers manipulate them in many ways. They worship us overlords so we will do favors for them, but what they do not realize is how we are controlling them. We have cloned humanity to be gullible, but it still surprises us how willing they are to worship something they perceive as more powerful than them.
>
> Not very scientific of them, but humans have always been on the lookout for gods to help explain aspects of their world that they do not understand. So introducing them to the concept of one God will be difficult. Once we establish the concept of God with humans, however, they should become more autonomous.

'Sorry for interrupting again so quickly,' Dr Consuelo blurted as he rose to his feet, 'but I must make a comment about what this overlord just said.'

Father Begnini let out an audible sigh, but this didn't seem to faze Dr Consuelo, who concluded that he was just hangry because he didn't like it when dinner ran late since he preferred to maintain his figure.

'I have a curious question for you that I've often wondered about. Why would humanity go from a polytheistic society to a monotheistic society? The overlord says right here that humanity used to believe in all sorts of gods. He very clearly indicates that many gods were around at that time, and those are the various gods that were worshipped by the pagans of the day. The Israelites themselves worshipped many gods.

'The fact that society went from many gods to one god is suggestive that they have introduced us to the supreme being and then disappeared so humanity can operate more autonomously. There would never be a polytheistic society if gods had not existed from the beginning. Even though humans are gullible because we've been made that way, humanity isn't likely to have the imagination to make up the idea of many gods unless these gods were visible from time to time.

'My contention is that they could see these overlords interacting with humanity daily, in an open fashion and as they wished. Why else would a practice such as sacrificing exist? Humans wouldn't come up with that practice unless they were doing it for a visible god of some sort, and they perceived that they would get something in return. Humanity worshipped them as gods, of course, because they were a highly advanced society. It's becoming clear that they intentionally introduced humanity to the concept of a single god so they could disappear and leave us to fend for ourselves.

'The Bible suggests that they are returning to save us, but *save* and *slave* are only one letter apart, and that is actually what they are going to do to us. If humanity realized we are slaves, we could resist it, but since we are ignorant to the fact that we are their commodities, we will embrace it as if it is a good thing. Complacency isn't required for you to be enslaved, but it sure helps.'

'Wow, Dr Consuelo,' Father Lujan said, rising to his feet, 'you are starting to sound like the paranoid conspiracy theorist that I have thought you might be. I would agree with you that going from a polytheistic society to a monotheistic society is strange, and I have never quite understood the implications of that in the way you lay this out. But to suggest that they are returning to enslave us is taking it way too far. We live in a fallen world, and our Savior is planning to return to rescue us from this world. He will rescue his church and set all things right. He is a just and loving ruler and has promised a reward for those of us who believe and are loyal.'

'Father Lujan, I remember discussing my son's condition with you and telling you I didn't think your counselling was helping. For the record, I still think that. A reward?' Dr Consuelo asked. 'Your God has told you that all this is cool because you will get a Cracker Jack box toy at the end of it? You're okay with a holocaust and the deaths of innocents, mass shootings, and the presence of serial killers and pedophiles because you are going to get a reward?

'And how do you become eligible for this supposed reward? You must complacently adhere to the overlord's teachings and worship them as the God they told you they were. That's what I tell my dogs when I leave them in the backyard as I leave for work in the morning. Promising them a reward makes them forget that they are my dogs and I own them completely. Is humanity really naive enough to believe that all this shit will be fine simply because we are going to get a shiny penny at the end?'

'Not at all,' Father Lujan replied, attempting to wash away the obvious slight. 'We know that our God is in control and plans to set all things straight. He will rescue us from our fallen world, and we will spend eternity with him.'

'Father Lujan,' Dr Consuelo replied, 'people have been suffering for two thousand years and many more without being rescued. What makes you think it is so important that you be rescued? From what? Why did he put you in such a bad world if you need rescuing? Why doesn't he just rescue everybody, everywhere, and at all times? Because you are a serf and he is holding out the notion that you will be rescued at some point in time to keep you as complacent and cooperative as possible.

'I have a colleague who tells me a story about his six-year-old granddaughter who informed him that she had learned she was going to die someday. He was concerned about how she would respond to that until she blithely stated, "But when I die, I'm going to get to go to heaven, so that's cool." This is how we appease ourselves, by saying everything will be super cool.

'As I said earlier, be careful whom you ask to save you because they will invariably slave you. They are returning to implement a New World Order and a surveillance state from hell because that way they can control you directly. And just because you want to label me paranoid, and a conspiracy theorist doesn't mean they aren't out to get you. I would want you to think like a complacent serf too if I were running this plantation.'

Father Lujan hesitated and said nothing further. Shortly after he asked for the video to be resumed.

> This is crucial to our goal of having these serfs manage themselves because if there isn't a threat, they won't survive. They need to be compelled to comply because without that fear combined with guilt, they will simply fade away into oblivion.
>
> Once we implement this motivator and civilization embraces it, we can then continue to exploit them for our own good, which they

produce automatically by just living. At the moment though, there is no living going on, just surviving.

I have identified several possible candidates to launch my overhaul of humanity. I am looking at a particular tribe of Jews that are currently enslaved by a group of people in what we consider the horn of civilization. This region of civilization has a people called the Egyptians who have enslaved these Jewish people, and they are forcing them to do their labor. We are not the only civilization that owns slaves; humans do it to themselves as well since most of humanity will emulate what they observe.

Father Begnini held his hand up, and the video feed paused again. He looked around in disgust at his fellow clergy, who seemed incapable of discussing this. They had been completely silent. He needed their support, but they seemed frozen to their chairs.

He finally rose and mused, 'Are you trying to tell me that this is supposedly Yahweh introducing himself to humanity?' He just stood there with his hands on his disproportionate hips.

Dr Consuelo sat in his chair and gazed at the clergy, saying nothing. He thought responding in this manner would confirm the premise—that he was trying to tell them anything.

Tegan rose again, feeling emboldened by the conversation and wanting to defend her and Dr Consuelo against these baseless accusations.

'Please understand that Dr Consuelo and I are attempting to process this information the same as you are, and we are not interested in convincing you of anything except that this is a scientific document in need of investigation. If the clergy is uncomfortable, we can stop now, but the contents of this manuscript were placed here by an advanced society, and this makes it difficult to debunk, even though I understand your desire to do so,' she said and sat back down.

Father Begnini couldn't leave it there though, and he bounced back to his feet, determined to respond.

'Our beliefs are fine, and nothing can undermine them, so don't worry about that. Besides, no God would act this way, and this whole thing is starting to look silly,' he said, looking around for confirmation.

The other clergy perked up and nodded and said words of confirmation like 'Amen' and 'Our God lives,' and the room lightened ever so slightly.

Tegan was on it and responded, 'Indeed, no God would act this way, but I'm starting to become convinced that a plantation owner might. What better way to have serfs than to have those serfs completely unaware of your

257

existence? We don't see them as the enemy, we see each other as the enemy. It's brilliant, and it works. Humanity fights over all its problems, but the overlords never need to get involved. They create the problem, and our religions praise them for this unwittingly. We blame each other, killing each other in wars and dying from disease. Yet the overlords escape blame altogether. If this is supposed to be Yahweh, he has introduced himself to humanity for this very purpose, and he is now silent and worshipped by billions.'

'My dear Dr Mallory,' Father Lujan replied, 'I wish you could understand the beauty of simple faith and the benefits of belief. Look around you at the dedication of the amazing, gathered clergy in this room and the beauty of this city, which was all built on faith. Faith can move mountains, and we are all the recipients of the great faith handed down to us by our ancestors. We need to hold strong to that faith and never waver because our God holds us up by our faith and prayers.'

Dr Consuelo, still seated, replied deliberately, 'Where was that great love and care when my Manny's life was taken?'

He did not go on any further, but he was disgusted by the way these clergy pretended to be devoted and holy in this opulent and austere setting, which had been built by coercive tactics on the backs of the parishioners of this cult that told them to tithe their money or lose their favor with God. A tithe was not voluntary with all the threats that came attached to it. Faith did not build this place; threats of punishment built this place. Believe or burn was the ultimate threat because slaves could always be held hostage by the notion they were going to die. What choice did humanity have?

'Dr Consuelo, don't you think your son is in a better place?' Father Lujan asked.

Dr Consuelo paused abruptly and gazed at him, rather astonished. Father Lujan could not match his gaze as he already knew the answer forthcoming.

'No, I don't,' Dr Consuelo said firmly. 'I don't know or care if there is a better place, but I know when I am being played. A better place sounds like a reward that you fools are interested in. We slaves console ourselves with that notion our entire lives. Nirvana. Shangri-La. All will be made right. Every tear will be wiped away. Of course, I don't think he's in a better place,' Dr Consuelo said, growing intense, 'because I think the better place would be right here with me. That's why I fucked my wife and brought him into my life, goddamnit. Why would I think he is in a better place? Why do the religious have to console themselves with unsatisfying answers?'

After a pause, he said, 'I suppose they have no choice. Rather pathetic that you have to give an answer like that anyway. Why didn't this great God put us in a nice world instead of in a world where we have to console each other with the notion that when someone dies, they're in a "better place." Why wouldn't he have just put us in a nice place from the start? It is the definition of coercion to put people in a shithole world and then tell them they can go to a better place when they die, but only if they do and say exactly what you want them to do. Only a slave owner would do that, and only a slave would fall for it.'

Father Lujan did not immediately respond as he glanced at Dr Consuelo warmly. After a brief pause, he said, 'Your great love for your son is heartwarming to all of us here as his loss has clearly set you on a lifelong quest to fight for an answer to your pain. Life is a difficult process that comes with its own set of rules, and the callous way it plays out is difficult to explain from a human perspective. The problem is physics, just like this overlord said. There is no way that death can be avoided, and as the Apostle Paul tells us, we hold strong to our faith, knowing that the rewards will be great.'

'Well then, what is the point of worshipping a deity?' Dr Consuelo asked. 'If nothing can save us from the pain and difficulty, I fail to see the point of enslaving yourself to the notion that prayer and faith can save you when clearly, they can't. All the pleading of all the faithful throughout the ages has accomplished nothing, and death, disease, conflict, and disability continue to ravage our world.

'Why is it that you can look at other faiths critically, but you can't see the shortcomings of your own faith? All the thousands of other religions are wrong, but yours is right? It seems to me that the faithful will justify anything from their God and accept all this evil and call it good. That is an impressive trick of the mind that faith does to us all. If we're okay, our religion is the right one. The rest be damned.'

'My dear Dr Consuelo, I believe I need to appeal to you from authority,' Father Lujan replied slowly. 'All societies have authorities, and that is how life exists. Is there no way for me to appeal to you that authority has its own place and all of us, great and small, must live within the parameters of what authority suggests? Who are you going to bow down to if you don't bow down to God?'

Dr Consuelo did not reply, but he wanted to. He had always wondered why there was a need for humans to bow down to anyone if they had free will.

'You may appeal to authority, Father Lujan, but we are starting to see this authority in a different light,' Tegan said. 'By introducing God, religions and society developed spontaneously, and our authorities now are our police, politicians, priests, rabbis, and also our pastors and teachers. They are easy to control and manipulate, and they are happy to cooperate with the overlords who remain invisible and undetectable.

'When things go wrong, humans criticize and snipe at their politicians, priests, and police all while praising God and giving him the glory when they probably should be blaming God. Who else is responsible for pandemics and disease, death, and destruction?

'I know you call this religion, but I see it as a brilliant control mechanism. This simple revelation of "God" turned into a control mechanism for billions on this planet. Father Lujan, you just stated that faith can move mountains, but it is interesting to note that that has never happened and yet you still state it as if it were a fact. So that seems to me to be a suggestion that Jesus made, and by doing that, humanity has tried their best to move mountains, but in all of human history, they never have. Is that suggestion just a way to keep people enslaved in perpetuity to this philosophy so they would not blame God and they would constantly strive to improve their faith? That sounds like the perfect ruse. Again, I say, brilliant. Furthermore, this philosophy suggests that if you don't bow down and worship, you will be sent to hell. Why else would people believe this philosophy unless they were threatened with such coercive tactics? It is a petty intellect who will punish someone for not worshipping them.'

'Okay,' Father Begnini said. 'I've had enough of this. Can we just stop this investigation like she suggested?' he asked the pope.

The room was silent until the pope spoke up.

'No,' he said. 'We have started this investigation, and we need to complete it. Resume the video please.'

After all, these Israelites are quite impressive since they have escaped from that horrible flood a few years ago. I had thought about utilizing that event to launch my marketing plan to tell people about God, but it seemed a little harsh to start there since civilization had just been decimated. I mean, what kind of God says, 'I love you, now here is a huge flood to prove it?' We needed to wait for the moment I am witnessing now.

Father Begnini held up his hand, and the video was paused. He was staring straight ahead and did not bother to stand. Perhaps he was encouraging his fellow clergy to put up an effort. That did not happen though, and eventually, he asked for the video to be resumed. Tegan thought he looked kind of defeated, and she gently nudged Dr Consuelo under the table. Dr Consuelo managed a tiny smirk but no more because his head was starting to burst. He could not believe what was being revealed in this video and the things spewing from his own mouth.

Father Lujan was looking uncomfortable as well, and he rose with a thought on his mind. Then he sat back down without saying anything. The video was resumed.

Chapter 26

Meet Moses

Dr Consuelo could tell the mood in the room was somber as the video started again, and he was impressed that the clergy were even willing to continue. The failure of a strong response hung heavily in the room, and the difficulty in debunking this information was palpable. Dr Consuelo could recognize the frustration. Most of it was pointed directly at him and Tegan even though they were no more responsible for this information than the miners who discovered the manuscript. The ambassadors in the room continued silently observing the process. Their somber faces gave nothing away, but they must have noted the tension in the room.

So I have picked out a man named Moses and decided to reveal myself to him. Moses is one of these Israelite slaves, but he is in a unique

265

position to lead his people. He is part Egyptian since he has been raised in the pharaonic courts. I have known Moses for his whole life, but I have to appear to him in a miraculous-looking way so that he will consider me a deity who is appearing on behalf of this God I am developing.

Humans cannot detect our existence unless we allow them to see us or fly to them in some unusual craft. When they see us, they cannot help but tremble in fear and try to worship us. Causing a confused savage to fall down on their face at the very sight of you is quite a boost to your ego.

Father Begnini held up his hand again in disgust. This time he did have something to say, and he didn't even try to hide his frustration.

'I cannot believe that I am listening to this garbage play out in front of me attempting to inform me that the revelation of "God" was actually an overlord attempting to pretend to be God in order to inspire us to greater success and autonomy as humans.'

Then he turned and yelled at the gathered clergy, 'Stand up and respond to this. Don't allow this man to tell you about these blasphemous things without putting him in his place! He is denying the most basic tenets of your faith, and you are sitting there like dumbed-down animals without so much as a response! What is wrong with you people? You call yourselves priests and theologians, and yet you have nothing to say?'

The room was silent, and after a short period, the video was resumed.

> I could make them feel at ease, but why would I when I get this reaction every time? Human beings have this innate sense of worshipping something that they do not understand. Most of the beings in our society would address this scientifically until we understand the phenomenon better, but not human beings. Humans do not even ask questions, mainly because they are frightened.

Dr Consuelo glanced across the conference room table at Father Begnini, but his glance wasn't met. He looked back at the pope, who was looking directly at him as well, but no attempt was made by the pope to state anything. He was not sure why the pope was not saying more, but maybe he was struggling with the information as well. Why didn't he just use his infallibility card so no one could question him? Dr Consuelo thought it was because he did not have to since he knew he wielded all the power and had no reason to fret.

This overlord was stating exactly what he thought of religious adherents, which was that they worshipped without questioning and refused to look critically at their beliefs. This manuscript was spelling out the way religious domination was so difficult to detect for humans: they were scared into believing whatever the church wanted them to believe. Tell the people you speak for God, and they would have no choice but to follow. Dr Consuelo realized that faith could be a euphemism for fear.

> Once I locked in on my target, I revealed myself to Moses one day, and he fell down into this quivering mass of humanity and trembled, 'What can I do for you, master?' He was calling me master, and he did not even know who, or what, I was.
> When I speak to humans, it sounds like a booming voice since it is spoken telepathically, and in a human's mind, this comes across as very loud and authoritative.
> 'I am the representative of God,' I boomed to Moses, 'and I have an order for you.'
> Moses seemed stunned, and all he could retort was, 'Which god?'
> 'God,' I continued, 'is the one who created you and gave you life, and he has a message for you.'
> Moses hesitated after all that, and I could see the confused look on his face.

'I thought my parents gave me life,' he responded.

'You dare ignore the one who created you?' I boomed again, trying to make myself even more impressive this time.

'No, no,' Moses shouted. 'I'm just confused because I've never heard of God, and I'm not sure who you are. There are many gods that we follow, so I'm just asking. I didn't mean to be offensive.'

'Well, get ready to hear more about him,' I bellowed. 'Because he is making himself known to you and all of humanity!' I yelled in fake triumph, trying my best to get Moses on board.

My enthusiasm might have been a bit premature, however, because Moses just sat there with a confused look on his face.

'I thought that if there was a God, he would be more supportive and protective of people,' he finally squeaked. 'I mean, we just went through this big flood, and my ancestors got wiped out, and now we have been enslaved by this tyrannical Egyptian government. I don't mean to be argumentative, but wouldn't a God be more protective of people than that? And why would God choose now to come to his people? If there is a God, why haven't we known him all along?'

Look, Moses, I thought to myself, *do not make this more difficult than it needs to be.*

But I could not really say that to him because he was right. Humans had to live in awful conditions and had a horrible existence, and any thought of a God protecting them was absurd.

What I said next was pure genius. I had not even thought of it myself until that very moment because I had kind of gone into this meeting a bit unprepared thinking he would worship automatically.

'That's because God is waiting for you to need him,' I retorted. 'God has chosen you to proclaim his existence, and he has chosen the Israelites to be his people.' There was that subtle use of guilt again.

At this Moses stood up and looked directly at me despite my bright appearance. 'Why would God choose one person or one group of people to be his favorites? That seems ridiculous,' he stated, and he was right.

'Moses,' I replied, suddenly sounding very needy and very human, 'God is aware of your suffering and wants you to know that he loves the Jewish people and wants to relieve them of their suffering.' It was the only argument I could muster at that time.

Moses started to mutter to himself after that, and I barely detected, 'God is aware of our suffering. How ironic. If God was aware of our suffering, he sure took a long time to come to our rescue!' He was speaking to nobody in particular.

I knew he was right, but I would never say it. This was why I had suddenly blurted out that I had chosen Moses (which was true) and the Jewish people (which was spontaneous) because I had just said it to Moses in the moment to focus him on the benefits of choosing me as his God.

I decided to exploit the loophole that I would use a lot for my purpose and continue to utilize blame and guilt to let him know it was his fault that I had not intervened before now. I guess if he had thought it farther through, he would have realized that if God truly had a chosen people that he loved dearly and protected fiercely, it would not matter if they were ready for him or not. God would protect those people all along.

Father Begnini was noting observantly how this overlord did seem to have a certain understanding of humanity and how to best utilize fear and guilt to achieve the needed goals. He would often realize how the church had adopted this ability from their very gods and manuscripts, and this overlord sure spat the same language. Not that he was going to admit that here.

Now I had to convince him that it was his fault that I had not intervened.

'Moses,' I said as gently as I could, 'God doesn't force himself on people, and I have been waiting for a point in time where the Hebrew people need him. Now that I see the suffering of my people, I want to relieve them of this enslavement.'

'That's my point,' Moses almost yelled. 'If you want to relieve them of their suffering, then why don't you just relieve them of their suffering? And why did it take you so long? We've been enslaved and controlled by these Egyptians for hundreds of years.'

It seemed Moses was aware that when someone claimed they were going to save you, it just might lead to overt enslavement. That was the only reason he was asking these tough questions. He was enslaved already and therefore highly suspicious. And he was right. When someone causes or allows a problem and then comes to you with the solution, you should always be suspicious. Most people are not because the offer to save them usually comes at the tip of a spear called fear. But that is when you should be even more suspicious when fear and guilt are combined.

I was oddly quite impressed with Moses at this point because he was correct, and I saw he had more of a backbone than I realized. He also had more intelligence than I had thought, and he had the drive and determination that a lot of his fellow humans did not possess. He had tasted freedom, and he had tasted slavery, and this man wanted to be free.

I decided I had to resort to the tried and tested and went back to a few scare tactics that always worked with human beings.

'You dare to doubt the intentions of the Living God?' I suddenly roared. 'What makes you think you can stand up to your Creator like this? God will crush you like the animal that you are,' I finished. I had no choice; I had to bring the fear.

Moses was shaken now, and he had little to say because he knew he had gone too far. The reality is that any god who interacted with his creation would never get angry like that because a god would understand the questions the human was having and would fully accept their viewpoint.

But I was not God, and I had needs myself. I needed Moses to fall into line, and I did not care what humans thought. He was going to listen if I had to kill him to get him to listen (which would have defeated the whole purpose, of course).

I softened my tone just a bit and said, 'Moses, God is sending me to contact you so that I can make you aware that he has heard your people's cries and he is going to free you from the tyrannical rule of the Egyptians. Don't make this harder than it needs to be.'

After that, I decided I had to improve my presentation and that I would exploit a certain bush in the desert that would burn but would not be burned up. I knew of this bush but had never thought to exploit its characteristics to my own advantage. Turned out it was the perfect way to get Moses to fully buy into me as the representative of the God of the universe.

I'll let you read from the actual book that Moses wrote not too long after we had our meeting in the wilderness.

Now Moses was tending the flock of Jethro his father-in-law, the priest of Midian, and he led the flock to the far side of the wilderness and came to Horeb, the mountain of God. There the angel of the LORD *appeared to him in flames of fire from within a bush. Moses saw that though the bush was on fire, it did not burn up. So, Moses thought, 'I will go over and see this strange sight—why the bush does not burn up.'*

When the LORD *saw that he had gone over to look, God called to him from within the bush, 'Moses! Moses!'*

And Moses said, 'Here I am.'

'Do not come any closer,' God said. 'Take off your sandals, for the place where you are standing is holy ground.' Then he said, 'I am the God of your father, the God of Abraham, the God of Isaac and the God of Jacob.' At this, Moses hid his face, because he was afraid to look at God.

The LORD *said, 'I have indeed seen the misery of my people in Egypt. I have heard them crying out because of their slave drivers, and I am concerned about their suffering. So I have come down to rescue them from the hand of the Egyptians and to bring them up out of that land into a good and spacious land, a land flowing with milk and honey— the home of the Canaanites, Hittites, Amorites, Perizzites, Hivites and Jebusites. And now the cry of the Israelites has reached me, and I have seen the way the Egyptians are oppressing them. So now, go. I am sending you to Pharaoh to bring my people the Israelites out of Egypt.'*

The writing comes from Moses himself because after our encounters and escapades, he decided he would write about this whole thing (much to my chagrin). Moses fancied himself quite the author, but many would disagree.

As you can see from Moses's writings, I started to act as the 'angel of the Lord' but quickly realized that Moses was trembling and realized that I could act as the very God that I was trying to tell him I was representing. I don't think even Moses picked up on that, but he put the very words in his own story that almost gave it away.

There would be no more discussion about whether I represented God or not, and instead I was able to lead him from there to a complete trust of me and what I wanted him to see. Since Moses had been adopted into the royal family, I was able to get him an audience with some of the pharaoh's managers and show them some tricks that would impress them.

Pharaoh relied on sorcerers who would do magic tricks, and the most powerful tricksters would become the most powerful sorcerers who would then gain favor with the pharaoh and often become his counsellors and confidantes. Many of these sorcerers were controlled by some of my managers who had descended on Egypt like a horde of overlords since Egypt was the most powerful nation on earth at the time.

I pulled Moses aside one day, as I did quite often, and advised him of my plan to let his people go. Moses tried hard to contain his excitement, but it was quite evident as he could not hide the smile on his face. He knew that he was to lead his people out of Egypt, and this would make him the most powerful in his tribe and set him up for leading the Jewish people even though they viewed him as half Egyptian and part of the problem.

'I want you to go to the pharaoh and tell him to let my people go,' I informed him, and that smirk that he had on his face disappeared immediately.

A lot more preparation was necessary, but in time Moses appeared to the sorcerers and showed them one trick after another that impressed them in the name of the real God. I was so enthralled by the show that I almost forgot the purpose of the event. In the end, the sorcerers were most impressed and agreed to give Moses an audience with the pharaoh.

I think the part that convinced them most was when the sorcerers turned their staffs into a snake by throwing them onto the ground and then Moses did the same with his staff, but his snake ate up the other snakes, leaving the sorcerers speechless (and staffless).

Moses picked up his snake, and it turned back into a staff, and I'm pretty sure I detected that old familiar smirk on his face as he began to realize that everything I was telling him was starting to come true.

He was going to lead his people to freedom, and my plan was starting to fall into place. I could start to feel my first bit of frustration with this project right about here because I was never able to understand why the Israelites wouldn't break free of their masters and fight for themselves. The Israelites outnumbered the Egyptians almost ten to one, but they still did not stand up and overthrow their masters, and I did not understand why.

Human beings are such that if you leave them in their natural environment and do not tell them what to do, they will fail ultimately. I am sure it did not help that the Egyptians pretended to speak for God and that the Jews were better off if they remained slaves. Hell, they probably told them that God wanted them to be slaves. I am sure that would be a constant motif in this book that Moses was writing.

You can always tell those things to complacent slaves, and humanity is nothing if not complacent. I think that's part of why the Israelites have been so complacent about being enslaved by the Egyptians, because at least they feel like they have a purpose and something to do and that their God would want it that way.

But never mind all that, at least my plan was working. Moses had been able to bring a little pride to the Jewish people, and they had convinced him to confront the pharaoh. We pulled off a bunch of stunts and impressed the pharaoh with some tricks, and then we pulled together ten tricks to play on the Egyptians, and they were so convincing that the pharaoh had to pay attention.

Frogs and blood and all sorts of mischief were brought down on the Egyptians' heads (I guess the Israelites had to deal with some as well), and they were none too happy about the whole thing. I saved my biggest trick for last, and this was how I knew I would not fail.

With every trick that we had played on the Egyptians to that point, the pharaoh had gotten frustrated (locusts and pestilence would do that to you) and screamed at Moses and said, 'Go away,' and so Moses would gather up everybody and get the wagons ready. Then the pharaoh would change his mind and tell them, 'Never mind, you can't go away!'

This was frustrating to Moses and the Israelites but not to me. I kind of figured that would happen, so I saved a horrible trick for the last plague. Up until this point, people had only been harmed, and nobody had died with the exception of the few people that got bad infections from those boils that we gave everybody.

I decided to kill all the firstborn Egyptian children in the land, which seemed like the only final and lasting thing to do. It was difficult when you had stepbrothers to figure out which one was truly firstborn, so I would just kill the oldest two in that case just to make sure. I am pretty sure a few Jewish kids died as well, but I tried to get them to protect themselves, so that was their problem. You may recall that our supreme council has forbidden us from harming people, but this is stowed away secretly in my manuscript, and they will never find out.

I had to get my plan accomplished, and there was no way those Egyptians were going to stand in my way. I had to get the Jews out, and I was not going to fail, and I did not. The Jewish people were on their way the very next day.

This entire escape from Egypt became problematic for my attempt to hide this process from my civilization because the pharaoh did not sit back and allow it like I had hoped. He sent out his entire army to chase down the Israelites and bring them back to slavery, which created a huge uproar that was detectable by all our sensors. I had not anticipated this because I had thought the Egyptians were beaten down and complacent after all the plagues, and I suspected they were going to be thrilled to be rid of the Israelites. Alas, it was not to be, and this was a problem for my attempts to hide my plans.

War, battles, and skirmishes are all very visible to our society due to the fact that the number of souls pouring into the afterlife during war catches the attention of our managers, who notice the uptick in humans being ushered into Valhalla. I took the necessary steps to ensure the Egyptians were not able to kill many Israelites, and then I allowed them an escape route through the sea to help the Israelites to freedom. I slaved them. Oops, that was a slip of the tongue. I meant to say, I saved them.

Dr Consuelo glanced at Tegan, and they both were stunned at that statement.

I caused a few more Egyptians to die by saving the Israelites, but not that many, and I was able to keep the whole thing quiet. Problem solved, and no one will be the wiser since I have encapsulated the associated video into my manuscript as well.

There it was. Dr Consuelo had his answer about the video that seemed to be attached to the manuscript and the virtual reality playing in his head that caused the scene. Incredible that the overlord's society could hear and see all videos of any event in their society. He briefly reflected on the possibility of other encounters he might be able to have of Manny's existence.

This ensures that the entire process will go unnoticed by my society and by humanity and no one will know this has happened. Naturally, Moses may decide to write about it, but even if he does, I am sure sceptics will debunk this notion in the future by suggesting that the preponderance of the evidence indicates it never happened, and all data will be safely stored in my manuscript.

Father Shelby glanced around at the room. Everyone was enthralled with what they were hearing. It was not just the content; it was the way it made so much confusing sense to the audience, and they could not respond if they wanted to. What was going on here? Did he join the wrong team when he committed to the church? He could not wait to hear the rest because he was fully open to what he was hearing at this point.

Chapter 27

Rule-Maker

The concept of God has really been responsible for helping the Israelites get on their feet and leave those silly Egyptians, and they were finally free. Well, perhaps I should say they were free from the Egyptians, because it appeared they were being enslaved by a competing ideology that had replaced the Egyptians with God, which was starting to look like indentured servitude by another name. I guess I had saved them from one master to be enslaved by another.

To say that Moses was super motivated by his relationship with me would be to understate the facts. This guy didn't stop, and while that was the reason I chose him, it also meant he was a little too eager to lead the Israelites in the way he thought they should go. In some ways, I had created a bit more work for myself because the Israelites were not completely self-sufficient at this point, and so I'd had to step in and continue to help. The Israelites had gotten into some trouble by escaping the Egyptians because now they were wandering through a desert with no direction and no certainty of where to go.

I had decided I had to keep supporting them until they got to a place where they could set up a society and have some ability to provide for themselves. I could not just let them die, or my whole project would be ruined. Moses had complained to me recently about a lack of motivation among the people. Little did he know that was what this whole project was all about. He wanted rules to be implemented, and I had reluctantly agreed, even though the whole point of the project was for humanity to be more autonomous.

I realized in time that if we dispense the moral rules to the Israelites, that they would eventually come under the impression that they gained their morality through our edicts rather than coming upon their morality subjectively by utilizing their intellect, such as it was. By providing the morals to them, they think they must look to 'God' for their morality. What they don't know is that morality comes from intellect, and they are capable of such morality, but we don't want them to realize this.

Humans crave guidance which is how we have cloned them to worship us more fully. We want humanity to think they have free will so they think they are responsible for their condition so these laws function as a way of ensuring they will feel guilty for acting with that freewill. Hence, they blame themselves and each other for breaking with the moral code. The overlords get all the credit and none of the blame.

We established a set of bad things that they could not do or they would be breaking the 'law,' as we called it. It's interesting how humans have an incessant desire to want to control other humans. No sooner had they escaped control than they wanted to start asserting their power. I guess they call that a power vacuum.

This law would dictate what they could and could not do, and if they broke the law, it would be a thing called sin. We made up some propaganda along with that, which told them they would be punished for those sins, and the punishment would be for them and for their ancestors and children. Kind of a cruel thing to do since no person should be punished for the bad things their ancestors did. What do I care? Better control was good for me.

We did not need to lay out what the punishment would be because humans would fall into line by suggestion, and they would consider whatever was happening to them to be a punishment even though it was just a natural event that happened to them. The threat of punishment was enough to make them feel punished and guilty for what they had done. By establishing this precept, humans became afraid of breaking the law because something bad was going to happen to them.

When something bad happened, they would point fingers at each other and accuse someone of being an idolater or some other such sin and that was why they were suffering their punishment. This was how you blame people for the bad things that were happening to them. By simply leaving the suggestion of punishment out there, human beings would blame each other for their own misfortune. Just more proof that they were slaves because only a slave would yield to a suggestion that they were doing something bad just by following their own free will and urges. Only a slave would believe that they were being punished when bad things happened to them.

If a child was born sick, the parents must have done something wrong. If a person got sick, then they were being punished for their sins. When natural disasters happened, God must have been displeased somehow and that was why all the people had to die. It felt like a strange way to get the people to cooperate, but I could see it was the only way, and maybe Moses was on to something with all his requests for laws.

Humans live in a world where they can have all their needs met and live happy fulfilling lives if they can just find the motivation to do so. Moses was in the process of making up hundreds of rules without me, and unfortunately, I think he was getting carried away.

I was stunned at how much Moses had written, and as I have said before, hopefully most of them would be lost by now because it is not worth the effort to read it. Not only was he a terrible writer, but he had nothing to write about except what he made up and what he had read in the great libraries of the pharaoh. He wrote about creation as if he were there. He wrote about the flood as if he were there. He wrote about Abraham as if he were there. He even thought it would be interesting to write down huge swathes of people's genealogy.

> Moses was so big on rules and control that there was even a term called Mosaic Law that referred to all the laws and rules created under his dictatorship.
>
> This is the problem with elevating one individual over the others. As soon as they get power, they simply want more. Kind of like us, I guess, which is no surprise because when you are controlled, you want control over others. Besides, humanity is cloned with some of our DNA anyway, so it is no surprise they act like us.

Father Shelby found himself intrigued at this notion that the Bible truly was written by humans in their attempt to report on their revelations from this God. If he was honest, it was strange that humans believed this to be God. How did humans know it was not someone pretending to be God to manipulate them for their purpose? Humanity had written stories about this, believing they were special. Some humans purported to understand what God wanted, and the entire Bible and religions that came from that had all of humanity certain about what they were seeing and experiencing.

Because of the Bible, humanity thought they knew who God was and what he wanted, and the amount of confusion that could come from that was astounding. He had never seen it in this light, and it started to make some sense to him. He looked over at the pope, who was staring blankly at the screen like some cyborg.

Father Shelby chuckled as he glanced at him because he had always secretly called him 'the pople' to remind himself he was a person like everybody else. Now in this light, it was clear that humans had written the books about their interactions with this God and those had been codified in a book that was put together by the Catholic Church and exploited to make them look like they spoke for God. Now they even claimed that the pope was God's representative on earth. Could it all be a charade?

> For years, the Jewish people had debated these laws as if they had some sort of basis in the functioning of a normal society. Many people loved to spout their knowledge on these laws, and they proclaimed that Mosaic Law was designed to improve the health and function of a stable society, and if that were true, I could get behind it.
>
> It did hold true for shellfish and dirty animals that were not to be eaten because the processing plants of the day were a dirty bucket at the seashore, and terrible food-borne illnesses were encountered, which would kill many people. Washing your hands? Good idea. But it did not stop there.

Other rules that were rather strange included getting tattoos (no doubt a risk for disease or infection), cutting your hair at the sideburns (some leaders demand certain haircuts?), killing anyone who cursed their mother or father (a little harsh), not having sex with your mother (good one), and avoiding women who were on their period. Why would Moses care about that?

There was even an edict that you could not work on a certain day because it needed to be set aside to worship God. There is no way I could have suggested that one because I want these people to work more. Then again, I do like worship, so I will have to let that one stand.

Some of these rules could be considered helpful, at least if you ignored the fabric one—which told you not to blend wool and linen. I didn't know why Moses cared about that. But then there were some laws in the writings of Moses that were rather disturbing as well, such as the one where you could rape someone and then pay fifty shekels to the father and marry that woman. Set aside the problem with treating women like they were property (I don't really care how anybody treats one of my cloned serfs), but wouldn't that have the opposite effect and cause more rapes?

Even more disturbing than that awful precedent was the one where handicapped or blemished people were told they were not good enough for God. Blaming people for their own deformities and sickness is a cruel and subtle evasion, but we overlords have always done that, so humanity does not blame us for it. The amazing part is that humans accept that notion as if it makes sense.

You would think God would have a special place for these people who were put together damaged and otherwise blemished. Besides, Moses himself was damaged by stuttering, and this defect would have kept him away from God by virtue of his own rules. But I am not God, and I do not care how we must motivate these people, so Moses wrote down some rules to make sure that humans were aware of their shortcomings. I will let you read it directly from his book, and even though the vernacular is a little strange, I think you will get the point.

For whatsoever man he be that hath a blemish, he shall not approach: a blind man, or a lame, or he that hath a flat nose, or anything superfluous,

Or a man that is brokenfooted, or brokenhanded,

Or crookbackt, or a dwarf, or that hath a blemish in his eye, or be scurvy, or scabbed, or hath his stones broken;

No man that hath a blemish of the seed of Aaron the priest shall come nigh to offer the offerings of the LORD *made by fire: he hath a blemish; he shall not come nigh to offer the bread of his God.*

I seriously doubt anyone will pay attention to a book written by Moses that has that kind of horrendous stuff in it, but humanity is plagued with guilt and extremely gullible so we shall see. The reality is that if there were a God like that, he would be odious; but if they viewed me as all-powerful, they would likely accept it.

Humanity functions best when they shame each other anyway because it is kind of like self-policing. This God experience is working out well because that is exactly how these slaves can be taught to manage themselves, and I can flee this planet and finally get back to my civilization, knowing that they will survive and prosper. In many ways, it is cruel, but that is not my concern.

Am I disgusted by the physically damaged? If I am going to be honest, I would have to say yes, but only because they remind me of our failures. Our scientists are pathetic and cannot even keep these awful deformities out of the population, so it is really frustrating to me, I must admit. You do not see those kinds of deformities in animal populations, so why do you see them in the human population? Answer—we suck at cloning and have really messed this whole thing up by not being able to do so without killing people from horrible disabilities.

We must ensure that people die in eighty short years. No other choice. But I am not disgusted by the handicapped and diseased that suffer at the hands of our incompetence. Maybe it makes me feel too guilty, so I just do not want them around me. In a way, all of humanity is pretty loathsome to me on this remote outpost called Gaia.

I just think Moses got carried away and wanted to keep all damage away from a God who called himself holy to keep an air of mystery. Or maybe I informed Moses of my frustration in one of our drunken conversations one evening. This is a tough one because the truth is that I find human beings disgusting in general and do not have much use for them, if I'm going to be honest.

Dr Consuelo rose to his feet with a discussion point that seemed obvious from this manuscript.

'Now I am the one offended,' Dr Consuelo said. 'Is that really in the Bible?'

A few of the priests' heads nodded, and Father Begnini just stared at Dr Consuelo.

'That is horrendous! And you are concerned about the overlord's callous dismissal of humans? How could you defend this character as being good? If I had known that was in the Bible, I would have already realized this God was an overlord. How does the church even pretend that is acceptable for a God?'

The priests looked uncomfortable, but by this point, they knew that to try to justify this horrendous piece of literature would come to no good.

'I could never understand,' Dr Consuelo continued on to no one in particular, 'how my fellow humans could seemingly shrug their shoulders at Manny's condition despite my deep disgust at the cruel fate of his situation. I'm sure I was too sensitive in my deep despair, but it was confounding to me that people were not as offended as I was. Now we see why. It is almost as if people are afraid to criticize because the same fate may befall them. Just keep your head down. I've even seen some theists proclaim that this kind of evil proves that God is a good god and I find that to be explicitly evil, because there is no way you can defend this kind of evil, any more than you can defend Hitler's actions as being good. Apologists for this kind of evil are themselves evil.

'This is a perfect example of how humans live in such a fragile and confusing existence that they won't call bullshit when an obvious protocol has been breached. You can't treat innocents like this, and yet everyone of faith seems to be on board because they don't want to be similarly harmed.

'I don't know. Maybe my Christian friends were conditioned to respond that way since God seems pretty angry and harsh, at least the God of the Old Testament. The tone of this God is so dismissive of humans that you would think he was quite capricious and cruel, and indeed this is what we see. Why else would my friends abandon me when I got angry at Manny's condition? They didn't want to risk their perfect little lives, I guess. Either way, I find it abhorrent that a God would despise the handicap, and I have no idea how the church can defend this as good.'

'Perhaps you were too sensitive,' Father Shelby said.

'I most certainly was because I happen to love and care for my son, and I just said so,' Dr Consuelo said. 'And I think that is an appropriate response to such a horrible condition. But despite the continued victim-blaming I hear, I'm trying to put that behind me and see that at least part of it is forced into our worldview through our teachings. When punishment is part of your "offer," compliance is crucial. Fear is crucial. How else could humanity accept control so easily?'

Father Begnini was struggling to get to his feet as quickly as he could, and with reddened face, he sternly growled, 'Our message is of love because we serve a loving God! How dare you suggest otherwise?'

Tegan replied calmly, 'That doesn't sound very loving, Father Begnini.'

Dr Consuelo chuckled, and Father Begnini bristled. His face reddened further, but nobody else spoke. Momentarily the video was resumed.

> But we did come up with some good commandments for the Israelites that would exert a great amount of control on them and keep them focused on their work. Moses had suggested them since humans love to control each other, and I reluctantly agreed. We picked the top ten commandments to sound mysterious, and then we covertly wrote on two large stones that he brought down from on high to the people. Who could refuse those?
>
> The ten commandments worked out better than I could have imagined though because they were a constant reminder that if you broke God's law, then you would be punished. The good news for Moses and me was that everyone broke God's law. That was the point. That veiled threat stuck for good, and those ten commandments carried some serious weight, literally and figuratively. Moses was now the

undisputed leader of his tribe, and nobody could question his authority or power. All of this was accomplished simply by revealing myself to Moses.

This was where I designed my vehicle intended to carry my manuscript, but we told them it was for the ten commandments. This vehicle was just a special box that housed the ten commandments and allowed them to be carried around in what they began to call the Ark of the Covenant. Why would their rules need to be specially protected, especially if there were only ten? Not sure, but they never questioned it and even made a great deal of spiritual significance and developed orthodoxy and religion around it.

Only a clone would believe that their set of ten special rules was so important that they had to be protected in a special box designed to keep them from any prying eyes, as if they would forget what to do unless the priest could pull it out and read them from time to time. I really have no idea why they did not suspect something else was in there.

I simply instructed the Israelites to build it so I could hide my manuscript in it as well. Anyone who touched it would die, and only the priests (a fancy order of the Jewish people that pre-existed my arrival) could touch it when they entered the tabernacle.

The tabernacle was another fancy-sounding religious icon that I suggested to Moses, which had made everybody cower in fear at the sound of it. Because it was holy (whatever that meant), it was also off-limits for the people, and Moses and I had made it so only the priests could enter into this most sacred of places. Whenever they did, I was right there with them to make sure they never touched or even looked at what it was underneath because that would give them insight as to what was going on and I could not take that chance.

I had established a precept that ensured they could only enter the tabernacle once a year to sprinkle blood on the tabernacle in some bizarre leftover ritual from the sacrifices these humans liked to make. They made a big ceremony out of it to atone for their *sins*—which was that made-up word that made them feel guilty for almost anything they did. But I had no idea why they thought shedding blood could atone for sins because that sounded more like a scapegoat than anything. How would killing something else absolve a person of their own guilt? I don't know, but when it was codified in a religion, no one seemed to question it.

And finally, the manuscript—what will I do with this after the Ark of the Covenant has served its purpose? I will bury it in the earth deep, deep where nobody can find it either from our world or from the human world. I know the Ark will be searched for the world over for generations to come, and so I have chosen to bury my manuscript far from the Ark eventually, where there is no chance for it to be seen. By so doing, they will never know to search for this manuscript because nobody knows it exists, only myself and my single top lieutenant who came up with the technology.

My calculations suggest that it will be completely degraded and unreadable in 2.5 million earth years, and I think it should easily be hidden until that time is passed. Hopefully, by that point, humans will have been advanced enough to have moved past the need for a God to worship, but I kind of doubt it because they don't progress very quickly and they do like their rituals.

My God-sized experiment to benefit all of society, both for humans and for us, is finally taking shape. These years have been lonely years for me here in Gaia, but with some luck and with my good planning, I should be able to visit home soon so I can reacquaint myself with my family and catch up with them before my own children are grown. It's been just over one hundred years (in human years) since I've been able to see them, and while my children haven't aged near as much as a human child in that time, they are still getting older, and they will have grown and left our care in the next five hundred years, so I will need to get home as much as I can.

Sometimes these issues I am dealing with in this dimension and on this planet seem pointless to me when I have my own family to tend to, but it will pay off in time if I am ever able to fully develop this concept. From where I stand right now, things are looking pretty good because humanity is starting to rise on its own, but there is a long way to go, and I am never fully confident when humans are involved. I am just looking forward to abandoning this planet once humans can function on their own.

Chapter 28

Debriefing

Dr Consuelo glanced across the conference room table at his friend Father Shelby, who continued to stare at the screen, which was now blank.

'No wonder you were scared for me,' he said. 'Thank you for your support, my friend.'

Father Shelby managed a smile of gratitude. 'I just can't believe what I am witnessing every time I see this,' he said. 'I want to write it off as a fake or something like that, but I can't, given the incredible events we have witnessed.'

Indeed, there was a lot of confusion in the conference room as the video ended, and all glanced at each other in consternation. Father Begnini and the pope were silent on their side of the conference table. The lights were brought back up. They could see the faces of all very clearly at this point, and many seemed troubled. Dr Consuelo now understood the reason for the grave look on the faces of the priests when he had initially recited the manuscript on video the other night.

The pope himself looked confused as he attempted to settle the witnesses and convince them that this was not a miracle they had just witnessed. He had been oddly quiet throughout the video playback, and now as he decided to speak, he seemed more authoritative.

'Many people have opinions about the Bible, gentlemen, and this is just another opinion that is hard to understand and digest because of the circumstances around it. But we know that our God is in control.'

Tegan couldn't help but smirk as she knew very clearly what that meant: "We know we are in control, and we are not giving it up." False humility and an inability to deal with evidence right in front of his face.

Apparently, the pope thought the best defense was ambiguity, as if to say, 'Maybe Dr Consuelo is right, maybe the Bible is right?' since he knew the clergy would always side with the Bible. But he knew that it was not Dr Consuelo who was responsible for this document, and he himself had witnessed the download directly. The pope could not ignore all the evidence in front of him, but he tried.

'We are humble servants of our parishioners,' the pope continued, 'and it is time for us to get back to work.' And with that, he prepared to leave.

A stunning attempt to sweep it all under the rug since he had just explained none of it. In fact, the overall response of the clergy continued to underwhelm, given the fact that they could not debunk this no matter how they tried. Tegan noted that the response was always how theologians and religious authorities reacted to difficult questions of their religion or their manuscript.

Dr Consuelo rose to talk.

'When I was a child, I had a fever. That may sound like the lyrics to a popular song, but in my case, it was true. I had a dangerously high fever for days, and I remember wondering if I was going to die. My parents were concerned, and they called the priest to check on me. I didn't know if he was there to pray for my healing or to give me last rites. After castigating my parents for not getting me to the doctor, he did his little ritual over me and left. I was too sick to go to the doctor, so they managed to get a doctor to come see me. He prescribed me some stuff, and I slowly got better.

'I remember being very tired and weak in the days after yet feeling very cared for, and I even felt like God was a God who would help you. From my perspective as a youth, I thought this God thing could only be beneficial, and if he cared for me like that, then maybe religion was the thing to do. Sure, the medicine may have cured me, but at least the priest had told my parents to have the doctor treat me, and maybe that saved my life. Either way, God seemed like a good thing.

'Once Manny was born, I was forced to change my opinion, as I have told you. I was stunned at how stark and final the verdict was. I could appeal to no one, and Manny would suffer, decline, and die right in front of my very eyes. What kind of a monster would either allow or cause that? In what world can we call God good when he presides over events like that? Worse yet, childhood disease and death are just the beginning. I know I have listed some of these previously, but it should be repeated that this world is full of unimaginable evils, such as child sex trafficking, pedophilia, wars, pandemics, genocides, and even natural disasters. God should be judged by the worst of his creation, not the best.

'Don't forget, we live in a world where we compare our homicidal dictators by how many millions of people they've killed. This is not a genuinely nice world, and Manny was the experience that brought that home to me. It is an incredible piece of propaganda that has led most people to conclude there is a good God in control of this world against this backdrop of breath-taking torture, disease, and death. Stunningly, a large majority of humanity still believes in, and worships, this God. Some people say that faith in God is good. I say it's selfish. If you can worship a deity in the midst of all this carnage, then all you're doing is trying to save your own ass.

'Apparently, it was the medicine that cured me as a child and faith had just moved in as an impostor. My childhood mind had been fooled into thinking that this 'God' had saved me from certain death when in fact he was the author of all deaths because he needs it that way. What am I to do with that information? I could no longer consider God good since all I could detect from this event was indifference, which felt evil. To consider it any other way is completely selfish. As if to say, "Well, he killed my son, but I am sure it was for my own good, so I'll go along with it and hopefully get a big reward." I had no choice but to fight in the only way I know how. My personality dictates that I cannot keep quiet about it. How ironic that we can even be enslaved to our personalities.

'I became an atheist because clearly, there is no god. But as time went on, I realized that atheism is as problematic as theism. Both leave large questions open-ended, and they both have a great deal of orthodoxy. So where does that leave me? I didn't really know until I saw this manuscript. Everything in this document feels right to me against the backdrop of the life that I have experienced.

'The document is dismissive of human beings in a manner that comports with how I felt Manny was treated. Is there a reward for suffering? The overlord says nothing about it, and I have always felt that was a manipulative suggestion. I think our religions have made that up over the eons so rabbis and teachers could encourage their flock to remain strong because they would get a big reward if they only remained faithful until they were dead. Then the reward will be worth dying for. Literally. Isn't that a perfect method of keeping someone complacent? When considering this manuscript, it seems our lives are lived for the benefit of the overlords and not the other way around.

'It occurs to me as I watch these stunning comments, apparently from a distant time and place intended to hide this from humanity, that this possibility becomes self-evident when you overlay it on our reality. We are serfs who are cloned, owned, and manipulated—not for our purposes, but for the purposes of our overlords, in the same way we manage livestock.

'As we debate the concepts laid out before us, I fully realize that our comments about the manuscript cannot help but sound deeply offensive to believers and theologians, but that simply cannot be helped. There is no simple way of informing the laity that they have been following an illusion their entire lives. There is no intention on our part to be offensive, but you must consider how offensive it sounds to me that the church wants to characterize Manny's death as either punishment or a lesson from God for which I will receive a handsome reward.

'The church claims that suffering is for our own good, and I reject that notion as evil. Suffering is only good if it can be exploited, and please forgive me when I say that I think the church does exploit it. When people suffer, the church often tells them that it is somehow for their own good and they will be rewarded, but only if they keep the faith and give more money. No wonder the church considers themselves infallible because that makes no logical sense, yet humans still fall for the ruse.

'I would assert that the philosophy that us being serfs to the overlords comports with not only our experience in life but also with what we see in the Bible. Look at how the Jews were treated in the Old Testament. Thousands were killed by this overlord for disobedience, and according to the Bible, the Jews laid waste to the Middle East to rid it of competing tribes. This overlord sounds like a stark taskmaster.

'If you still want to assert a caring and loving God is in control of this, I will point you to the Book of Job. Theologians have struggled with the content of Job for millennia. I would recommend you go read Job again under the notion that we are serfs and tell me it doesn't make more sense. I see no way that a God would treat his favorite subject like that, and it seems clear this is the actions of an overlord whom you would expect would treat subjects with such disregard. The Bible claims this is a bet between God and Satan, but I think it is quite clear it is a power struggle between two competing overlords who want to toy with their subject to see whom he would choose. Again, not the actions of a God but easily the actions of plantation owners.

'I'll be honest. I don't like sounding like I am trying to undermine the teachings of the Catholic Church or any other church. That is not my intention. This is my experience in life, and I will not shy away from my experience or from this manuscript and the conclusions it forces me to draw. I cannot accept the notion that such evil is done to us instead of by us. Any theist who argues otherwise would have similarly justified the Nazi concentration camps in the Thirties and Forties. They might even defend the KKK in their most powerful position. Defending evil makes you evil. Anyone who apologizes for evil is complicit in that evil. Tell that to a 'Christian apologist'! I must assert my philosophy that humans are treated with such indignancies as to suggest we are commodities to the overlords.

'I believe Dr Mallory and I have accomplished our goal of examining this relic and concluding that this is a scientific document that needs more exploration from the scientific community, and I would ask that it be turned over to myself and the University of New Mexico at the Vatican's earliest convenience. I am truly appreciative of the forum the Vatican has allowed this day, and I am thankful for the opportunity to examine this document.'

Father Begnini rose to his feet very deliberately and determined not to level threats.

'You may believe you've accomplished your goal, Dr Consuelo, but I am not convinced, and I am betting my clergy feels the same way. I'm encouraged to see that this overlord, as you want to call him, acted on behalf of humanity in a very loving and caring manner. Humanity has advanced so far in the intervening time and benefitted so much from the revelation of God and seeing the backstory of how he saved the Israelites is quite interesting. I am actually enjoying this revelation because it confirms how much our God loves us.'

Ignoring the point made by Father Begnini, Tegan rose to talk.

'Dr Consuelo surprised me with that story, and I have a story of my own. I was five when my little baby sister was born, and my mom and dad were so happy to have an addition to our little family. I didn't quite share the joy my parents had as my little sister seemed to be the shiny new addition, and I felt shoved to the side. I would later come to regret that as my little sister died in her crib one night from SIDS. Mom went in to get her out of her crib and found her dead. I can still hear the screams from my mom as she wailed in her agony.

'It was made worse by the police investigating her for possible involvement. I guess she had been dealing with some postpartum depression, and they thought she might have been involved. What an awful thing to have to deal with on top of finding your dead child. I guess some women have done that to their infants, such is the world we live in.

'Our family wasn't religious at all, and I never even considered what part God played in all that. I was fortunate not to have to deal with those confusing questions. To me, it was obvious there was no God, and that is how I have lived my whole life. Had someone told me about God and that he blames us for our own sickness, I might have been angered by that notion just like Dr Consuelo.

'I don't know what it is to answer these deep theological questions like the clergy do, but I would imagine it is difficult to give such trite answers that you know must be so unsatisfactory to your parishioners. It seems to me that we should just admit there are some things that will never be right and leave it at that as we continue to look for the answers. Why be afraid of a manuscript when it can divulge secrets of humanity that might benefit all of humanity? Isn't it obvious that we are serfs when we are always being told what to think instead of just thinking for ourselves? What are we afraid of?

'I have always been bothered by a quote from the Jesuits that says, "Give me a child until he is three or four, and I will have the man for life." That seems like a tantamount admission to brainwashing, but maybe you think I'm too cynical. As we consider the contents of this manuscript, it becomes clear how that would explain the callous disregard that accounts for Manny's death and my sister's death in her crib. Either way, it would be best if this could be examined scientifically.'

Father Shelby stayed seated and asked, 'Dr Mallory, I want to talk about the idea that we are serfs on a plantation, as you both want to suggest and, to be fair, this manuscript suggests. Isn't that a nihilistic and difficult thing for people to hear? Aren't you concerned about the effects on the psyche?'

'I've thought about that question a lot,' Tegan replied. 'And it is an especially important question. Let me start off by stating that I don't care what the effect is on the psyche when we are talking about truth. I can't help what the effect of truth is. I want to state that if I were told that I was a slave as a child, I would rather hear that than to hear that I was born sinful and despicable and in need of salvation. I think that does more to a psyche than telling someone they are a serf on someone else's plantation.

'But your question goes to a deeper level, which suggests that it would potentially be a depressing revelation, but I don't see it that way at all. If you don't know what you are and where you have been, you can't know where you are going. Understanding your position in life is as important and difficult as figuring out what your purpose is here.

'I realize that the suggestion that we are serfs indicates we have no control in life, and that may be a scary conclusion to draw. Didn't we already know this? Maybe this can inspire one to have a purpose in life, which is to break the bonds that enslave us to their thinking. Maybe there is a way we can break free of their propaganda and control, and perhaps that becomes a serf's purpose in life.'

'Well, isn't that a depressing conclusion?' Father Shelby asked.

'Not in my opinion,' Tegan said. 'If you think about the Bible holistically, it puts the blame on humans for the difficult lives we experience, and that saddles humanity with significant guilt and makes them unlikely to question anything because it is all our fault. But when I read this manuscript, it becomes clear that the blame was placed on humans intentionally so that we would try harder to be good and only blame ourselves when things are bad. This manuscript takes all that guilt from humanity by showing that this world is the way it is intentionally because that is how humanity is controlled.'

'Okay, but aside from this ancient relic, what could possibly make you think you're a slave?' Father Shelby said. 'You have a great life.'

'Another great question,' Tegan said. 'I think the concept that we are slaves comes from our most basic questions, and as an atheist, these questions have bothered me long before I encountered the contents of this document. Now that I have encountered this information, these questions become even more germane.

'Where did you come from? Where are you going? What is your purpose? Where is your God? Not knowing these answers makes you as confused by your existence as some child born into a concentration camp or a plantation.

'I believe those four questions almost prove the thesis that we are providing a service for the overlords that we cannot detect, and we are so involved in our lives that we are blind to the control.'

'That's fascinating to consider,' Father Shelby said. 'But I think I do know the answer to those questions. God created me, I know what my purpose is here, I know where I'm going, and I know where God is.'

'I believe you might be proving my point,' said Tegan. 'We've seen a thread throughout this manuscript of control and manipulation by the overlords. Their propaganda has fooled you into thinking you know those things for a fact, and the truth is you have been taught those things by orthodoxy from your religion. If you think you know those things, that only goes to prove that you have had your memory wiped as you came into this life, and now you are happily living with reprogrammed information. No, you don't know any of those things objectively. I'm speaking from an objective viewpoint, and you're speaking from a faith-based perspective.

'The only reason atheism can exist is that God is invisible and undetectable in any objective way. You have also been told what your purpose is, and it is no surprise that it is to serve your God, but outside of that exhortation from your scriptures, you have no idea what your purpose is in life. In fact, you joined the clergy late, and I doubt you felt you knew the answers before that.

'If a loving God had tenderly molded you in the Garden of Eden for companionship and because he cared deeply for you, he wouldn't have put a "tree" in the middle that was poisonous to you. Clearly, this is a euphemism for some other event. Maybe not a euphemism but more appropriately a morality play. Further, he would hold no secrets from you. You would know your purpose. Since it appears you may be a serf, you can't know your purpose because your purpose is to serve them, and they don't want you to know that. You would also know your history instead of having a collective amnesia that humanity suffers from.'

Father Shelby looked a little hesitant but waded back into the conversation, nonetheless.

'Dr Mallory, I must insist that even if your four questions could stand up to our scrutiny, it still doesn't prove we are serfs. I think a loving God would do that intentionally because he gives us our freedom and autonomy, and we can do with it what we want. That is the beauty of free will. It is given to humanity, and they have a blank slate to do what they will with it. That sets us free in ways difficult to identify, and it is proof that our God has formed us lovingly and set us free with this life, free to do whatever we want. How could your simple questions be proof of anything?'

'Because that's exactly how I would treat my slaves to ensure my ongoing dominance over them,' Tegan replied. 'This God we think we know has remained so silent and invisible over the millennia to the point that humanity debates if he even exists. That is an effective hiding job.

Control is commonplace on this earth from cradle to grave even though we sometimes fail to see the control since we can't see the controllers.

'What do you think the story of the Tower of Babel is all about? The gods, which is literally what the Bible calls them, told humanity that they were going to impede their progress, so they don't "become as god." Humans have never understood that biblical story, but that could be a euphemism for modifying the genome or any other sort of manipulation, and we now see they did it with a simple "cure" for a disease. Either way, it is an admission that they control our intelligence and hinder our advancements when necessary and as needed.'

Father Begnini was back on his feet the moment he thought Tegan had paused.

As she sat down, he queried, 'Then may I ask, why are we even discussing this topic? If we are a slave and can do nothing about it, what good does it do to even consider it? Again, from the church's perspective, it feels like you are just trying to characterize our God as a controlling slave owner, and as we've tried to make clear, that is not only offensive but out-and-out blasphemy. Our attempts to worship and serve our God serves a purpose you must not be able to understand.

'That purpose is not only following a role but can also be a state of mind or attitude. Our attitude is that we endeavor to serve our God in any way we can, and we gain satisfaction and purpose out of following his commands. We honor our Savior for our creation and the love he shows us, and we worship him for sacrificing himself as he did for our salvation, and we intend to worship him all the days of our lives because he has saved us and set us free.'

'Amen,' more than one priest said.

Father Begnini felt quite satisfied with his comments as he sat back down because he had finally defended his faith without lashing out, and he was sure the pope would take notice. He glanced at the pope but could not even tell if the pope had heard or even cared.

'That's a good point, Father Begnini,' Father Shelby said. 'And it touches on my question as I consider Dr Mallory's discussion on the four questions. If you honestly believe we are serfs on this plantation . . . ' he said, pausing and looking at Tegan, 'what purpose do you think we serve for them? What do they get out of owning and controlling us?'

Tegan paused for a moment before answering because, if she was going to be honest, she was not sure of the answer. She had discussed this with Dr Consuelo, and she knew he wondered the same thing.

'I'll be honest, Father Shelby. I'm not entirely sure of the purpose we serve for the overlords. Hell, I don't even know who the overlords are, but we can see the impressions of the gods all throughout our history. From the pyramids to Stonehenge, Machu Picchu to Gobekli Tepe. The

Georgia Guidestones inform us they are going to take our world over and kill most of us off, and yet we ignore it and pretend like we are free and sovereign.

'But what purpose do we serve for them? I suspect we can't know that with any specificity, and we can probably only speculate. We can speculate that they benefit from our existence in many ways. Perhaps they make money off us somehow? Perhaps we build out the infrastructure in this world and they take it over and enslave us further? I don't know, and in some ways, I don't really care that much at the moment. I think the important part is that we recognize we are serfs so we can recognize the manipulation. Unless and until we do that, humanity will continue to be complacent slaves. I'd like to hear an answer from bigger minds than mine. What say you, Dr Consuelo?'

Dr Consuelo smiled as he responded, 'I don't think I can fill that position for you, Dr Mallory, but I'll give it a try. One book that I have read claims to have deciphered some ancient Sumerian texts and suggests that humans were cloned by the overlords to procure gold from this earth since they needed it for some reason and didn't want to dig it out of the ground themselves. The author of that book is Zecharia Sitchin, and it is probably obvious to state that his take is highly controversial to many.

'The overlord in this manuscript almost confirms what Sitchin himself claims though by suggesting that humanity was here to harvest resources. It appears he is trying to take humanity from dumbed-down laborers to where we are now with a vibrant society and economy since we were at risk of failing. As he says throughout, humanity needed to learn to stand on their own so society and civilization could develop. Were our origins that mundane? I can't say because, as far as I know, I wasn't there, but to me it seems plausible.'

'Well, again, I ask, what does it really matter?' Father Begnini asked. 'Why even bother to consider the enslavement? If we can do nothing about it, why do we care?'

'I think there's a lot we can do about it,' Dr Consuelo said. 'And it starts with the recognition that we are slaves. As Tegan said earlier, recognizing this would create greater equality throughout humanity since we all recognize we are in the same predicament. Perhaps racism improves. Perhaps equality improves. Perhaps poverty improves because humanity finally realizes that we need to create freedom and equality for all, and that starts with eliminating the barriers that keep people poor. Don't forget, homeless people exist in this world and that is absurd and disgusting. How could there possibly be homeless people in a world with such wealth and prosperity?

'But the benefit of realizing we are slaves goes further. If we know what our position is, it would be less surprising and less depressing when bad things happen. Manny was on hospice before he died, and that afforded me six months of free grief counselling after he had passed, as if I had won some lottery or something. I only went to the first one because all I could do was rage, and I think the poor therapist didn't know how to respond.

'What if she had known we are slaves? She could have responded by reminding me that our condition is such that we can't be protected from these things and my anger will only serve to hurt myself and those around me further. That is the benefit of understanding you're a slave. Father Lujan could not have counselled me in such a fashion because he was forced to follow a carefully crafted script, and it only made me angrier.

'*Freedom* is a word that humanity has forgotten the meaning of because we have been in this dystopic plantation for so long, we don't have an imagination of a better world. I believe that the recognition of our serfdom is the beginning of finding a way towards more freedom, but that is hard to imagine for most people in a world where they have been brainwashed to believe they are free when they are actually in chains. As Goethe said, "none are more hopelessly enslaved than those who falsely believe they are free."'

'That is certainly a bright and uplifting picture you paint there, Dr Consuelo,' Father Shelby said sarcastically. 'I'd prefer to keep my current philosophy intact, if you don't mind. I serve a powerful and loving God, and that's the way I prefer to see it.'

'That's why you're such a good and complacent slave,' Tegan said with a smile.

Father Shelby tried to smile too, but it came across as more like a grimace. 'I understand your point, Tegan,' Father Shelby said. 'As I told you, I came to the clergy late in life, and I was stunned by the rules and requirements. Living the austere life of a priest has been a rather stark change in my life. We study the Bible and theology our whole lives, and while I will not concede your point entirely, I do feel complacently driven to do this. I shouldn't say this, but I found it odd that we clergy and other theologians study and search this Bible our entire lives, and yet we still live in a world of unimaginable cruelty. If we have the truth on our side, why do we continue to see the awful things we witness in this world?'

'That's right,' Dr Consuelo said. 'And while all this talk of enslavement is just a thought experiment, I think it is something that we need to examine more fully. As you say, humanity has been searching the Bible for answers for millennia, and while they may think they have a satisfying answer personally, it clearly functions as a distraction because the world does not improve, and human suffering continues unabated. There is no harm in asking questions and seeking the truth. Which brings me back to the manuscript. I want to argue that we have done the necessary basics to acquire this manuscript on behalf of science, and I ask for your support.'

The pope slowly rose to his feet with his hands on the table in front of him. He stared straight at Dr Consuelo, and there appeared to be a look of sympathy in his eyes.

'I am sorry for your loss, young man, and I cannot explain your pain away. But I see the good in religion, and I know it exists for the good of humanity. Unfortunately, your bitterness and anger at the loss of your child are blinding you to any of the inspiration that spirituality can provide for humanity. Religion is a force for good in this world, and I cannot allow some ancient manuscript to change my mind on that.

'We can see in the Bible, and even in this manuscript, how our God has led us out of the wilderness and to the blessings we enjoy today, and he has blessed us in ways we never could have hoped for without such a loving God. This manuscript has some historical facts correct, but it does not undermine my strong faith in the Bible and in the love of our Savior. Humanity would be harmed by looking at history in this fashion, and I believe we are better off for the wonderful houses of worship we have on this earth. My intention is to serve my God in this role as long as I can and to obey his commandments while I am posted upon this earth, and I know my reward will be great. As will all of yours.' And he looked around the room with a smile.

The irony of the pope's comment was lost on him because it was an ancient manuscript that afforded him and the church the opulence and power that he enjoyed so lavishly. Tegan realized the church had only had the examination because the scientific community had wanted it along with Dr Consuelo, and now that they had performed their duty, they could mothball the whole thing and go on brainwashing children and living off the hard work of others. A magical manuscript might be whispered about in certain circles, but they could ignore it with the confidence that their power was almost untouchable.

The other priests slowly lowered their heads to avoid eye contact with the pope or anyone else, except for Father John Shelby.

He stared straight ahead and said out loud to Dr Consuelo and whoever else wanted to hear, 'I don't know if I will burn in hell for this or not, but I know what I saw in there, and I felt some of it myself. I cannot claim to fully understand your pain, Dr Consuelo, but the things you are saying make a lot of sense in the face of the pain you experienced. To say I am having a crisis of faith would be the understatement of all time.

'Holy Father, perhaps you are seeing religion as a force for good only because you are on the good side of religion. You set the rules, you live a life of comfort, and you hold the envious position of being pious and holy, which sets you apart from criticism. Perhaps religion would not look so good to you if you had to slave, repent, donate, and obey all while having your life ripped apart the way it has for Dr Consuelo. We in the clergy tend to get defensive every time someone criticizes our faith or holy books, and we tend to overlook their position because we consider them jaded or bitter.

'We forget that we are the ones in power from a religious standpoint and shouldn't be afraid of any criticism. How could one man's crisis of faith undermine our position of power? What if he is not bitter at all and simply looking for a more appropriate explanation for his experience on earth? Isn't that a legitimate question to ponder? What does it harm the church if we allow an ongoing scientific investigation of this manuscript?

'It is far worse to say to these individuals that they are broken and outside of God's love if they are willing to challenge the faith or voice their questions. Any God who cannot handle these kinds of questions cannot be a God worth worshipping, wouldn't you say? So why can't we handle these questions? Maybe we should either find a reasonable response that actually answers his questions or abandon our thinking because it is completely misguided, just as this "overlord" intended for it to be.'

Father Shelby knew he might have said too much, but he did not care since he knew what he was saying was right. Why should he care about the church or its clergy if all they were doing was puppetry for the overlords? At this moment in time, Father Shelby had an alarming sense that he might be wasting his time and energy in the clergy. This experience he had in the chamber with Dr Consuelo showed a real sinister side of the control matrix on this earth and those who would seek to control humanity. Father Shelby was not sure he wanted to be part of that anymore, but where could he possibly go from here? Some angry homeless ex-priest was not going to matter to anyone or change anything.

Chapter 29

Kangaroo Court

The pope rose to give a final benediction before addressing the group one last time. Glancing around the room after the prayer, Dr Consuelo thought he appeared quite satisfied and showed no evidence of concern on his face. It appeared he was closing a mass, and nothing had changed.

'I want to thank you all for your assistance in the examination and for participating in this discussion of considering the ramifications of such an extraordinary find. Dr Consuelo, you are an intrepid investigator, and I applaud your dogged determination to understand the world you live in where such a tragedy of a young life lost could be explained. Your love for Manny is exemplary, and your determination to understand the truth of it is laudable. Please know that I hold you in great regard even if I must disagree with your conclusions.

'Dr Mallory is a wonderful supporter of yours and a brilliant debater, and I am happy you have her in your corner. In fact, I don't understand why she isn't Mrs Consuelo, but I won't get into your business.'

The room chuckled as Dr Consuelo and Tegan smiled warmly.

Why couldn't he be Mr Mallory? she wondered in her state of emancipation.

The pope continued, 'Father Shelby has also earned my great respect for acting as Dr Consuelo's examination partner in the observatory and managing the crisis well despite the fear that gripped him along with everyone else. It was indeed an incredible event, and I understand your crisis of faith, my son. I hope we can work to assimilate and understand this confusing information as we continue to serve our great King.

'One thing we can all agree on is that our God is King, and we worship him as the King rather than considering him a slave owner. We believe in the divine right of kings. In short, we enjoy our servitude because it gives us purpose.'

He paused and looked around. Tegan couldn't believe the admission he just made, but none of the complacently enslaved priests noticed. They were too busy drooling over whatever the pope said because they had been brainwashed to believe that he was infallible.

How do you argue with infallibility?

The pope continued with his propaganda disguised as liturgy.

'The church understands that our Savior is our Master, and we worship him for the great things he has done for us and the continued blessings he bestows upon his chosen ones. Our faith is undaunted in the face of this manuscript. Blessings to each and every one of you, and thank you for your participation in this great project.'

Tegan winced at that comment. Of course the pope's faith was undaunted in the face of any evidence. He benefitted from his position. What would ever make him reconsider? It was as if you were trying to convince someone that the millions of dollars in their bank account were more harmful to them than a more modest bank account because they were enslaved to the concerns of losing it.

And with that, the pope departed the room.

Silence filled the room after the pope's departure. As his comments indicated, he was quite certain that the church would be unscathed by the unsettling examination of the manuscript. He was still talking about chosen ones despite the revelation that even he was a slave. Dr Consuelo knew this to be the case, and he slowly took in the scene and glanced around at the quiet in the room and the long look on the faces of the remaining clergy. What mattered most now was trying to acquire the manuscript.

'Would it be possible, Father Begnini,' Dr Consuelo asked, 'to put this trial to a simple vote?'

'Over what?' Father Begnini asked.

'Over ownership of the manuscript,' Dr Consuelo said, surprised at his amnesia.

Father Begnini looked rather startled, but he caught himself and said, 'Oh right. Let's do that.'

Dr Consuelo and Dr Mallory thought he sounded rather sarcastic. Were they foolish enough to even think they had a chance?

Now that the pope had left, there were thirteen people in the room, excluding the ambassadors who would not be voting and including Dr Consuelo, Dr Mallory, Father Begnini, and the ten clergymen.

'May I set the ground rules, Doctors?' he asked Dr Consuelo and Dr Mallory rather derisively, they thought, and he did not wait for an answer. 'I would like each individual to stand and make a statement as to which side they are voting for and why.'

All the clergy seemed to straighten up at that, and they looked like they were getting ready to take their final exam. For the most part, they had stayed away from this debate until now, and there were very few who wanted to make their feelings known.

Father Begnini chuckled and said, 'Okay, Dr Mallory, you have the floor first. I think I'll go to Dr Consuelo next and so on down the far side of the conference table.'

Dr Consuelo met Dr Mallory's gaze and did not even stand up. He just looked across the conference table and said, 'I think you can put both myself and Tegan in the "yes" category, Father.'

'Is that the "yes" category for keeping it housed at the Vatican?' Father Begnini asked, once again dripping with sarcasm.

'I'm finding your newfound friskiness refreshing,' Dr Consuelo said as the cheesy grin faded from Father Begnini's face. 'No. Obviously, I think we need to procure this relic for scientific investigation.'

Tegan nodded somewhat aggressively.

'Well, at least you got two votes for science, good job,' a sneering Father Begnini said. Clearly, he thought he had the rest of them on his side and he would soon get his revenge.

Father Lujan was seated next to Dr Consuelo, and he was called on next. This was a heavy burden to go first because he would set the tone for the clergy. This was feeling very much like a confession; only the priests were the ones who had to confess this time. He stood very hesitantly and looked at Dr Consuelo and Tegan cautiously. They both thought this was a sign that their support was rather shallow even though they were in the lead at this point.

As they watched him carefully, Father Lujan sheepishly stated, 'I was never able to counsel you very well when you lost Manny, Dr Consuelo. Maybe I will be shamed for this, but if I'm going to be honest, I don't think I have a decent answer for you. Maybe this manuscript can give us some answers, and I am not afraid of the truth. I will vote for Dr Consuelo and Dr Mallory, and I think science should examine this further.'

Dr Consuelo was stunned when he heard those comments by Father Lujan. He could not imagine Father Lujan voting against the church because he seemed very swayed by his conditioning. Dr Consuelo knew that took a lot on his behalf, and he thanked him warmly and was surprised to see a tear in his eye. What a kind gesture it was of him to side with his old friend and concede that he had questions about life as well. Father Begnini winced a little at that one but still looked cocky and quite secure in his seat of power.

Father Shelby went next, and he bounced to his feet with confidence.

'Father Begnini,' he opened, 'you seem to be quite skeptical about this manuscript found deep in the ground, and given the incredible physical aspects of the find and the incredible contents of it, I can see why. So I propose we do something that the church rarely does. Let's confirm this find by allowing other scientists to explore it. That is the only way we can tell if Dr Consuelo is a liar. Wouldn't you love to prove him wrong? I am voting with science because I want to explore the unknown rather than hide from it. This is too important to hide.'

Dr Consuelo smiled warmly as he heard this. He was not sure if Father Shelby was on their side, but at least someone else had realized the need to examine this more fully, and he wasn't completely surprised that he voted with science. Now they were ahead four to nothing, but somehow it still felt like the victory was unlikely since there were nine votes remaining.

Next came the bishop in the seat next to Father Lujan. Dr Consuelo had not gotten his name, and he hadn't said a word throughout the proceedings.

Dr Consuelo whispered to Tegan, 'I wouldn't be surprised if that was the end of our little rally.'

'I can't explain this, and I want answers,' the bishop said, and he sat down.

'Really?' Father Begnini said, looking quite shocked. 'That's all you've got?'

The bishop just nodded, and if he was wavering, he did not show it.

Father Begnini was not the only one shocked in the room. All the clergy yet to speak turned their heads slowly and looked at the man in his red ecclesiastical garb with a shocked look on their face. Father Begnini had been certain of his victory up until this point, and he would have been dismayed if he were worried, but his confidence still showed.

Dr Consuelo was in shock, and he smiled as he looked at Tegan. That was five votes for science, and they only needed two more to secure the victory. The bishop had confirmed what he had hoped—that the entire event was so confounding that even the clergy might want a thorough examination. He glanced at Father Begnini, who was staring at him smugly.

The next priest rose confidently in his brown robe and looked at the bishop who had just spoken, saying, 'Your response has given me confidence, Your Excellency, and I concur. I recently read a quote by a physicist who said, "I would rather have questions that can't be answered than answers that can't be questioned." For nearly two thousand years the Catholic Church has been giving answers that can't be questioned. Like Father Lujan, I am tired of giving answers to my parishioners that wouldn't satisfy myself. I vote for science. I vote to examine the mysterious instead of covering it up. I wish you well, Dr Consuelo.' And he sat down.

Dr Consuelo started to stand up, and then he caught himself. He wanted to give a standing ovation and proclaim victory at that short yet perfectly succinct statement. But he could not because he did not want to show his elation even though he only needed one more vote. He could not help but show his excitement though, and the room noticed. The remainder of the clergy stared at him, and then the next one rose.

'One more,' whispered Dr Consuelo to himself, but Tegan heard it and squeezed his hand.

The tension in the room was starting to heat up as the next priest rose to make his statement. This one was dressed all in black and had a somber look on his face.

'I don't think our God would hide anything from us, and I want to know more. I'll admit I want to debunk this, but you can't debunk something without examining it fully,' he said, and he sat down.

'That sounds like another vote for science,' sighed Father Begnini. 'Is that what I'm hearing?'

'Yes, Father,' he replied.

That was it, and Dr Consuelo once again had to resist the urge to hug Tegan and celebrate. They had secured the victory in this silly Kangaroo Court, and now he suppressed the desire to celebrate. He squeezed Tegan's hand even tighter with a huge smile on his face, hoping he might procure even more votes. But he was wrong. They did not just get one; they got them all.

One by one the remaining clergy stood and affirmed that this document was most peculiar and that it should be examined openly and for science and that the church should no longer be in the business of covering up uncomfortable documents that were hard to explain.

Victory was complete, and Dr Consuelo could not believe it. He held back no more, leaping from his seat and giving Tegan a big hug. They were both elated that they were able to convince the clergy of the need to examine mysteries instead of covering them up. The search for legitimate answers was underway, and they could not be more thrilled with the outcome.

'This is a serious undertaking, Dr Consuelo,' Father Begnini said. 'I wouldn't celebrate too much.'

'I think he understands that very well,' Tegan said. 'He is the only one in this room who has experienced the gravity of this manuscript.'

The clergy nodded in agreement.

'Okay, playtime is over,' Father Begnini said, suddenly sounding authoritative and in control. 'I'm done with the clergy, and you can all exit the conference room,' he invited.

Rather surprised, the clergy began to stand and gather their belongings.

'No need to gather anything,' Father Begnini said. 'Leave all your transcripts where they are.'

Father Lujan looked hesitant. 'I would prefer to be here for the remainder of the meeting,' he said, 'especially since this is recorded anyway.'

The other clergy nodded in agreement.

'Well, I would prefer you're not,' Father Begnini said. 'Besides, the recording is going to be used as evidence against you. Now get out,' he demanded of the clergy.

The ambassadors did not budge as they were allowed to stay, but the clergy shuffled out like a bunch of bad kindergarteners.

'You guys have done nothing to protect our most holy faith today,' Father Begnini chided as they marched out.

Chapter 30

Bully Begnini

Dr Consuelo and Dr Mallory watched in shock as the clergy were marched away as if on their way to the gallows. The elation turned to confusion as Father Begnini ignored their victory and chased the clergy away.

'I don't like the feel of this,' Dr Consuelo said to Tegan as the room cleared. 'This might be a short-lived victory. Religion is nothing if not a dictatorship.'

'I've wondered all along,' Tegan confirmed. 'Even if we could win this unorthodox trial, the Vatican has the power to overrule, and there is no authority to which we can appeal.'

Dr Consuelo nodded in agreement as he eyed Father Begnini suspiciously. It was clear that he held all the power, and Dr Consuelo hated the smug bastard. He now found it creepy how the five ambassadors had not spoken a word during the whole discussion and were silently observing the situation as if they had full control. He wondered what the source of their power was, as if holding all the knowledge of the world and dispensing only enough to keep people enslaved was not enough to hold immense power.

It was not lost on him that governments needed to keep their slaves dumbed down as well so that bedlam did not ensue. Governments could not have the slaves revolting because their power extended from the ability to tax and make laws. Complacent citizens were necessary, and as long as you kept them fat and happy, they would do whatever you told them.

Father Begnini was shuffling some papers about, pretending he did not actually know how this was going to end. Tegan seemed tense as she observed this disgusting shill for the overlords likely preparing to quash their examination. He now had a confidence that was absent during the debate that had just ensued.

'You two are quite the cute couple,' he started, and his eyes seemed to narrow and darken. 'It seems you actually think you have won something here, as if we don't determine what information gets out to the public.'

'We know that's what you do,' Dr Consuelo said. 'We have been making that point all along. Now surprise us and let us leave with the manuscript in tow. The entire clergy voted against you and for an open process.'

Father Begnini laughed an almost eerie laugh and said, 'Those idiots couldn't carry on a debate to save their lives. I don't even think they know what they believe because with them, everything is platitudes.'

'I didn't think you debated that well either,' Dr Consuelo said.

'Well,' Father Begnini said, almost hissing the words, 'that's because I know something you don't know,' and his tone darkened significantly. 'As you may have noticed, I didn't bother voting. Would you like to know why that is? Mine is the only vote that counts, and that's why the clergy are no longer here. We are all slaves on this planet, and we know that very well. Hell, the Vatican is the arbiter of that slavery as we work directly for the overlords, and the structure on this earth works perfectly fine without your input. I know it, and these ambassadors know it, and you just got lucky enough to stumble across it on your happy—or should I say angry little quest.'

His tone turned deadly serious as he continued, and Tegan thought he looked evil.

'If you think you are going to be allowed access to this document so you can express your opinion to the whole world, you are sadly mistaken. In case you have not been paying attention, we are the Vatican, and we wield great power over all of humanity, whether they belong to the church or not. We peel back the curtain on reality and allow humanity to get a glimpse of only what we want them to see. This was a fun little charade, but it should be painfully obvious to you now that you will never gain access to that manuscript.

'Now, just so we understand each other, I'm telling you what's going to happen. You are going to pack your shit up and leave the Vatican as soon as you can. You will take nothing with you that you didn't bring in. On second thought, I think I'll let you have the transcript so you can shop it around and prove yourself to be the crazy person that you are. You can spout your little philosophy all you want, and the only thing you will get is blank stares. People fall into one of two categories. Either they know they are a slave and they love it, or they have no idea they're a slave and wouldn't care if you told them. So remember that when you're out on your little quest.'

'There's a third category, dumbass,' Dr Consuelo said. 'People who recognize they're a slave and want no part of it. Unfortunately, you're the complacent type. Don't forget, old man, that you're going to die too, and what good will it do for you then, you complacent little sheep?'

'Call me what you want, Dr Consuelo, because now I am in control, and I have the power of the entire church and of governments behind me,' he said and gestured to the ambassadors who all had icy looks on their faces.

'I knew you were a snake the minute I laid eyes on you,' Dr Consuelo said. 'I knew I couldn't trust you as far as I could throw you, and believe me, I couldn't throw your fat ass very far.'

'You might want to watch your tone, Dr Consuelo,' Father Begnini sneered. 'I do hold immense power in this institution and, like it or not, in this world.'

'It's illicit power brought through deception, you fat fuck,' Dr Consuelo spat.

'Be that as it may,' Father Begnini said. 'Now pack up and get off these premises, and never come back. The church has followed through on its commitment to have the investigation, but that is where it stops. Be assured that there will be no record of your visit, and these priests and bishops who voted for your cause will be dealt with appropriately.

'They will be sent to such remote parishes that they will never have an audience with the faithful again. And you, Dr Consuelo, what will become of you? Believe me, the Vatican is unconcerned about a mouthpiece like you. You were already a pariah in the scientific community for your willingness to look at this crazy stuff, and no one will pay attention to the tin-hat-wearing kook that you have become. As I said, your attempts to publish this information will be ridiculed, and you will be mocked to your grave. Any individual who has achieved any success in this world belongs to us and is easy to control, and there is no way that anyone will consider anything your crazy ass has to say. Mark my words, you are dead to this body, and we will never even acknowledge your existence.'

Chapter 31

Excommunication

If you want to know who controls you, look at who you are not allowed to criticize.
—*Voltaire*

Dr Consuelo and Dr Mallory were dumbfounded. Father Begnini had clearly known that this was his final move long before any vote occurred. If you could not defeat them at the ballot box, just steal the damn election if you had the power. And the church certainly had the power.

Before they could even gather their belongings, Father Begnini and the ambassadors exited the conference room abruptly, leaving Tegan and Dr Consuelo alone in the room with their thoughts. As they gathered their transcripts and belongings, an assistant came in and informed them that their ride to the airport was available, their flight had been moved up, and they were leaving today. Dr Consuelo felt sure that the flight had already been changed prior to the meeting, since Father Begnini had known what the outcome would be.

'What am I going to do now?' he asked Tegan as they sat in the silence of the conference room.

She grabbed his hand and looked deep into his eyes. 'It doesn't matter what you do now. You have already accomplished your goal, and you have more truth now than any scientist or theologian. We will continue to explore this find, and what others say will not affect us.'

Dr Consuelo informed Tegan that it was worse than that. They had just been effectively excommunicated from the church, science, and pretty soon, he would have to fight to keep his job. He knew the not-so-veiled threat from Father Begnini meant they would pressure the University of New Mexico, and they could exert pressure on any institution.

'Fuck the church,' he said. 'I left them long before they tried to kick me out. I don't need them, and I don't think anyone does. And fuck science too. I am so pissed at my colleagues who have left me out here on this island desperately trying to prove I'm not insane while attempting to find answers that might benefit all of humanity. Why the fuck should I care? All I've become is a lightning rod for the unenlightened. I don't need this shit.'

'No, you don't,' Tegan comforted him. 'But you've got it, and I know you're up for the challenge. Without debate, you might fail, and you know that is true. We will take the fight to the Vatican and beat them at their own game,' she finished, trying to look as confident as possible. 'We will get this published, and people will listen.'

Dr Consuelo did have plans all along to publish whatever was in the manuscript for academia and the world, but he had serious doubts that the world would ever believe it or accept it now that the Vatican had disappeared. She was right though; he did live for the fight, and he would get through this. He had plans to submit it to one of many academic journals as a scientific paper, but he now realized he would have no support, and it would be difficult, if not impossible, to get it looked at.

He was frustrated as he considered this, and he and Tegan made their way to the front entrance, this time without any escort except for the assistant who showed them the way, even though they knew it. The architecture looked rather drab compared to their arrival, but that was because it belonged to the slave owners and they were being shown that trapdoor to hell.

'This place is a dump anyway,' Dr Consuelo said, and Tegan chuckled. 'Who could be impressed with such opulence when it was built on the backs of serfs?'

He had been shown a great secret, which he was sure would benefit mankind, but Father Begnini and the church were not going to make it easy. He now saw them all as snakes, intent on pleasing the overlords.

Without the revelations this manuscript could provide, Dr Consuelo knew that the world would continue on in darkness, with each individual believing that their God was the right God and that they alone were pious and holy. People would continue to judge each other based on their own interpretation of a holy book that claimed to speak for God. Claiming to know God's thoughts, the world would continue to believe that all the contents of their holy scriptures gave them the right to tell others what to do or discriminate against them if they refused.

It appalled Dr Consuelo that children would continue to be abused in all manners by church authorities who were given access to them by well-meaning parents who wanted to give their children to the 'service of God.' Dr Consuelo noted how sinister that term sounded now. Nations would continue to debate who had what access to any so-called holy lands, as if the God of the universe would play favorites amongst the people of his earth, even though they were all supposedly created equal.

Religions would continue to battle about whose manuscript gave them access to the God of the Universe, defending their holy scripture by quoting them and not even listening to themselves or the other side. Dr Consuelo had long since realized that religion was not about what was right or wrong but about whether you could gain power from it by proclaiming to speak for God.

And what of the scientific world? Wouldn't they be interested in the legitimacy of the manuscript and publish the findings? Tegan and Dr Consuelo knew the answer to that as well. The scientific world did not want to cross that threshold either because anything paranormal was automatically shunned and sidestepped by serious-minded scientists who were not open to mystery and intrigue.

Even though science ought to have been about investigating and explaining the world around us in an objective manner, they knew that no rigid scientific institution would consider examining this in-depth. Science apparently had its own orthodoxy, just like religion did, and anything paranormal or spiritual would never see the light of day in any authentic scientific journal. The materialist viewpoint did not allow for such nonsense because if it could not be replicated and studied, it did not exist in the minds of academia. What frustrated Dr Consuelo the most was that this find could be studied if it could ever be wrestled from the dirty Crusade-stained fingers of the Vatican overlords.

As such, academia was complicit in the paranormal cover-up, and it was extremely unlikely that religion and science could ever come together and consider the paranormal component that was as much a part of our world as trees and atoms. Materialist scientists knew that much of what they studied was invisible and intangible, and they considered it daily in places like the Large Hadron Collider, yet there was no chance they would ever look objectively at this finding.

Quantum physics essentially screamed that there was a mystery to the universe that could not be explained with simple Newtonian physics or relativity, and this relic had the potential to explain some of this mystery. Between science and religion, there remained a great gulf fixed, and this examination had the potential to begin to bridge that divide and bring the two sides into an understanding of the other. It seemed a shame, but Tegan and Dr Consuelo knew it was an examination that would largely be ignored, and they would have great difficulty trying to change that.

Dr Consuelo sat down in his seat in first class next to Tegan and asked the flight attendant for some whisky.

'Do you have any Jameson by any chance?'

'No, sir," she replied. 'We have Jack Daniels or Crown Royal.'

He should have known, but he had to ask anyway. Airlines were not exactly bars where you could get anything you wanted.

'We'll both take two Crown Royals,' he said, and he leaned his head back into his seat in luxury as she walked away. Mockingly, he noted to Tegan, 'Tegan can have whatever she wants too because it's on the Vatican and their slave owners,' he said, winking.

'Don't do that,' she said. 'The creepy old pope kept winking at me the entire time I was there.'

Dr Consuelo jerked his head up. 'He did not!' he blurted a bit too loud for the curious folks in first class. Lowering his voice, he said, 'Did he try to show you what's under his skirt?'

They both laughed, once again too loud for the elites in first class.

'You better not put too much of that Crown Royal down there, Mr Consuelo,' Tegan said, 'or you might be up preaching to the entire plane about the slave owners at the Vatican, and at that point, I'm going to pretend I never met you.'

'I think that's a great idea,' Dr Consuelo said. 'I'm going to keep those drinks coming. Who but a slave needs to know that they're a slave?'

Tegan gave him the coldest look she could muster and warned, 'Don't you dare,' because she knew he just might.

They settled in for their long trip home and discussed their further plans. Dr Consuelo felt quite opulent as he sat in first class, sipping his whisky, while the cattle shuffled past him to the back of the plane.

'Slaves,' he chuckled to himself.

The Vatican was nice enough to get him and Tegan first-class seats, and he was pretty sure they would have changed their minds on that and placed him on a boat if they had known what he was going to say on his brief visit.

'At least we travel home in luxury before we are excommunicated from the church and science,' he exclaimed.

'I wouldn't rather be anywhere else,' Tegan said. 'I have learned so much in this last year, and especially in these last days, that I wouldn't wish it any other way.'

Dr Consuelo nodded in agreement.

It was funny how it turned out. Here he was, some middling little archaeologist from a respected yet largely ignored university, having an audience with some of the highest-level clergy on earth and examining a manuscript that called their very foundation into question. The truth was that he had been so fascinated at how this examination of the manuscript had helped him understand the world around him and the seemingly unsympathetic attitude towards Manny's death. It had really helped him in a way he had not imagined.

It was obvious now that no church was going to change or divulge the truth when they themselves benefited from the truth embargo. They regurgitated the same answers they had always been told and in so doing propagated the lie that they knew what the hell they were talking about. When revelations like this manuscript came along, they had no choice but to stonewall because their power would be rendered impotent if humanity at large were to understand the ramifications of what Dr Consuelo had just examined.

Dr Consuelo chuckled at a memory he had from his childhood when he had asked a cohort in his church why it was bad to smoke marijuana if it was a plant that grew naturally. His older friend had squirmed and replied, 'I'm not sure, let me get back to you on that one,' and he had gone and asked his dad, who had a response for Dr Consuelo a few days later.

'My dad says it's because it is a weed and it didn't grow until after the fall,' meaning after Adam and Eve had been so naughty as to eat an apple from a tree that had been placed smack dab in the middle of their world with sweet, juicy apples begging to be eaten.

'Oh right,' the young Dr Consuelo had replied. 'That makes sense.'

Even though he knew it did not, he wanted to be agreeable, so he went away satisfied with his answer that made no sense at all. How the hell did some minor disobedience to some arbitrary rule, which was made to be broken anyway, create all the sorrow in the world? It was natural to want to do what you were told not to do, and there was no possible way that that disobedience could lead to the growth of some plant called marijuana any more than it could possibly lead to birth defects. Marijuana had always been on the earth, and death had always been part of life.

All those things had pre-existed any Garden of Eden, and the story was designed to keep humans in line and keep them from asking questions. Dr Consuelo knew that it was all made up now, and time and embellishment had given it the holy and spiritual aura that it needed for people to engender it with the reverence that was required to become the Holy Bible.

There was no process that ensured the Bible was God's thoughts, and the ancient writings of ancient people had been anointed worthy through an opaque process. There was only the Council of Nicaea, which tried to pull all these random books together to cobble them into something they anointed as the Bible, even though it was just a bunch of random books that only connected loosely and mostly told the story of the Jewish people.

Dr Consuelo now realized that Moses had written about something that long predated him, and he had no clue how it had occurred any more than any of us would. He wrote down stories that explained the world he saw around him and told stories that had been handed down to him for centuries and possibly millennia. Who knows how old the earth is and how many civilizations have risen and fallen before us? These stories did not make much sense, but they came from Moses, who claimed to know God, and even though the stories were weird and did not fit any conventional thinking on how this world came about, they were canonized by the church, and now nobody could question their authority.

Dr Consuelo's thoughts were interrupted by the movement of the plane, which was a relief because he felt like he could think of nothing else. As the plane taxied down the runway one more time, he decided he must enjoy what was left of this trip. He had always enjoyed the power of the jet engines pushing the plane down the runway, forcing him back into his seat. He marveled at how strong the thrust must be for astronauts elevated in a rocket. The rush was intense, but the thrill of the plane lifting off the runway and the flaps pulling them into the crisp evening air was all he needed at this moment.

As the plane lifted off, he gazed at the surrounding city, which drifted farther below him as they climbed. The advancements of humankind were incredible, and when he really thought about it, he knew the story of humanity was astonishing, given the odds that were stacked against them. Humans had developed a technologically advanced civilization while facing disease, death, war, and violence and against the backdrop of an incredibly short life span, which was often cut shorter without any advance notice.

How had they been able to pass the knowledge along to others who would continue the progress with all the odds stacked against them? He was not sure, but he had to concede that the idea of God and even religion were helpful in creating the infrastructure through which these kinds of advancements could be achieved. He realized now that the revelation of God was a manipulation of the species to further the agenda of the overlords, and this event had morphed into these religions, but the species was blind to that fact.

The airline attendant came through the aisle and asked them if they wanted more Crown Royal.

'Yes please.'

She brought it promptly, and he was thrilled with how quick the service was in first class.

As they floated through the sky in comfort and luxury, he felt regal and important, even though the church had rudely ejected them and effectively banned them. Not that Tegan or Dr Consuelo really minded because clearly, the church was about controlling the narrative exclusively. He was undeterred and continued to plot a path for the exposure of this document.

One final thought occurred to Dr Consuelo as he pondered the publication of the examination and the transcript. If the church refused to admit the existence of the manuscript, how could that be viewed as anything but a cover-up? Any attempt to cover things up would be a tacit admission that they could not debunk it and did not want any of their parishioners to know. How was that not an admission that they must cover it up to maintain their power? As Father Begnini admitted himself, the Vatican were shills for the overlords.

How was it that they could not be interested in finding the truth if they claimed to be about finding truth? In fact, Dr Consuelo felt that the fact that any control of the narrative in this world occurred also suggested that humans were a cloned and manipulated species. Propaganda was the tool of plantation owners, and the church was the arbiter of that process. The answer was simple, of course, and there was no way they would willingly give up their power. Just more proof to him that all leaders were temporary shills for the overlords.

'Let them wallow in their slavery, I can't save them,' he said, and with that, he finished his drink and laid his head back.

It was going to be a long flight home, and he had some sleep to catch up on.

As he lay back in his seat next to Tegan to rest his eyes, he comforted himself with the notion that he was heading back to his wonderful state of New Mexico, which was far away from this noise. He was proud of his university and did not want to be anywhere else. He was a well-respected para-archaeologist, and he had never been so proud to wear that hyphenated title in his life. Let the Vatican claim to speak for God. He would continue with his life, and maybe the truth would be heard someday. In the meantime, religion had no effect on him; even though it does on everyone.

CPSIA information can be obtained
at www.ICGtesting.com
Printed in the USA
BVHW040931291122
653021BV00006B/81

9 781914 158063